CHACO

Peggy A. Wheeler

DMP

CHACO

Peggy A. Wheeler

CHACO

ISBN print 978-1-988256-75-7

ISBN ebook 978-1-988256-76-4

www.dragonmoonpress.com

Acknowledgements

A ton of appreciation to my husband, Steve Wheeler, for your keen eye, patience, unconditional love, and steadfast belief in CHACO. Thank you to the Hemet Writing Group. Best critique group ever. Big hug to my one-time agent, and still good friend, Chila Bradshaw Woychik, for wonderful editing on an earlier version, and most of all, for loving this book and taking a chance on me.

Thank you Marylou Knapik for proofing the first seven chapters of the re-write. Thanks, Kathleen Saubrbrei for taking a peek, and making a suggestion that made me rethink the entire first page. Also, many thanks Michael Gonzales for your tremendous help on the introduction.

Gratitude to my long-time friend, Frank Ivan, for taking time from your gnarly schedule to beta read CHACO, for your astute observations, and great feedback. Your suggestions on the science sent me back to the heliophysics sites for additional research, which made the story so much better.

And…a bucket of gratitude to Gwen Gades with Dragon Moon Press, my publisher.

For the love of my life, my best friend, and my most ardent supporter, Steven D. Wheeler.

CHAPTER 1

Chaco Erhard Rodriquez hid with his maternal grandmother in a dense copse of white sapote trees. The old woman crouched on her heels, grabbed the boy's arm, pulled him to her, and whispered, "Get down, *mijo!*" Once Chaco dropped and curled into a ball, she concealed him with brush and dirt. Only a bit of his face poked through a halo of leaves. The old woman scooted close to her grandson, and best she could, she pulled additional shrubbery around them both.

When the soldiers approached so close they stood only three meters from their hiding place, the old woman put her forefinger to her lips, "Shhhhh." Grandmother and grandson watched as men torched the old woman's birthplace, the Pipil Indian village of Tunal, El Salvador.

Flames engulfed the village, and the sky filled with sepia clouds that turned the sun's color from brilliant yellow to dull bronze. The soldiers passed bottles of *Tick Táck*, laughed, talked, and occasionally shot or hacked to death the few villagers who had somehow managed to escape the initial massacre but dared run from their hiding places. The killing and burning continued until little remained of the village but the blackened skeleton of the church, and the charred bones of innocent people.

The smell of blood, mingling with the stench of scorched human flesh and burned buildings, so overwhelmed the little boy he held his hand over his mouth and retched into it. The boy did his best to be silent, but he could not help himself. One soldier squatting on his heels over a corpse, machete in hand, froze and turned to them. He stood, motioned to the other soldiers, and took a step toward the sapotes. He halted and tilted his head to listen. Chaco, vomit dripping from his chin and hand, buried his head into his grandmother's breast. The soldier took another step closer, and the boy dug his fingers into the folds of the old woman's shawl. Tears ran down his cheeks. *"Dios, mio, Dios, mio,* (Dear God, Dear God*),"* the boy prayed in silence. But when a lone Curassow lifted from the branches of the sapote with a cry and a rustle of feathers, the man turned back to his work of hacking the limbs off the body of a small girl, barely older than Chaco.

Eventually, the soldiers departed. The little boy and his grandmother remained in their hiding place until certain the murderers would not return. Their muscles ached, their throats closed with thirst, and ants bit into their skin. The moon rose high and higher still. Unable to hold it any longer, the boy urinated in his pants.

Chaco's grandmother, a half Pipil Indian, later told him she would never forgive herself for thinking it a grand idea to take him at such a tender age to meet his Indian relatives, especially during a known time of violence. "I am so sorry. So sorry. I promise to keep you safe forever, *mijo."*

Twenty-Eight Years Later, Southern California

Chaco handled the hedge clippers as though he'd been using them for decades. The shrubbery delineated the property between his employers, the Walkers, and their neighbors, the Pennymons. Leaves and blossoms rained down on the lush Walker lawn on one side, and the stiff AstroTurf on the other. The pale flowers settling into the grass like tiny moths reminded Chaco of ash flakes from that long-ago fire in Tunal, forever burning in his waking thoughts as well as his nightmares.

He clenched shut his eyes until the memory faded, then with renewed vigor Chaco returned to his task. Once finished, he inspected his handiwork, picked up a rake, and stepped over the line to extricate the debris littering the Pennymons' yard.

Rocky Pennymon charged out of his house in his tighty-whites, his bare stomach jiggling, and his eyes frantic with outrage. "What the hell you doin' here? This is *my* property."

Chaco hefted the rake for the man to inspect. "I'm removing waste from grooming the hedge, Mr. Pennymon. I'll be done in a moment."

"You're done now. I'd prefer not to have you people on my land. Nothing personal, but too many Americans out of work these days to have your kind takin' jobs."

Chaco set his jaw and gritted his teeth. "Excuse me?" He dropped his rake and stepped forward, fighting a powerful urge *to pound the goddamn ignorant white bastard into pupusa meat* even if it meant losing his job, or getting himself arrested, deported and executed. *It would be worth dying to kick this puto's fat ass.* Rocky's eyes widened. Chaco advanced another step, took a breath and willed his tension to ease. "I apologize for any inconvenience, Mr. Pennymon. With your permission, I'll get these leaves off your property, and I'll be gone."

Margo Pennymon, teetering on six-inch red stilettos, emerged from the double doors of her glass and steel monstrosity of a house. The fabric of her snug leopard print leggings crammed into her vulva revealed a distinct camel toe, and she'd applied her mascara with such a heavy hand it looked as though she had pasted tarantulas to her eyes.

Born and raised poor in a ratty little town near San Antonio, she spoke with a Texas twang so shrill it hurt Chaco's ears. "Git in the house, Rocky, put some clothes on fer gawdsake, and leave Chaco alone. Whaddaya think he's gonna do? Hold us up with that rake and steal yer new big screen TV?" She motioned toward the door with one hand as though batting a gnat. "Now, I mean it. Y'all get inside and eat yer tuna casserole before it cools off."

"Okay, enough. Shut up already. I'm coming." As Rocky retreated, Chaco marveled at the tangle of dark hair covering the hulk's back. *That aberrant dundo's mother fucked a bear, I'm sure of it. No full-blooded human could be that hairy. Qué feo. Ugly.*

That evening, Chaco opened a bottle of chilled Spätburgunder imported from the Reingau. Because of its hefty price, he rarely purchased this particular wine, but he kept a few bottles on hand for special occasions and emergencies. His late afternoon encounter with the truculent demon-beast, Rocky, qualified as an emergency.

He poured the pale liquid into a glass and headed to his small redwood deck. He removed the dust cover of his Takahashi telescope and aligned the finder, orienting it to the northern sky where light pollution would be least intrusive. He star-hopped, loosening, unlocking and locking the axis, turning magnification up and down, searching the skies.

Chaco would have stayed out longer, but when hunger gnawed at his stomach, he replaced the dust cap and went inside. He'd intended to make an early dinner, but first he flipped open his laptop and checked the helioscience sites once again. He signed onto a forum. The threads went on forever, the comments excited, and what he read delivered a kick to his gut.

"The Sun's going crazy," one scientist said. "Monster Class X flares look like they're headed right for us."

By the time Chaco completed his online search the clock on his desk read midnight, but Chaco had to talk to Dr. Javier Ruiz. Chaco's old mentor and former colleague had earned the reputation as one of the most venerated scientists at the National Center for Atmospheric Research in Boulder, Colorado.

The last time the two men spent time together had been years before at a convention they attended after visiting NASA's Solar Dynamics Observatory. Over tapas and wine, they enjoyed a lively discussion on the Quebec Blackout in March 1989 that occurred when a solar storm a third the size of the 1859 Carrington Event discharged a Coronal Mass Ejection (CME). The CME slammed into Earth, generating a powerful geomagnetic storm that damaged Montreal's electrical grid.

"If that happened today with as many satellites launched since then," Javier said, "we'd be screwed."

They discussed the solar storms that hit Earth after Quebec, and speculated over the many near misses. Javier refilled his tumbler from an earthenware pitcher of Gama Reserva Tempranillo. "We better drink up, *hermano,* because a monster X-class direct hit is not a matter of if, but when."

CHAPTER 2

Most white Americans in the town of Green Lake knew Chaco as "The Walkers' Mexican Gardener." But, before he'd fled his country to escape execution, and entered the U.S. to hide under cover as a simple handyman and gardener, he'd been known in El Salvador as *Professor* Rodriquez. Students and faculty at Universidad Tecnológica de El Salvador liked the young professor, although sometimes he got under the skin of the Administration, who urged him to be more scholarly and authoritarian, and less congenial with his students.

Chaco earned his PhD with the highest honors from the prestigious International Graduate School of Mathematics, Physics, and Astronomy, in Bonn, Germany, the hometown of his maternal grandfather, Rolf Erhard. When he returned home, he secured a position as the youngest professor ever hired in the history of the Salvadoran university.

Besides Spanish, Chaco spoke a smattering of Nawat, the Pipin language, fluent German and flawless English except for pronouncing his "Y" as "J," and his "J" as "Y." In this moment, Chaco only cared to speak in one language to one person. "I'm calling Javier. I *have* to know what's going on."

Chaco pushed the buttons on his cell.

Javier answered on the first ring. "Thought you might call."

"Sorry, it's so late."

"No problem. We're all awake."

"I've seen some big storms through my SolarMax over the last few mornings, and the heliophysics sites are busy. What's going on?"

"Massive events in active regions all over the solar surface. We've never seen anything like it."

"Which regions?"

"NASA Space Radiation Analysis Group reports Class-X storms on 12324, 12364, and others. These will make Carrington look like a picnic."

"They're going to slam right into us, aren't they?" Chaco's heart fluttered against his ribs. "What about our early warning system, 'The Buoy'?"

Javier paused. "We've lost contact with The Buoy, and the other satellites monitoring the Sun."

"What?"

"We think a flare took them out."

"And now?"

"Light a candle to the mother of Jesus, *mi amigo*. If God is with us, the storms will miss."

***

The next day proved uneventful, and the Sun's activity had calmed. *The storms had to have missed. Everyone overacted, that's all.* He'd planned to use his SolarMax to revisit the Sun's activity, but by the time he finished his daily chores, evening had fallen, and hunger set in. Chaco used a metal spatula to scrape crisp, fried *platanos* from a cast iron skillet onto a plate half-filled with steamed basmati rice. From his childhood in Soyapango, El Salvador, even over Abuela Erhard's *pupusas*, his favorite meal had always been *platanos fritos con arroz*. Back home, his family employed two maids, but his grandmother loved to cook and spent hours in the kitchen. Her doe-eyed grandson perched on a stool and watched her every move as she made *tamales de elote, sopa de pata, yuca frita*, and other fine delicacies. Before his tenth birthday, Chaco created traditional Salvadoran and Pipil dishes like a pro.

Right when he lifted his fork to take his first bite of the starchy fried fruit, the electricity cut out. "Damn. Where's that pinche flashlight?" He felt along the cool backsplash. When his hand made contact with the handle of the plastic light, he grabbed it, switched it on, and stepped out of his cottage into the summer night air.

Electrical outages were a common event. Chaco stretched and yawned. "Probably just another overload to the circuit." Although charming, the guest house he'd called home for over four years was almost a century old, and the electrical system had not been upgraded in many decades. The circuit breaker tripped occasionally, usually at the most inconvenient moment. He'd lost electricity several times when frying *platanos* on the old electric stove that sucked so much energy that sometimes all he need do is turn up the heat and, bam, no power.

Chaco went to the shed and flipped the circuit breaker switches. Nothing. The lights at the main house where his employers lived were also off, as were the lights of Green Lake's commercial district nestled in the valley below. He pressed the power button on his cell phone. Dead. "Please let it be a spent battery."

The southern California summer blessed the hills with balmy gardenia-scented breezes. Nevertheless, the hair stood on his arms and the nape of his neck, and his shoulder muscles seized. Chaco looked to the sky. A solitary shooting star arced beneath the Big Dipper and disappeared behind the San Padrino Mountains.

He swallowed a lump of panic, plaited his long black hair into a thick braid securing the end with a rubber band he kept on his wrist for that purpose and slogged through the wet lawn blanketing the acre between the cottage and main house. Chaco could not be certain if his reason for going to the Walkers was to see if they were all right, or because he simply needed to be around other people just now.

He found Abigail Walker in a dove-colored chenille robe, hair wrapped in a towel, padding barefoot over the flagstone patio. She carried a lit oil lamp in one hand. The flame cast a luminous glow over the wet stones. Two Waterford crystal champagne flutes and a half empty bottle of high-end Prosecco perched on a low table adjacent to the built-in hot tub. The Friday night ritual for the Walkers, going back to the beginning of their marriage thirty-eight years earlier, was to relax in their hot tub listening to Mozart or Sibelius, sharing a bottle of imported sparkling wine. Chaco never appeared unannounced at the Walkers, but his since cell phone had cut out, he had no choice. The presence of the older woman gave him comfort, and the tightness in his shoulders eased.

"Hello, Chaco. Looks like a town-wide blackout. Russ went to check the circuit breaker, and he's going to see if Rocky and Margo's power is off, too. This is all rather romantic, don't you think?"

"I came by in case you need anything, Mrs. Walker." He snapped off his flashlight and set it on a patio table.

"I don't know how many times I've invited you to call me Abby, but you still call me 'Mrs. Walker.' Why?" She put her hands on her hips and tilted her head to one side. "C'mon Chaco, you've lived here so long you're practically family."

"My mother taught me to be respectful. If I call you Abby her ghost will haunt me for the rest of my life."

"Okay, do whatever makes you comfortable. I don't require you to be so formal with me, though."

Chaco glanced skyward again. "If you and Mr. Walker need me, call out. I'm headed back to the cottage, but I'll hear you."

"We're fine, thanks. Personally, I find with the power off, the world is more magical, soft and mysterious. It's so quiet now, too, lovely. I imagine a hundred years ago the world was much like this at night, silent, and dark. Look at that magnificent sky."

Abigail set the oil lamp on a table and gazed into the moonless expanse. "Usually, there's so much light pollution you can't see even a fraction of those stars. Beautiful."

Chaco liked Abigail Walker. She treated him with respect, seeking his advice on gardening, demonstrating an authentic interest in Salvadoran culture, and she never pried into his past. He even taught her to make *pupusas* the way his grandmother made them with corn meal dough called *masa*, stuffed with shredded pork, cheese, and beans, fried and topped with Salvadoran style cabbage salad. Abuela Erhard would have been impressed by the ease in which this white American woman, this *chele*, took to *pupusa*-making. Abigail also made the effort to pick up a few phrases in passable Spanish, but what made Chaco like her the most is she talked to him as though he were her trusted friend rather than her handyman.

Pretty in an unexpected way, Abigail's russet colored hair streaked with silver hung below her shoulders. With eyes so blue they were nearly purple, and her pale, translucent skin, she could have been the subject of a Pre-Raphaelite painting. Chaco had seen photos of her when in her late-twenties, newly married to Russell, and others taken later when their daughter and son were toddlers. No surprise she'd been a beautiful woman back then. She carried maybe another twenty-five pounds on her frame than before giving birth to Fiona and Jude. She forever dieted, but Chaco thought she looked fine, particularly for a woman in her sixties. He liked women with soft, plump hips, thighs and breasts. Mirabella, his girlfriend back home, *may her precious soul rest in peace,* had been gorgeous. She could have starred in the *telenovelas*, the Latino soap operas, starring voluptuous women. But by U.S. standards, she would be considered overweight and unappealing. He never understood why American men preferred angular, bony *flacas* to fuller women.

Chaco picked up his light and switched it on for the walk back to his cabin. As he stepped off the patio and onto the lawn, Russell Walker, wearing a pair of leather slip-ons and a heavy dark blue robe, rounded the corner of the house bearing a flashlight. A man who had to stoop to get through most doors, with a lion's mane of white hair, Russell cut an imposing figure. To those who did not know him, he seemed tough, humorless, but like his wife, Chaco knew the older man as a kind and decent human being.

Although not as affable and warm as Abigail, Russell treated Chaco with respect too, and not only provided a furnished guest house and a nicely restored 1965 Ford pickup, he paid a good salary. In less than two years, Chaco saved enough to purchase top-of-the-line telescopes, a Takahashi Mewlong for night sky viewing, and the SolarMax Double Stack for observing solar activity. Chaco stepped back onto the patio. "Good evening, Mr. Walker."

"Good evening, Chaco. Some blackout we're having."

"Well?" Abigail asked her husband. "What did you find out?"

"Not the circuit breaker, that's for sure. Some drunken jerk probably ran into a major power pole." Russell pulled out a deck chair and plopped into it. "Rocky will be here in a bit. We're going to crank up the generators."

"Mr. Walker?"

"Yes, Chaco."

"I'd go easy on the generators."

"Why is that?"

"Depending on how long the electricity is out…. you won't be able to pump gas, that's all."

"I'll syphon from the cars if I need to."

"You might…well…I think the newer cars are full."

"What did Margo and Rocky have to say?" Abigail asked.

Chaco was grateful Russell had not asked him to go to their neighbors' home. Abigail had once told Chaco she felt sorry for Margo because severe endometriosis had left her uterus such a scarred mass of tissue that at age twenty-four she had to undergo a hysterectomy. Chaco didn't say so out of fear that Abigail would think him lacking in compassion, but he thought Margo's infertility a good thing. *People like that should not breed.* Tonight, right now especially, Chaco was in no mood to deal with the Pennymons.

Abigail lit a row of citronella Tiki torches and placed additional oil lamps on the glass top patio tables. "You still haven't told me, Russ. Did Rocky and Margo have any news on the blackout?" She picked up the bottle of now tepid Prosecco, poured a glass and handed it to her husband.

"They don't know anything." Russell took a sip of his drink, screwed up his face, and set the flute back on the table. "This stuff is vile when it's warm. Once the power is back on, we'll open a chilled bottle. Let's dump this one." He picked up the container and spilled the remaining contents onto a patch of grass. "Rocky said he'd planned to head down the hill to check things out, but when he turned the key in the ignition, the car wouldn't start so decided to have a beer instead, I guess."

"Sounds like Rocky. Did anyone think to call the power company?" Abigail asked.

"Sure did. While at their place, we tried several times to phone them. Odd thing, cell phones don't work either, not mine, not the Pennymons'. I tried yours, too, Abby. What about your phone, Chaco?"

Chaco shook his head—and that's all he could manage because his throat had clenched tight and he couldn't speak.

Russell stood, yawned, and carrying his flashlight, strolled to the edge of the patio. He flicked on the light and aimed the beam at the town beneath. "I only see lights in the supermarket and hospital. Probably running backup generators. Rocky did mention he'd heard an explosion down the hill seconds before the blackout. I'm thinking rather than someone hitting a pole, maybe because of all the air conditioners running full blast an overloaded transformer blew. I have no idea about what might have happened to the cell towers, though."

The Salvadoran blanched and dropped his flashlight. It clattered against the flagstones like rocks tumbling in a cement mixer.

"Are you okay, Chaco?"

"I'm fine Mrs. Walker. I must have…. I don't know why the

flashlight slipped from my hand. Sorry." He bent to retrieve the flashlight from the stones, his mouth dry as a tender box, his chest constricted. As he stood, he had to staunch an urge to vomit.

Days before he'd called Javier, Chaco observed through his SolarMax a frightening disturbance on the Sun, a colossal geomagnetic storm. The Sun's surface resembled a blazing wonderland covered with massive glowing plasma hoops that stretched out like gelatinous octopi tentacles looping back on themselves, enthralling and mesmerizing. The maelstrom released a series CMEs, each one, Chaco calculated to be larger by far than the 1859 Carrington Event that knocked out telegraph service for months over Alaska-sized swaths of North America and Europe. Chaco had hoped for the best, that the solar storm would bypass Earth, but after what he'd seen on the forums, and following his talk with Javier, he feared the worst.

Now, Chaco knew for certain what had happened. No. It wasn't a drunk jerk who had hit a power pole. No. Air conditioners had not caused a transformer to blow. Earth had taken direct CME hits, possibly the most powerful in recorded history. Life on Earth, as the Walkers, the Pennymons, and many others on the planet had known it, could be over.

CHAPTER 3

Chaco dragged himself home from the Walkers' and dropped into bed exhausted, but no matter how many times he changed positions or flipped his pillow, he couldn't get comfortable. He recited Pablo Neruda's *El Amor* by memory, counted backward from 500, and mentally replayed the hits and runs of his softball games as a boy in the streets of Soyapango.

He tried to remember Mirabella's face, her even white teeth, her delicate ears, her inquisitive black eyes. Chaco could not remember her smile, not exactly. His memories of her seeped into his thoughts like a vapor, then, poof, they disappeared. He recalled the dress, though. The last time he'd seen her, she'd worn a bright yellow sundress printed with ridiculous huge red poppies. When she walked, the dress rustled as though made of crepe paper. Yes, he liked that dress with the silly flowers very much.

Mostly, though, he thought of the woman he now loved, different from his Mirabella as any woman could be. How is it he had fallen so hard for this tall, leggy, robust American girl with light sea colored eyes that squinted shut when she laughed? What might she be doing right now in this dark world? Sleeping and dreaming of angels? Maybe she'd been awake turning in her bed thinking of him, too.

Chaco rose, ventured outside and considered the night sky. Great swaths of blue and green swirls lit the darkness, mesmerizing him. "The Aurora Borealis in southern California? Jesus." He watched for a long while, took dozens of photos with his cell, then out of habit, shut it off to conserve the battery. Exhausted, Chaco returned to bed. On his back, with his comforter pulled to his chin, he absorbed the absolute blackness of his cabin. He thought about what it would be like to be blind. "How could I live if I could never see the stars again?"

A few minutes before dawn, he gave up on sleep, climbed out of bed, poured water from plastic bottles into a basin, and washed his face. Chaco lit an oil lamp, retrieved the camp stove from its place under the sink, and made a pot of strong coffee. After pouring a cup, he stirred in one level teaspoon of raw sugar.

With full mug in hand, he stepped outside, removed the dust cap from his Coronado SolarMax, adjusted the aperture, and scanned the Sun's surface. He took a sip of coffee, cranked up the magnification to get a better view, and that's when he choked. Electro-magnetic pipes the size of Earth appeared as giant sunspots, releasing millions of tons of plasma. "Shit no. These are even larger than those I viewed a few days ago. I've got to talk to Javier again. Man, if these others hit, too, we are triple-screwed."

The solar disruptions Chaco observed were monsters, but without more sophisticated equipment, he couldn't be sure how large they really were. With the power out, he couldn't get on the helioscience sites. He reached for his copy of "The Sun, The Earth, and Near Earth Space Guide," but changed his mind. He needed to talk to Javier. He picked up his cell and had begun to key in the digits when he remembered *no service*.

***

The Pennymons, Walkers and Chaco gathered on the Walkers' patio, the atmosphere heavy and muggy. Although nearing 4 p.m., the outside temperature gauge registered 101 degrees. Without air conditioning, the covered patio by the pool seemed the only place to escape the punishing heat. Incredulous that Margo and Rocky were intent on finding a way to still host their annual "Cowboy Jamboree Brew and Bones Barbecue," Chaco's neck muscles constricted.

In their early forties, neither served any apparent purpose. The couple spent much of their time in five-star resorts on Galveston Island. They dined in chain steak restaurants at places called *The Texas Meat Cleaver* and *Big Hunter Steakhouse*, which to them, represented the epitome of haute cuisine. In the summer, they threw catered barbeques for which they ordered cases of Lone Star beer, brought in hay bales for seating, and hired Country Western bands dressed in corny outfits complete with felt cowboy hats and red bandanas.

Margo, wearing a peacock blue spandex dress so short that with each step she nearly flashed her privates, clip-clopped across the Walkers' patio in her snakeskin Prada heels. She plopped on one of the patio chairs, took a swig out of her longneck Bud, her hand wrapped around the amber bottle. As she crossed her legs, Chaco caught a glimpse of what might have been black lace panties. *Probably moscas, flies.*

"Fer the party this weekend, if the lights are still out, we kin start an old-fashioned bonfire, and we'll use lotsa oil lamps and Tiki lights. Would you mind if we borrowed yers, Abby?" She uncrossed her legs and moved forward. "Gawd knows how we'll keep the Lone Star cold, and a 'course, even though I got invites out nearly a month ago, with what's goin' on, I have no idea who might even show up. But, I'm thinkin' with all this darkness, a party is jist what folks need right now."

She took another long pull off her Bud. "We're gonna give everyone a hell of a fun time even if we have to drink our beer warm and have a sing-along for music. 'Sides, those ribs ain't gonna last long in the freezer with no electricity. Not much gas for the generator, either."

Rocky threw up his hands and looked to the sky as though pleading to an invisible superpower. "What about that freezer full of other meat we just spent a thousand dollars on? You're really planning a party while all that prime meat rots? Why don't you think about that?"

Margo gave a reassuring nod. "Don't you worry. If it looks like this thang is gonna last for a while, or we run outta fuel fer the generator, I'll put some of the other meat in salt and hang it in the wine cellar, and I kin fix jerky with the tri-tip, but the ribs…salted pork ribs ain't so good. We're havin' a barbeque, dammit." For emphasis, she slapped her bare knee. "It would be good fer everyone. Right, Abby?"

"I can't really think about a party now. I have no idea what's going on down the hill since we can't call. I don't know if Jude, Bethany and my granddaughters are all right. And, what if this is big and lasts a long while? There's no way we can check on Fiona and the boys up north. Aren't you concerned about your family, Margo?"

"Hell, no. Texas folks kin deal with anythin'. Yer son 'n daughter 'n their families are jist fine. They're probably makin' a camp-out of it. Any time now the lights will be on, and once everything is back to normal, they'll be talkin' 'bout what a fun few days they had. Honey, don't you worry."

Abigail paced, chewing her nails.

Chaco moved close to Abigail and whispered. "I'll go down and check on Jude, Mrs. Walker, and Fiona will be fine. Her community is off-grid and self-sustaining." Nonetheless, his shoulder muscles contracted with worry. *I must find a way to get to Fiona. Wish I could tell Abigail. She would be all right about us, might even bless us.*

Fiona's husband went crazy after she filed divorce papers. He looked for any reason to take their two boys. An affair with his mother-in-law's undocumented hired help would have—that is until the world's power shut down—not only guaranteed Chaco's deportation and certain execution, it would give the husband the necessary ammo to take Fiona's children from her. Even if the catastrophe might be less widespread than Chaco suspected, to protect Fiona, he thought it prudent to keep their relationship secret.

Chaco observed the activity down the hill through a pair of Zeiss binoculars. Things appeared quiet in the small town. The only incorporated "city," if you could call it a city, for the larger suburban area, Green Lake, was the County Seat. The courthouse and DMV were located there, as well as a decent medical center. Although because of the surrounding communities, Costco put in a smaller warehouse, besides a few grocery stores, churches, bars and chain restaurants, there wasn't much else around. The residential areas sat close together. Green Lake had one k-through eighth-grade school, and the district bussed the high school kids out of the area. Just outside of town, a small industrial area grew where apricot orchards had once been. The lake, a small reservoir in the only park, served as a rainwater catchment. The National Guard would deploy to the large population centers first. No help would arrive, not for a long time.

Other than a few pedestrians, and an occasional older car or motorcycle, little moved in the streets. Chaco knew what to expect. In a day or two, pandemonium. Soon, people will realize what's going on, and mass hysteria will take hold. No one can call 911. The power company can do nothing. It could be weeks or even months…no one is coming to the rescue. Chaco wiped his forehead with the bandana he kept in his back pocket.

Russell and Rocky huddled together in one corner of the patio sipping room temperature gin and tonics. The more they drank, the louder and more bellicose Rocky grew. "You can't trust him! You're a goddamn fool if you do. I'm telling you, that wetback is up to something."

"You're overreacting. I'm sure there's a rational explanation. Let's talk to Chaco and get this thing sorted out."

The two men approached the Salvadoran with their half-empty glasses in hand.

"We need to talk," Russell said. "Rocky says he saw you stockpiling food in the shed. What's up?" He took a drink of his cocktail.

Rocky sneered and his eyes morphed into malicious dark holes. "What were you doing at Russ's shed, boy?"

Chaco didn't know what galled him more, being addressed as 'boy' by a man only five years his senior, or the fact that an ignorant *hijo de puta,* not fit to lick dog crap off his feet, could be so impertinent.

"I don't know what you mean, Mr. Pennymon."

"You know exactly what I mean." Rocky thrust his jaw.

Chaco set the binoculars on the fence railing, and stretched as tall as his five-foot nine-inch frame could extend.

Rocky stepped closer and glowered at the smaller man. "I'll tell you what's up." Addressing Russell, his glare fixed on Chaco, "This Mexican of yours has been stealing food and supplies to send down to his family in Tee-Ah-Wana or Haw-Lee-Scoh, or he might be planning to sell it. You all do that to make a little extra cash, isn't that right?"

The tendons in Chaco's neck throbbed. He clenched his jaw until he thought he might crack his molars. "How would you know what I'm doing at the shed?"

"I've been keeping a close eye on you, believe me. And as soon as the phones are working again, the first thing I'm going to do is make a call to our local immigration authorities." Rocky jabbed his finger toward the smaller man's chest, and grinned, displaying a row of browned teeth. An imprint of a round can was visible in his shirt pocket. *Snuff. No wonder that miscreant's breath stinks.* Before yesterday, Rocky's threats to call inmigración mortified him. But today he felt only anxiety over Fiona and her two sons. If the CMEs and solar flares bombarding Earth were as powerful as he believed them to be, deportation would no longer remain a threat…the only upside to the world ending.

"Chaco, is it true you removed all the contents of the work shed to make room for storing food and other goods?" Russell asked.

"Yes, Mr. Walker, but it's not because I've stolen anything."

Rocky spoke through gritted teeth. "You lying little…" From

down the hill, a distant explosion caught his next words in his throat. He snapped his head toward town, and his jaws moved up and down like a big-mouthed bass hooked by an angler.

Chaco brought the binoculars to his eyes and adjusted them. "No, no, no." Smoke billowed from what appeared to be a bank or office building. From the entry way of the Costco where he'd gone after observing the first solar storm to purchase supplies as a precaution, a series of flashes appeared accompanied by the popping of gunfire.

"Gunshots!" Rocky said. "What the Hell is going on? Russ, you got any idea?"

"Not a clue." Russell extended his hand to Chaco. "Give me those binoculars. I want to take a look."

"Mr. Walker, we need to gather everyone together." Chaco handed the field glasses to the older man. "I've something important to discuss with all of you."

CHAPTER 4

"You're a Ph.D.?" Abigail asked Chaco. "I knew you were educated, intelligent, but I had no idea." She leaned forward in her patio chair, her eyes fixed on the Salvadoran. The warm evening breeze heated Chaco's skin, but Abigail pulled her sweater around herself as though to stave off a chill.

"You mean to tell me the handyman who lives in my guest cottage is a university professor?" Russell took a sip of water from a plastic bottle. "How in the hell did you end up here?" He stood and paced the flagstones.

"He's here because he's an illegal alien. You hired him without even checking his papers, didn't you?" Rocky grinned at Chaco. "He's running from something. He's bullshitting us, can't you tell?" He scanned the faces of the others. "I don't know what he's up to, but he's making this up, and I can't believe any of you are buying his crap."

"Oh, fer gawdsake, pipe down and let Chaco speak. Y'all aren't lettin' him get even one, single, solitary word in edgewise," said Margo.

"I'll answer all your questions in time," said Chaco. "But we have more important matters to discuss first. I'm afraid we are confronted by a dire situation. We need to formulate a plan, and if we're to survive, we must stick together.

"What do you mean we must stick together?" Rocky shook his head. "I don't have to 'stick' with anyone if I don't want to, least of all you." He stood his ground, his legs wide apart, feet firmly planted, arms crossed.

Chaco's back stiffened. *Ignorant hijo de puta.* He kept his voice low, steady. "This is what we are faced with. A few days ago, and again this morning, I observed a series of solar prominences so large they expanded way beyond my telescope's viewing capacity."

"What the hell's a 'solar prominence'?" asked Rocky.

"A giant eruption on the Sun's surface that releases superheated gas called plasma composed of electrically charged hydrogen and helium. These prominences are natural occurrences. Most are harmless, even beneficial in that they 'charge the Earth's batteries,' you might say. But what concerned me about the ones I observed—their size."

"So what?" Rocky asked.

"Even a small M-6 class eruption has been known to create severe electrical disturbances on Earth, such as the one that hit Canada in 1989 knocking out power to six million people in less than two minutes. If a large enough electrical particle wave resulting from a plasma surge, known as Coronal Mass Ejection, CME, as we call it, strikes Earth it can do quite a bit of damage. The prominences I observed were hundreds of times larger than an M-6 class CME."

"And you know about this how, exactly?" Rocky asked another question, then another.

Chaco put up his hand to halt the other man's string of inane questions. "If you give me a moment to explain…. I completed courses in heliophysics, and participated in postdoctoral fellowships over several summers in El Salvador and Colorado."

"What exactly is 'heliophysics'?"

"The science of the Sun-Earth connection, and it includes physical processes found in laboratories as well as in our solar system and the universe as a whole."

"What do these CMEs mean to us?" Russell ceased his pacing and scooted his chair across the flagstones closer to the verdigris wrought iron bench where Chaco sat.

"In 1859, two amateur astronomers in England, one named Richard Carrington, and another, Richard Hodgson, observed two bursts of light within a group of Sunspots that Carrington had been mapping. At the same time Carrington observed the flashes, a measuring device called a magnetometer located in London's Kew Observatory registered a wild disturbance. Carrington and Hodgson had witnessed a massive solar superstorm, the largest ever recorded. The storm launched tons of charged particles toward Earth, and when those electromagnetic waves collided with Earth's atmosphere, several strange things happened."

"Like what?" Rocky asked. "And when exactly do you get around to answering Russell's question about what all this claptrap has to do with us, that is if you can actually answer the question." The hairy man snorted, still standing legs apart, spine rigid.

Margo crossed her legs and bounced one high-heeled foot. She held her arms tight over her abundant breasts and threw her most withering look at her husband. He ignored her.

"Give me a moment. I'll get to that," Chaco said.

"You better get to it," Rocky said. "Right about now I'm beginning to wonder if you didn't make up all this baloney to avoid my calling Immigration once electricity is restored. I guarantee you, I will figure out what game you're playing, even if everyone else here has their head stuck in the sand."

"Rocky, we've all had enough of your attitude," Russell said. "Let the man tell us what he knows, or I'll have to ask you to leave."

"It's your house and your boy. You do what you want, but I'm done listening to this bullshit. I'm outta here. C'mon, Margo. Let's go."

"No, Rocky. You go right on ahead." Margo's foot ceased bouncing. "I ain't goin' nowhere. I'm stayin' here and listenin' to what Chaco has to say. You got the manners of a peckerwood, and I'm ashamed of how rude yer bein'. I'll come in and fix supper later." She unlocked her arms and motioned him away with both hands. "Go on, now."

"Suit yourself." The hulk of a man turned heel and stomped off toward his glass mansion.

"Please, Chaco, continue," Abigail said.

"When the magnetic wave of 1859, known as the Carrington Event, slammed into the planet, it knocked out power to telegraph lines over large areas of North America and Europe. Oddly, though, some stations disconnected their batteries and could resume operations using only geomagnetic power. Some telegraph operators even reported the signal as clearer than it had been with battery connection."

"Fascinating. I don't recall hearing about any of this."

"There have been many articles in scientific journals about solar flares and CMEs, and there is quite a bit of information available on-line and in print about historical solar disturbances, but if astrophysics or heliophysics are not topics you are fervent about, you probably would not have taken notice, Mrs. Walker. According to various articles, and other accounts I've studied, people reported seeing the Aurora Borealis as far south as Hawaii and Central America. In Colorado, campers observing the northern lights thought it morning and rose to make breakfast."

"What do northern lights have to do with them CME thangs you're talkin' about?" Margo asked.

"CMEs create the Northern Lights, Mrs. Pennymon. I saw them the other night."

Margo's jaw dropped. "You mean to tell me there was Northern Lights right over Green Lake? You shudda woke us up. I would like to see that."

"I got some good photos with my cell. I'll show them to you when cell service is restored. Besides, there may be more. You very well could still have a chance to view them yourself."

"If a CME that size hits Earth now…I mean," Russell said, "with our reliance on technology, electricity…I can't even imagine. What, exactly, *would* happen, Chaco? I'd think the results would be devastating."

"Until now, no observatory or solitary astronomer has recorded a solar storm nearly as large as the Carrington Event so it would be difficult to ascertain what a comparable impact would do. But you are correct. It's a certain bet the results would be catastrophic. Depending on where the CMEs hit, power grids and circuit boards with microelectronics could be destroyed throughout half or more of the planet. Hundreds of nuclear plants would run out of diesel fuel for their backup generators. The result would be mass nuclear meltdowns rendering vast plots of land uninhabitable for centuries." Chaco held up his hands and counted on his fingers. "Any vehicle with a computer chip will most likely not run. There would be no lights, no way to pump fuel, no potable water, no sewage disposal, no cell phones, no land lines, no computers, no satellites, no way to get prescription meds, no banking, no radio service, no police or fire services, no...you get the idea. Mr. Walker, I'm going to take the truck down the hill and see what's going on."

"I'd rather you not. If what you say is true, we've got to conserve fuel." Russell sat forward in his seat. "How long will it be before we can expect power?"

"If we received massive CMEs, some scientists speculate it could be years, even up to a decade, before full power might be restored. When the Carrington event occurred..." "My God!" Russell bolted out of his chair. "Is that what you saw, then? Solar storms as large as the Carrington Event?"

"No, Mr. Walker. I'm fairly certain each of the storms I observed were several times larger."

CHAPTER 5

"The violence is escalating fast. Looters and… damn it! People are killing one another." Chaco took the binoculars from his eyes and handed them to Russell. The Sun had set and the air had finally cooled, relieving the summer heat, but the increase in gunfire, the killings fueled by panic, and the blush from buildings on fire in the town below put the Salvadoran on edge. *It has only been a short while since the CMEs hit. How can civilization have broken down so completely?* He knew what would come next. "At least we don't have to confront a chupacabra, right?"

"What in the hell is that?" Russell asked.

"A supernatural blood-sucking beast. My grandmother told me the stories, and as a boy, those tales scared the crap out of me, and still do. The only real things that frighten me are venomous snakes and coyotes, but I'm embarrassed to admit there are things not real from those scary tales Abuela Erhard told me of flying ghosts searching to capture souls for the Devil, and the chupacabra, who leaves nothing of its victims' bodies but dry husks."

He did his best to shrug away all those fears, but often, when Chaco confronted real danger, or through his nightmares, they'd well up into his chest and throat from within his guts like toxic sludge. Throughout his life, whenever he found himself in a precarious situation he'd say, "At least I don't have to deal with coyotes, evil wraiths, vipers, or the chupacabra."

Chaco gestured for Russell to look through the glasses.

The older man squinted through the lenses, adjusting the viewfinders. He took the glasses away from his face, shook his head, and handed the binoculars to Abigail. "I've got to get to

Jude, Bethany and kids right away," he said. "I'm going to bring them up here to be with us. They aren't safe in Green Lake."

Abigail gasped. "What about those nuts with the guns?"

"I'll take side roads."

Without having looked through them, Abigail put the glasses on the bannister.

"I don't want to see what's going on down the hill right now. I just can't."

"That's understandable, Mrs. Walker. I know how worried you must be about your family." Chaco stuck his hands in his pockets and leaned back on his heels. "Mr. Walker, may I make a suggestion?"

"Sure."

"You'd have a much better chance of getting through late at night. Plan on leaving when everyone is asleep and I'll go with you. The two of us can get Jude, Bethany and the kids out safely." He lifted the binoculars, put them to his eyes, and adjusted the viewfinders. "Right now, while the rioters are in such a panic, they may not even realize who they are shooting at. It's far too dangerous."

"I know you mean well, but I'm not letting my son and his family stay down there one more hour if I can do anything about it. I don't even know if they have food or water…we're sitting up here sipping gin and tonics…who knows what's happening to them!"

"I'm not suggesting you leave them there, sir. But you cannot help them if you are injured or killed attempting to rescue them."

Abigail put her hand on her husband's arm. "Chaco's right, Russell. I couldn't bear it if…please, wait until later."

Russell drew his eyebrows together. "I don't know, Abby. I can't stand by and do nothing."

"No one is expecting you to 'do nothing', Russ. But Chaco brought up a good point. For everyone's sake, we must consider your safety. We need you alive and kicking so we can help our son, and afterward, I need you to get to Fiona and the boys and bring them here. Please."

Chaco took a step closer to the older man. "Mr. Walker, have you eaten anything at all today? You could get some food, lie down for a bit, and after, we'll head down together."

"I couldn't possibly eat anything right now, Chaco, but… maybe a little sleep…I'll take a short nap. Abby, wake me in an hour." Russell looked at his tired wife, her face drawn with worry and exhaustion. "Better, yet, let's both take a short snooze. I can set the manual alarm." He put the back of his hand to his mouth stifling a second yawn. "Chaco, I'll meet you back here at, say, midnight, and we'll get this done. Thanks for offering to help. It means a lot to both of us."

Abigail put her arms around her husband and smiled at him. He stroked her forehead, brushing a stray piece of hair from her eyes. "Chaco and I will bring Jude, Bethany, and the kids back to you. I promise we will. And, Fiona and the boys, too. We'll all be together soon. Count on it."

"I never doubt you." Although still pretty, to Chaco in the few days, she'd aged ten years.

The Walkers clasped hands, leaned against one another; and walked in slow steps across the patio to their home. The moment they closed the door, Chaco sprinted for the garage. With a massive CME, Chaco knew only three cars on the hill would work, the old Ford pickup, the Walkers' 1957 Chevy Belair, and the Pennymons' 1954 Lincoln Capri. The CME would have knocked out onboard computers and electronic starters, so the late model Mercedes and Lamborghini sitting in the garages would not run.

From Chaco's perspective, the Pennymons and Walkers had only four things in common. They were white, they were wealthy, they lived adjacent to one another, and they loved cars. Chaco concerned himself now with only the last commonality, and he didn't want anyone following him to town.

He popped the hood on the Chevy, removed the distributor cap and pulled the rotor. He crept across the lawn to the Pennymons' Astroturf, careful to keep a low profile, flashlight in hand but switched off, on guard for Rocky. *I'm sure that loco maje has guns. That son of a bear fucker will shoot me then tell everyone he thought me a prowler, pendejo.* Chaco pressed against the Pennymons' house hoping in the dark they would not see his figure against the glass. He slipped around back and tried their garage door. Locked.

The Pennymons' sliding back door opened. Chaco ducked behind a wall of bushy buddleias dense with foliage and blossoms, and held his breath.

"Fer gawdsake, Rocky. Yer acting like a damn fool. I don't know what you've got yer panties in a wad over, but I'm tellin' ya, Chaco knows what he's talkin' about. You weren't there to hear ever-thang. I were, though. So, don't go tellin' me he's full a' shit when it's *you* that's full a' shit."

"Why would you take that little wetback's side? Do you have any idea of how that makes me feel? Well, do you? Never mind…of course you don't."

"Jesus Hallelujah Christ. I ain't takin' no one's side. I jist know when someone is tellin' the truth, and Chaco ain't lyin'! Why would he? Rocky, you know I stand by you, I luv you, honey, but you simply gotta stop this hatin' and start thinkin'. I don't understand why you've got it in for this boy, but he ain't done nuthin' to you. Nuthin'. And, he ain't got no reason to lie about a thang like this. Now, I'm goin' in, are ya comin'?"

He turned his head away from her. "I'm not ready yet. I think I'll stay out here for a while."

"And do what outside here in the dark all by yerself? Pout? Besides, yer wastin' good flashlight batteries. C'mon in and we'll play checkers or somethin'."

Chaco took a small step back and, *crack*, he snapped a dead twig with his heel.

"What the hell?" Rocky said, and wheeled around to aim the beam of his Maglite at the buddleia. "Whoever's there, come on out!" He moved toward Chaco, who crouched low, held his breath, and crossed his fingers. *Please.*

Rocky came within a few feet of Chaco's hiding place, and advanced another step.

"Ya know we got tons of coyotes, rabbits, and feral cats around here, Rocky. It's nuthin'. Yer bein' plain silly."

"Yeah, probably a rabbit. Let's go in."

As the big man's footsteps receded, Chaco's heart rate slowed to normal. The second the Pennymons disappeared into the house, he released a rush of air from his lungs. He stooped low, crept out from behind the bush, and mounted a frantic search for something to pick the garage door lock with. No luck. He had an hour, tops, before Russell awoke. He crept back to the Walkers' property line. Once safe, he ran full speed for his cottage to look for a tool to break into the garage.

***

Five minutes and the Walkers will be expecting me. Jesus Cristo! Chaco had returned from his mission to the Pennymon's garage just in time and dumped the rotors into an empty coffee can. He stuffed a backpack with his coat, a .38 and a box of ammo that he'd taken from Russ' gun safe in the garage when he realized a direct CME hit could be a real possibility. Relieved Russell had trusted him enough to give him a key to the safe "in case of emergency," Chaco reached into the pack and felt the cold barrel of the gun and nestled it further into the material of his coat. He also dropped in his binoculars, a hunting knife, and wedged in a few bottles of water. On the way out the door, he grabbed his flashlight and raced for the Ford.

As he peeled out of the driveway about to drive passed the Walkers' house, Russell called out. "Stop! Where are you going?"

Chaco slowed the truck and rolled down the window a crack. "Don't worry, Mr. Walker. I'll bring your family to you, and I promise to keep them safe."

"No! No! I'm going with you." The older man approached the passenger side of the truck.

"I'm sorry, Mr. Walker, but you aren't coming. I'll bring your son and his family here as soon as I can." He gunned the engine and started down the hill. In the rearview mirror, Chaco watched Russell run behind the truck, struggling to catch up. The beam from his flashlight bounced off trees and boulders in a frenetic pattern. As Chaco came to a turn, he braked and glanced back at the older man caught in the red glow of his rear lights and the illumination of the waxing moon. The older man leaned against a tree, his eyes cast upwards, gasping for breath. Chaco's heart hurt for Russell. *Sorry, amigo.* He depressed the gas pedal and made the turn toward Green Lake.

Certain Russell no longer followed, Chaco pulled over to the side of the road to gather his thoughts and formulate a plan. All he could think about was Fiona.

He'd met her a year earlier when, after a nasty row with her soon-to-be ex-husband, she had come alone to visit her mother. She'd left her boys in the care of a trusted friend at the commune, Moonforest Sanctuary, where she'd lived for the past eight years. Abigail had asked Chaco to pick up her daughter at the airport.

Chaco waited outside of the baggage claim area. He parked the car and stood near the exit holding a sign, *Fiona MacDougal.* When a tall pretty hippie-looking girl approached him, Chaco didn't know what to think. He thought she might be a panhandler. She wore torn blue jeans, a gauzy white top with Guatemalan embroidery on the sleeves, and a pair of ratty brown Birkenstocks. Her sand colored hair hung longer than his, but like Chaco's, she wore it plaited into a thick braid. She carried only a cheap, worn backpack. Fiona hardly resembled the photo hanging on the wall of the Walkers' den with her hair pulled into a severe bun, wearing red lipstick, and a prim navy blue skirt with sensible black pumps. She appeared younger than he'd expected, almost childlike. Hard to believe her a married woman with two children. Before she spoke one word, he noticed her eyes. Not green, not blue, but the color of the Caribbean ocean. Lovely. And, then she smiled, and in that instant, she had him.

"I'm Chaco Rodriguez."

"I'm Fiona. Nice to meet you." She extended her hand, and as soon as he touched her, he knew with certainty he was utterly screwed. He'd not been in love, nor wanted to be, since his fiancé Mirabella had been lost to him. But Chaco fell in love, or something like love. At the very least he felt overwhelming attraction, and there wasn't a damn thing he could do about it.

"Where's your luggage?"

"This is it." She handed her pack to him. "I never travel with more than I need."

Chaco could not recall what they discussed on the drive to Russell and Abigail's home. That evening, after dropping her off at the Walkers', he went home and fried *platanos*. He took one bite and pushed the plate away. He poured a glass of wine and picked up *The Feynman Lectures on Physics, Volume 2*, read a few paragraphs, closed the book and stepped out onto his deck. He settled on some mindless star gazing, anything to keep his thoughts off Fiona. As he focused in on the rings of Saturn, he felt someone near him, and when he turned, there she stood.

"I don't mean to bother you, but my parents are sleeping, and I'm not quite ready to go to bed. I decided to take a walk around the property and thought I'd see if…well…I saw you here at your telescope. Do you mind if I look?"

"Please do." Chaco helped her adjust the viewfinder and showed her Venus, then he'd focus on the scope on another celestial body, and moved over to allow Fiona to step up closer to the telescope. "Can you see all right?"

"Yes, thank you. The sky is spectacular. I never expected there would be so much color."

In this way, together they jumped from star to star.

"Would you care for a glass of wine?" he asked her.

"I wouldn't say no." She smiled again and melted him.

He produced an unopened bottle, a decent Pinot Noir, and two juice glasses. They sat on a wooden bench talking until dawn. She told him of her love of the mountains, her studies in herbology, her failed marriage, and how the first divorce attorney she hired turned out to be a snake in a suit. Fiona spoke of her sons, her friends, how she'd fled a soul-eating corporate job to find herself living in an idyllic commune.

He hardly knew this woman, but somehow felt with her he could release all his contained caution, so when she asked about his life in El Salvador, he decided to tell her his story.

"You were a rebel fighter?"

"Yes. El Salvador has a bloody and violent history and is still among the ten most violent countries in the world. In 2009, when the Frente Farabundo Martí para la Libaracíon Nacional won the presidential election, things became somewhat calm. Life was good. I had a cushy teaching position at a prestigious university in El Salvador. I was young, about to be married to a beautiful woman, my sweet Mirabella. Then the coup happened, and everything changed overnight. When the soldiers arrested my colleagues, executed some, tortured and jailed others, I joined the resistance. I proved to be a good tactician, and a crack shot with both a rifle and a pistol, so General Jimenez promoted me to Commander."

"So how did you end up here?"

Chaco sipped his wine. "You won't like what I tell you."

"Please." She put her hand on his thigh, and right then he would gladly give up his secrets to her, all of them.

"I killed many men, and even some women and children, Fiona."

"You were at war for your cause, for your people. It's a terrible thing, I know, but…"

"In my country, I am a wanted criminal, a murderer."

He told her of the bombings he'd ordered, the people he'd shot. He told her that after he'd killed many opposing troops and a few politicos, his face became a common sight on the television news programs, on posters, and billboards. He told her of the $100,000 bounty on his head. "In a country as poor as El Salvador, most people would sell their grandmother for $500."

Fiona shook her head. "What you've been through…"

"They arrested my parents. Confiscated their property, and their money, but when the bastards executed them in cold blood, I was intent on revenge. Killing General Pablo Juarez, the leader of the opposition, the man who had ordered my parents' arrest, became my obsession. I didn't care about anything or anyone else. My spies observed his movements for weeks, and once I memorized his routine, I ordered a bomb planted in his car."

He looked into the sky then back to Fiona. "I watched through binoculars as his driver opened the car door to admit the general. I watched his driver circle the limo, enter and close the door. Then I watched as the car blew into a million pieces. Fire, smoke, metal shards everywhere. People screaming in the streets. Chaos. Exactly what I'd hoped for. What I didn't see through my binoculars is the general's wife, his two small children, little girls, five-years-old and 18-months-old, along with their 19-year-old nanny also in the limo."

"Oh, Chaco." She covered her mouth with her hand to muffle a gasp.

"I had no idea they were there. It expected the general and his driver, no one else. What's worse, although the general lost a leg, and suffered third-degree burns, through some twisted miracle, he ended up the sole survivor. The country hailed him as a hero. Rather than assassinating him, and ending his regime, ironically, I furthered his cause."

Chaco bowed his head, and let tears spill. For the first time since he'd left El Salvador more than five years earlier, he wailed like an infant in front of this *chele* who he'd only met a few hours before. It all came out. She put her arm around him and he wept harder. He recovered from his crying jag enough to talk. "The bounty on my head went so high after that, I knew I had to leave El Salvador. My grandmother, my *abuela*, gave me a sizable bundle of paper money she had stashed, and all her gold jewelry. 'Get out of the country now, *nieto*, my grandson. Stay safe and live well. Remember always, I love you.' Those were the last words she ever spoke to me. She handed me a bag with some sandwiches, a bottle of orange juice, and kissed me good-bye."

"How did you manage to make your way to the United States?"

"It took me weeks to get to the North on foot, sticking to side roads, walking through the countryside. I had more than one close call, narrowly avoiding capture on several occasions. I travelled only at night, sleeping out in the open in dangerous country by day, eating very little. When I finally arrived in Tijuana, I paid one of those people who take people over the border for a price, a 'coyote,' $20,000 and all the gold I had in my pack to smuggle me across. I arrived in the Land of the Free with less than $68 in my pocket, a small bundle of personal belongings, and the clothes on my back."

"Why didn't you ask for political asylum?"

Chaco wiped his sleeve across his eyes. "I'm wanted in El Salvador as a child killer, Fiona, but beyond that, the American government backs the Juarez regime, which now controls El Salvador. If caught, I will be arrested, deported, and executed the moment I step off the plane. The United States will never grant asylum."

"What happened to Mirabella and your grandmother?"

"Until he disappeared I had one trusted friend left in El Salvador, a professor of mathematics at the University, who had gone into hiding. He sent correspondence to me at a P.O. Box. We never texted, phoned or e-mailed. Too easy to trace between the U.S. and El Salvador. Through him I learned the soldiers tortured my grandmother to death. She never gave me up, never, not even when the soldiers burned holes into her back with their cigars." He told her about the massacre at Tunal, and how his abuela had blamed herself. "It was not her fault. God rest her precious soul. She didn't do anything wrong. She saved me when I was a child, and again when the soldiers... what they did to her because of me...and...Mirabella...arrested, gang raped, her legs broken. She died in the worst, most filthy rat hole of a jail in all of Central America." He gazed once again into the darkness of the sky and bit his lip.

"While I remained safe, my family, my friends, and the woman I loved died because of me. I will live forever knowing I killed innocents, that I issued an order resulting in the deaths of a guiltless woman, a teenage girl, two babies, my family, and Mirabella. I lost everyone I loved as a consequence of my behaviors, my stupidity, and there is not punishment enough for what I did. If there is a God, he will send me to Hell."

"Don't say that, Chaco. What happened—a horrible, tragic accident, but you certainly didn't intend to hurt those innocents."

"I will never feel good about the choices I made, Fiona. I can never forgive myself."

"You have gone through so much. I hope one day you can put this behind you, Chaco, and be happy again." She squeezed his shoulder. "How did you end up working for my father?"

He told her about how after strawberry picking season had ended, he and several other men who he'd worked with in the fields, including his good friend, Alberto, made their way inland to Green Lake. Russell hired a few of the men to work around the property, but kept Chaco on, not only because he proved an excellent worker, but because of his fluency in

English. Russell never asked for a green card, never questioned Chaco about his past. "Your parents have been good to me, and I'm grateful to them."

"They are good people, and you are a good man, too, Chaco."

That's when he kissed her the first time. They contrived ways to see one another afterward. She came down for visits every six or seven weeks on the pretext she had to escape the stress of her pending divorce. He asked to accompany the Walkers when they visited their daughter at the commune to "help in the orchards." The last time he'd seen her had been several weeks earlier when she'd come to visit. She'd met him at his cabin after the Walkers retired for the evening, and they made love all night. Between their infrequent visits, they texted, wrote long old-fashioned love letters by hand, hers always scented with lavender, called each other late at night and talked for hours. Once she had her final divorce papers in hand, they would make their relationship public, and he would ask her to marry him.

Chaco broke from his reverie. *Must find Jude and his family, then get to Fiona if I have to walk the entire way to her in my bare feet.* He turned the ignition, eased out onto the road. As he rounded the next corner, he encountered a roadblock.

CHAPTER 6

Three men stood in front of a pile of rubble blocking the compacted dirt road into town. All appeared to be in their late thirties to early forties. Chaco studied their faces and their positions.

The thin one with a black beard wore a pair of dirty jeans and a stained t-shirt. He aimed a Remington 798 at Chaco's face. Another, a heavy-set blond with a gut hanging at least eight inches over his belt buckle, aimed an AR-15. The third, a bald man with a pink baby face appeared unarmed except for a fixed blade survival knife stuck in a sheath strapped to one leg. Baldy directed the beam of an enormous yellow flashlight into the cab of the truck and motioned for Chaco to roll down the window. Chaco complied.

"Where you comin' from?" Baldy said.

Chaco smiled and spoke in his best Northern Mexican broken accent, hoping the men would believe his English poor. "Yust up the heel."

"Oh yeah? Whereabouts?"

"I leeb in a shack next to a beeg empty house."

"How many houses up there?"

"Maybeee four." Chaco shrugged.

"Four?"

"Jes, Señor, *Quatro.* I theenk. All emptee a long time, maybee for sale or son…thing. Emptee."

"Where you headed?" Baldy spat a glob of mucous that clung like a lump of greenish gelatin to the truck's side mirror.

"*No entiendo,* Señor. My English not so good."

"I said, WHERE…ARE…YOU…GOING?"

Why do ignorant fuckhead Americans think if they yell they can be better understood? "To find my cousin, Arturo.

Maybeee heez got son food. I'm beery hungree."

"Well, let me tell you what we are going to do, Beaner. You get on out of the truck. We are going to take it, along with anything you got in there. You can walk down the hill to find your fucking cousin. Understand? Nod to let me know you understand."

Chaco nodded.

"Good boy. We are going up the hill to check out these 'emptee' houses. If you're lyin' to us, we will find you and shoot your brown ass. How's that sound?"

"*Repetir, por favor.* I no understand." Chaco shook his head.

"GET...OUT...OF...THE...CAR."

"Okay, Señor. Whatever jew say."

"Now."

Chaco hesitated long enough to assess the men's positions. Two in front with their weapons, and one without a gun adjacent to the door. Easy.

Baldy turned to Fatty. "Shoot him."

"No, no, no, I'm comin' out now, Señor." Chaco eased open the door. "Don't shoot, pleez. I gotta wife an' five kids in Tijuana." He put his hands in the air. "I yust only want to find my cousin and go home, pleez, señor."

"Step away from the truck and get over there." Baldy motioned to the side of the road with his flashlight. "Take off your shoes and your jacket." The bald man paused for a second. "Your pants, too."

"¿Mis pantalones?"

Skinny snickered. "Hell, make the beaner strip completely. Let's see how long a naked Mexican running around town in the dark lasts."

"Yeah, do it." Baldy grinned. "Take off everything, you little brown bastard."

Chaco moved toward the roadside. *No sudden movements.* As he bent over as though to untie his shoes, Fatty let out a guffaw. He would never make another sound. In a quick, smooth movement, Chaco pulled his concealed .38 and shot him through the forehead. Skinny set his Remington against his shoulder. Chaco pivoted and shot him through the chest. Baldy peed himself as he dropped his flashlight, but before the bald man regained his senses enough to pull his knife, Chaco shot him through the heart.

Chaco inspected the fallen. Skinny was the only one breathing. Chaco dispatched him with a bullet through the eye. He gathered their weapons, removed Baldy's knife from its sheath, picked up the dead man's flashlight and flipped it off. He dragged the corpses to the side of the road, leaving wide blood swaths in the dirt.

He stowed the captured weapons in the cab of the Ford and searched for the men's vehicle. Chaco found their battered old truck a short distance behind the roadblock. The doors were unlocked, but the key—not in the ignition. *Damn.* Chaco rifled through the cab and found four unopened bottles of water. He opened one and took a long pull. On the passenger's side, he found a six pack of Budweiser, one can missing, a jean jacket with a Leatherman in one pocket, a jar of partially eaten peanuts on the floorboard, and two unopened Hershey bars. In the bed of the truck were three sleeping bags, a tarp, and a packet of bungees, but the greatest treasure: a hose and a gas can for siphoning. He loaded the goods into the Ford, he returned to the older truck and siphoned its fuel.

After hoisting the full gas can into the cab of his truck, he searched the dead men's shirts and front pant pockets. Nothing. Chaco rolled the men over one at a time. In Baldy's back pocket, he found a set of keys and a brown leather wallet. He tucked the keys into his shirt in case he may later want to take the truck, and flipped open the wallet. Inside, he found a driver's license. William Davis. He rifled through the contents. Besides the driver's license, there were credit cards, a Blue Cross insurance ID, and a few wrinkled dollars. *Useless.*

As he drew back his hand to toss the wallet, a photo slipped out and landed at his feet. In front of a lit fireplace stood William Davis dressed in a pale blue suit, his arm around a sweet looking woman. Kneeling in front were two little boys. One might have been seven, two front teeth missing, the other a year or so older. Chaco sighed, tucked the photo into William Davis' palm, closed the dead man's fingers around it, and gave the hand a tender pat. *Vaya con Dios. Go with God.*

CHAPTER 7

Chaco kept watch for escape routes off the road to avoid encountering another block. He drove with his lights off, creeping along the road to muffle the noise of the engine, and to staunch dirt clouds. He glanced at his watch. One ten a.m. He planned to find Jude, Bethany, and the girls, then detour to Alberto and his family, scoop everyone into the truck, and make it back to the Walkers before daybreak.

Less than a mile from town, a volley of gunshots assaulted him, and his side view mirror shattered. He spied an opening between the trees, jerked the wheel, switched on his lights and gunned it. The Ford bucked and jostled down the steep hillside. Chaco wrestled the wheel first one way and the other to avoid boulders and trees, gunshots popping from behind. His tires kicked up rocks and the truck lurched forward as he ran over a tree limb.

When the gunfire ceased, Chaco rolled to a stop, shut off the engine, and stepped outside. He filled his lungs with the crisp air, grabbed one of the bottles of water from the cab and took a swig. His hand shook so hard that some of the water dribbled down his chin. He wiped it with his sleeve, then fished his binoculars from his backpack.

He searched the sky, got his bearings from the location of the stars, and sought out Green Lake. Chaco had to get to Jude's family. No time to waste. He glanced at his watch, climbed back into his truck and eased along a level hiking path abutting the river, one set of wheels on the path, the other in the brush to the side. Time crawled like an ant with a broken leg. It took forever to reach the main highway into town.

Abandoned cars and trash littered the road. One nude male corpse, missing a face, lay twisted in a gutter. The body looked as though someone had fashioned it from wax.

A scruffy man in a torn t-shirt and jeans sat on the hood of a car, dangling his bare feet over the side. He threw back his head and upended a bottle of spirits into this mouth. The man drank in profound gulps, spilling liquor down his chin, drenching his shirt and jeans. "There's monsters around here," he said to Chaco. "Yeah, yeah, I know. I'm drunk. But, I've seen 'em. Monsters everywhere. They're even killing children." He threw back his head and laughed, then sucked on the hooch like a hungry infant at his mother's breast.

People crowded together in darkened doorways. Their expressionless eyes followed Chaco. Their facial features were indistinguishable, pale and androgynous. Tucked into the shadows, their forms were barely visible. Each of these tortured phantoms appeared stripped of even the faintest trace of humanity. The man swilling the hooch might have been the most human of them all.

Chaco turned into an alley, slow, easy, then made a right onto the street where Jude lived and pulled into the driveway. He didn't know Jude or his family well. He'd seen them a few times at the Walkers' and had been to their home to make deliveries. Like his father, the younger Mr. Walker stood an imposing man. But his wife, Bethany, with her delicate frame, curly light brown hair, and turned up nose was built like a little, bony, mouse. Their girls were no more than tiny birds.

Jude and his family were fastidious, neat, and their front yard usually looked like an image on a gardening magazine cover. Not tonight. Blossoms and slender branches scattered across the ruined lawn like fragile bones and pale pink bruises. Someone had beheaded and disemboweled the peonies, hibiscus, and azaleas. The beds of pansies were trampled. Garbage spread across the lawn, and someone had stripped bare the old growth peach tree in front, which had been laden with fruit. Whoever had done that had taken an ax to the limbs and hacked away in a herky-jerky fashion to get to the fruit at the top, or to cut branches for firewood, leaving a mangled scarecrow in place of a lovely tree that for years had gifted humans and wildlife with its shade and fruit. A dead tabby was on the ruined lawn, eyes open. Rigor mortis had already set in.

Looters had smashed the main door, along with the windows at the front of the house. Chaco grabbed his flashlight and exited the truck. He pocketed some rounds and drew his .38. He crept along the side, flashlight off until he reached the side gate. Usually, when Chaco lifted the latch, Rufus, the pit bull mix, bounded to him, tail wagging. This time, no Rufus.

The sliding glass door into the dining room gaped open. Chaco moved in cautious steps, his finger on the trigger of his gun. Looters had turned the kitchen inside out, ripped doors off cupboards, strewn pots, pans, and utensils across the floor. Someone had dropped an opened bag of flour, leaving fine white powder spread over the tile. Footprints tracked flour into the remaining rooms of the house. The pantry door stood ajar, and except a single dented tin of garbanzo beans on the lower shelf that a looter had most likely left by mistake, Chaco could not find a single food can, jar, or bag.

Except for some furniture, bedrooms were nearly empty, clothes thrown haphazardly across the floor, bedding gone, every room of the house tossed.

Jude worked as an accountant for a high-security manufacturing plant on the edge of town. Chaco guessed he might find the family there hunkered down behind high brick walls. Chaco grabbed the garbanzo beans, picked his way through the rubble, climbed back into the truck. As he backed out of the driveway, *bam*! Something cracked hard against his passenger side windshield. He grabbed his .38.

As he raised a tire a tire iron over his head to deliver a second blow, the man screeched at Chaco like a wild animal. "Get out of your truck, or I'm going to kill you!" The man grimaced and brought the tire iron down on the windshield, but before it made contact, Chaco pulled the trigger. The bullet passed through the window, spraying the hood with beads of glass, and struck the crazed idiot mid-chest. The man grunted, dropped the tire iron and slumped over the hood of the truck. Chaco stomped on the gas pedal and the truck peeled out of the driveway. The corpse slid off the hood and collapsed onto the concrete.

A woman let out a shrill scream. "You shot my husband! You bastard. You killed him!" Chaco didn't bother to look or slow down. He jammed the truck into gear and sped away.

Chaco skirted the town driving through parks, jostled over golf courses, speeding down narrow alleys, until he reached the factory a few miles away from the panic. The fires from downtown cast a malevolent glow, the eeriness punctuated by an occasional volley of gunshots, and now and again, a pitiful cry. A surrealistic demonic presence had claimed the peaceful and bucolic small city of Green Lake. Chaco could not fathom that only a few days before, women enjoyed their weekly facials and pedicures in the local spa, boys played baseball in the park, teenagers in baggy pants raced down the streets on skateboards. *By now, the panic-stricken population knows for certain there is no rescue. No hope.*

Silence shrouded the industrial park. Apart from a possum with glowing yellow eyes scuttling across the street, there were no signs of life. Now and again, a shadowy figure darted between the buildings. Dog? Coyote? Chupacabra? A chill took hold of Chaco's gut. He parked, turned off the engine, went for his flashlight and the .38. He approached the gate and tried the latch. Locked. He walked the perimeter calling, "Jude, it's me, Chaco. Are you there?" No response. He called again, "Bethany, Jude, I'm here to take you and the girls up the hill. Answer me. Are you inside?" No response. He whistled, and whistled again. Then a sharp bark followed by another. Rufus!

From a second story window, Jude shouted. "Chaco, come around front! Quick!"

Chaco sprinted to the massive front door. The latch clicked, and Jude, his hair, and collar of his polo shirt drenched with sweat, stuck his head outside and looked one way then the other. "Get in here."

Once inside, Jude slammed the door and bolted it. "My God, how'd you find us? Where're my parents? Are they all right? Jesus, Chaco, what are you doing here? Why hasn't help arrived? Where's the National Guard? The sheriff?"

"Your dad sent me to get you. Everyone is fine, and they are waiting for you. I'm afraid to tell you I'm the only help coming. There is no National Guard, at least probably not for a long while. I'll explain later, but right now we have to get Bethany and the kids, and go."

Bethany, in a sundress, ripped at the shoulder, her curls matted, ran from behind a wall clutching her purse to her chest, her two little girls in dirty pajamas and mismatched flip-flops close behind. "Thank goodness, Chaco. I'm so glad to see you. They were going to kill us. We barely had time to get out of the house. What's going on? I don't hear sirens. Where's the police?"

"It's all right. I'm going to get you to safety, but we have to go now."

Chaco brushed broken glass from the seat, and Bethany and the girls piled into the front. Jude climbed in the truck bed, and Rufus hopped in with him. Chaco handed Jude a bottle of water and the AR-15. "I hope you know how to use this."

"Two tours in Iraq. I've got it covered." He checked over the AR-15, stroking the barrel like he might pet a cat, grinned and nodded his head. For a moment, Chaco thought the weapon held some secret transformative ability. Jude, the rational accountant, morphed into Jude the possessed.

"Stay low. If anything goes wrong, don't negotiate. Pull the trigger, you can't hesitate to…"

"…don't worry, buddy." Jude grinned, his eyes glassy and bright.

"We're going to make a stop out of town to pick up another family, then we're headed to your parents' home. Hang on tight." Chaco banged twice on the side of the truck.

***

As Chaco drove toward the edge of town, his thoughts turned to Alberto, and to a better time. Since entering the United States, besides the Walkers, Alberto Sanchez had been Chaco's only friend. The last time he'd seen him they bumped into one another in Costco the day Chaco had observed the first of the solar storms and had gone into town to load up on survival supplies "just in case." It seemed it had been years ago rather than days when the Mexican approached Chaco with a grocery cart half-filled with food.

"*Hola, hijo de puta,* you son of a bitch. What's up? *Qué paso?*" Alberto said. He worked as a *bracero* now, but he'd attended medical school in Guadalajara before his family had fallen on hard times. Despite his education, and diligent practice, Alberto's English skills were halting. But besides intelligence, he possessed a sharp wit and enthusiastic sense of humor. Chaco found him good company. The two men had gotten to know one another when they worked side-by-side for a season in the Oxnard strawberry fields.

"*Hola!* Good to see you, Alberto. Long time." The two men embraced and clapped each other on the back. They spoke to one another in their own private blend of English and Spanish, sprinkled liberally with good-natured insults. "How's Juanita and the kids?"

The slightly chubby Alberto stood five foot four with cropped black hair, with a thick unibrow over onyx eyes, and a smile that consumed his entire face. "All good, *gracias a Dios*, but those five boys are going to eat up my *pinche* salary before I can pay the rent. Man, I gotta make this food last all week. It'll be gone in a day. I can't even afford to buy no beers."

When California re-implemented the Bracero Program, Alberto had been one of the first to apply. He did his best to help Chaco by securing for him falsified papers showing Mexican citizenship, qualifying him for the program. A suspicious farm worker noticed Chaco's Salvadoran accent and questioned him about life in Mexico, but when Chaco stumbled over the answers the worker ratted him out to the foreman who fired the Salvadoran on the spot. In solidarity, even though he had a family to feed, Alberto quit his job. "We'll go inland," Alberto told Chaco. "Plenty of work for everybody. If the émigré stop us, I'll show em' my papers. They won't question one more Mexican in the truck with my family. I'll tell 'em you're my ignorant cousin, a goddamn idiot who can't talk. They'll believe that for sure." The Mexican laughed so hard his entire body shook.

Chaco had been headed for the check-out line, but he turned back and picked up another twenty-pound bag of beans, one the same size of rice, and two cases of bottled water. He steered into the liquor aisle and picked up a case of Alberto's favorite beer, *Modelo Negro*. He rushed to pay for his purchases then ran length of the parking lot to catch up before his friend departed. Chaco found Alberto loading his remaining few groceries in the back of a beat up old Toyota pickup.

"What's all this, man?" Alberto said when Chaco hefted the additional food from his trolley into the Toyota. "I'm no charity case and we drink tap water, *pendejo*, not this fancy shit. We don't need this stuff. Maybe I'll keep the Modelos, though." The Mexican laughed.

"It's not for you. It's for me. I'm coming for dinner, and I want Juanita's beans and rice."

"These bags will make enough for ten years of dinners, *cabron*."

"Then you better invite me to your house for ten years. Besides, it's always a good idea to have a little extra food and water on hand for emergencies, understand, *sabes?*"

"I get it, *entiendo.* You come next Sunday, *Domingo.* We'll be expecting you. We'll fire up the barbecue, make *carne asada,* and drink some of these beers."

"I'll be there."

"Boys got baseball. Gotta go, my brother, *mi hermano. Gracias* for the food, *por la comida,* eh?"

"*De nada.* You're welcome. See you later. *Hasta luego.*"

"Hasta Domingo, cabron."

Alberto climbed into his truck. Chaco made sure the Mexican couldn't see him lob a package of flashlight batteries and a four-pack of duct tape into the pickup bed.

***

Chaco headed for the farm workers' quarters bordering the vineyards. Almost three in the morning, he pulled the Ford into the compound where the Sanchez's lived. The atmosphere hung heavy, black and silent. A bad feeling like a soggy wool blanket dropped over Chaco, chilling him. "Bethany, you and the girls stay here. I'll be right out."

He circled to the bed of the truck. "Jude, stay in the truck but keep your eyes open. I need you to cover me if anything goes wrong."

"I've got it."

Rufus attempted to jump out and follow Chaco, but Jude grabbed his collar. "Stay here, boy."

Keeping a firm grip on the handle of his .38, and with the flashlight in his other hand, Chaco approached the door of the cabin. "Hey, Alberto. You there?" He waited a few seconds for a response. Nothing.

He pushed the door with his foot and it swung open. Inside he found Alberto, his wife, and all five boys huddled together on the floor. Alberto had a protective arm around his wife, who still held the youngest boy in her arms, a child not quite three, his mass of curls now plastered to his scalp with thickened fly-studded blood. She had covered his face with her shawl. Whoever shot the family had blasted a hole through the little boy that exited his mother's back leaving a gap the size of a grapefruit. With Alberto's lifeless arm still around her, the pretty Juanita slumped, clasping her little boy to her breast.

Chaco knelt beside his friend and crossed himself.

***

Even desperate men must sleep sometime. By pre-dawn, most of the looters, murderers, thieves, and reprobates were dreaming, snoring, or tossing and turning half-awake in their beds. It would be another hour before sunlight crested the mountains, and if gracious Lady Fortune lived in Chaco's corner of the world, he'd have Jude, Bethany, the girls, and Rufus at the Walkers in time for everyone to witness the sunrise above the San Padrinos.

Bethany and the girls slept, arms and legs tangled together. One of the children, Olivia, the six-year-old, leaned against her mother snoring. Her little sister, four-year-old Lacy, slept curled into a ball in her mother's lap. A slight bit of drool slipped from the corner of her mouth. Bethany rested her head against the window. Her eyelids fluttered, and now and again she moaned in her sleep. The windshield, shattered when Chaco fired on the crazed man in Jude's driveway, admitted a rush of cool outside air. Bethany and the girls seemed oblivious to it. Jude and Rufus sat upright in the bed of the truck, backs against the cab, keeping a watchful eye for any threatening sound or movement.

Chaco decided on the shortest route, which meant driving on Main Street. *At this hour, not much chance of danger.* The town looked like a scene from a zombie apocalypse movie complete with the requisite shattered storefront windows and abandoned cars with doors ajar. In the recesses of a dark, narrow alley, men huddled under a makeshift tent. A solitary woman, wide-eyed and befuddled, hair hanging in tangled strings over her face, weaved in a drunkard's Z pattern down the sidewalk. She cried out for someone, maybe a husband or child. As Chaco passed her, she stretched her arms toward him. "Please, please, help me. I don't know where they are. Don't leave me here. I can't find them. Please."

Some buildings were gutted by fire, others still smoldered, and others remained intact. As though some giant unseen sword had cut the store neatly in half, part of Costco lit the sky in a blaze, and an equal part had collapsed into a charred heap. And there were the bodies. Mostly men, but women and children, too, their corpses splayed in grotesque poses in the streets and sidewalks, their skin milky blue in the moonlight. Chaco glanced over to the girls, relieved and grateful to see them still asleep.

As turned onto the street leading to the hill where the Walkers and Pennymons lived, something crashed into the passenger side window startling Bethany, the snoring Olivia and her sister, Lacy. The three bolted out of their sound slumber. Lacy let out a wail and clung to her mother. Then…another crash, and splintering glass. Chaco jerked his head to the back of the truck. "Someone's throwing bottles!"

Jude kneeled and shouldered the AR-15. Rufus snarled and barked, his hackles at full attention.

"Get down and hold tight. I'm flooring it," Chaco yelled as another bottle bounced off the hood of the truck.

"No, wait." Jude fired a volley in the direction of the bottle thrower. "I got the motherfucker. Yahoo!" He pumped his fist into the air.

"Oh no," Bethany said.

"What?" Chaco asked.

"Post-traumatic stress disorder. This violence could cause him to…"

Several men charged the truck with baseball bats. Bethany gasped. Jude let loose another volley, mowing the men down. He rocked back and forth in the bed of the truck. "Yeah, baby! Yeah, baby!"

The little girls screamed. Chaco yelled again. "Hold on!" He jammed the accelerator, and the truck lurched and sped away.

No one rested for the remainder of the mercifully uneventful trip. All went well… that is until they reached the site of the roadblock. Skinny, Baldy and Fatty's truck was missing, but something else alarmed Chaco…*Hijo de puta, where are the bodies?*

Chaco stopped and switched off the ignition. "I have to check something out," he said to Jude. "Stay put." Bethany nodded and pulled the girls close.

"I'm comin'," Jude said. "I'll waste anyone who comes at us." He blinked repeatedly as though midges invaded his eyes. The muscles of his face twitched.

"Look, buddy," Chaco said. "I really need you to hang in the truck and watch my back."

"Yeah, okay." His shoulders slumped.

Is Jude disappointed? Really? Maybe PTSD, or maybe adrenalin?

Chaco hopped out of the truck with the flashlight in hand, squatted and aimed the beam at the road ahead. *No no no no, Dios mio.* There were not one set of tire tracks between the hill and the site of the roadblock, but several—the tracks headed down the hill, and another set of fresh tracks led directly toward the Walkers' and the Pennymons', and back again.

CHAPTER 8

Chaco pulled his truck into the Walkers' driveway, but before he even rolled to a full stop, Abigail and Russell appeared at the driver's window. Jude and the dog leapt from the truck bed. Abigail nearly tripped herself running to her son. "Thank God you're okay." She grabbed him in a bear hug. Jude kissed his mother on the top of her head, then he and his father embraced.

Bethany and the girls piled out of the cab and the family huddled, arms around one another. Russell broke away. "Thank you for bringing our family back to us, Chaco."

"My pleasure, Mr. Walker. But I'm afraid we are in imminent danger. We need to get everyone together right away."

Russell's expression shifted from gratitude to concern. "What danger? And, what the hell happened to the windshield?"

"I'll tell you about it when we get inside, Mr. Walker."

"All right. Let's get the girls something to eat. The Pennymons are here."

***

Once the little girls were fed and deep into dream time, Chaco talked about the roadblock, the missing bodies, and the tire tracks. "Those men were not acting alone. My sense is whoever they were working with showed up to either relieve them at their posts or to check on them. After discovering their three missing comrades and the dismantled road block, they most likely understood right away what had happened. That's why they headed up this way, and will…"

"Wait! You think they are coming back? My dear God. And, you *killed* people?" Abigail asked. "Chaco…I would never think you would be capable of…"

"Mom, stop. Chaco did what he had to do, what we all may have to do," Jude said. "There are people out there now who won't think twice about killing us all just for our cans of tuna."

Abigail shook her head. "What's happening to our world? It's as though everything has turned upside down. People murdering other people. All of this is incomprehensible to me. Even Chaco?"

"You would do the same, Mom, if your life was in danger or the lives of any of your family."

"No, I don't think I could kill anyone, Jude. I'm not sure…"

"If someone intended to shoot Lacy or Olivia, you would. Anyone coming back here could hurt them. Do you understand that, Mom?"

Chaco studied Jude's face. The man seemed calmer, more himself.

"Yes, I know they are coming back, and I'm scared to death, but about killing people? I really don't think so," Abigail said. "I could never kill anyone."

Russell cleared his throat. "Let's hope we never have to find out. Now, back to our immediate threat. Where do you suppose these men are, Chaco? You say you saw tire tracks coming this way, right?"

"I'm guessing they ran a reconnaissance. It's obvious that two houses are vacant, but they probably figured out that the Pennymons and you are here. They probably went back down the mountain off-road to gather more support for an assault. These guys are ruthless. Desperate. We can only assume they plan to raid the houses for any food or supplies they can find, and will not hesitate to kill us all. I'll look around to make sure they aren't here now. We'll have to post a 24/7 guard."

"You pissed them off when you shot their buddies, too. If you hadn't done that, they may not have even bothered to come up here in the first place." Rocky pointed his finger at Chaco.

"This is on you, little hombre. It's your fault we're in danger."

"Will ya jist shut up?" Margo punctuated each word in a hammer-like cadence.

"I think we would be safer if we combined our resources, stayed together in one house. Easier for the six of us to protect one property than two," Jude said.

"My thinking exactly," said Russell. "What do you think, Chaco?"

"Strategically, we'd have a better chance if we all stayed here, Mr. Walker."

"What about my house?" Rocky said. "Why not there?"

"Mr. Pennymon, your house is literally made of glass walls. The Walkers' house is rock faced," Chaco said.

"I don't give a shit. I built that house practically on my own. I'm protecting it. You all stay here if you want. Let's go, Margo."

"Rocky Pennymon, you listen to me. This is what's gonna happen. We will git on back to our house, fetch our guns, and our ammo. While you do that, I'll empty the pantry and the liquor cabinet and find anythin' else that might be useful, and we are gonna hightail it back here. We are all scared to death. No tellin' how soon those thugs will be back, and we're gonna stick together in this rock house."

"Don't you tell me what to do, Margo."

"Yes, I *will* tell ya what to do. 'Cause if I don't, you're gonna git yourself kilt, and maybe me, too."

"Honey, it's my job to keep our home and you safe, and I only want…"

Their voices trailed off when they were part way to their property. Margo's Prada heels gouged divots in the lawn.

"Mr. Walker, Jude, after we check to make sure we are safe for now, I need some help with getting some things over here," Chaco said.

"What things?" Russell asked.

"I bought shelf-stable food, water, camping gear, first aid

items, and other necessities. The work shed is filled with supplies, enough for all of us for quite a while."

"When did you do all this, Chaco?"

"The morning I observed the first solar storm. I didn't know for certain if the CMEs would hit. I bought supplies as a precaution."

"That's what Rocky saw you doing at the shed, then?"

"Yes, Mr. Walker."

"Thank you," Abigail said. "I…don't…know what to say… only…thank you."

Bethany slept in a lounge chair, her arms crossed over her stomach.

"Let her rest, poor dear," said Abigail. "We four can unload the shed."

Russell, Abigail, and Jude headed to the far end of the property. After Chaco climbed onto the roof and scanned the area for intruders or approaching vehicles, he climbed down and joined the others. As they neared the guest cottage, Chaco said, "Go on, I'll catch up." He entered his cabin, loaded into his rucksack a few cans of food, some clothes, a bottle of water, his last few bottles of good wine, and the rest of his ammo. On the way out the door, he hesitated. He turned back and grabbed a framed photo of his family, his Grandfather and Abuela Erhard, his mother, and father. It had been the day after his fifth birthday. Chaco wore his Superman t-shirt, and held in one hand his Superman action figure, a gift from his father. He straddled his mother's lap, his bare legs dangling like those of a little cricket on each side of her thighs. Her arms wrapped around Chaco, her hands clasped around his chest as though to ensure he'd not slip away. His smiling grandparents and father stood behind. Chaco stuck the photo in his pack, then perused his bookcase, pulled off his four favorite books, a journal, some writing pads, a handful of ballpoint pens and pencils, stuffing them into the bag. On the way out, he grabbed his work gloves off the kitchen counter.

When he caught up to the others, they were busy unloading the contents of the shed into a utility trailer they'd hooked to the Ford. He set down his rucksack and pulled on his gloves.

By the time they'd returned with the loaded trailer, Bethany stirred oatmeal in a cast iron pot over the flame of a propane stove. She looked haggard, her clothes wrinkled, but she had managed to pull her hair back into a clip. A few strands had escaped and hung in wisps along the sides of her face. All the times Chaco had seen her before, Bethany bounced and flitted about like a nervous midge, a flighty beetle. Today, no bounce.

"Grab a bowl, everyone. Oatmeal coming right up."

"Where are the girls?" Abigail asked.

"Still sleeping inside with Rufus." Bethany beckoned with a clean ladle. "Come on. Get something to eat."

Russell took over guard duty to give Chaco a break. The Sun had risen casting a pale pink light on the flagstone patio. All remained quiet. For the first time in a long while, Chaco allowed himself to relax. His stomach growled with hunger, so much hunger he wouldn't have cared if Bethany had boiled socks for breakfast.

"You all eat. I'll get back on the roof with Russ to help keep a look out," Chaco said.

The other adults sat down to a meal of camp coffee, oatmeal with raisins, and sliced apples sprinkled with cinnamon. A few minutes later, Abigail appeared on the roof balancing a cup of coffee and a large bowl of oatmeal in one hand for Chaco. "I knew those days of waiting tables in college would come in handy."

"Thank you, Mrs. Walker." *Qué deliciosa*. "I understand from Russ that Jude suffers from PTSD?"

"He endured horrendous ordeals in Iraq. Two of his close buddies were gunned down in front of him by an Iraqi soldier," she said. "One of them lived for a short while. The only time Jude talked about it with his father he told Russ the soldier's intestines spilled out onto the dirt. My son tried to stuff the intestines back into his body cavity as he screamed for a medic. The boy had turned twenty the day before, not even old enough to buy a beer. My boy held his friend as he died. He'd seen other things, too, but that was the probably the worst. Jude doesn't talk too much about what happened." Abigail shook her head. "I feel for my son and his family. Bethany has been a real trooper, though, sticking by him."

"Do you think Jude is going to be okay?"

"He spent a few years in therapy, and he's been on anti-anxiety meds. Some things trigger memories and he suffers from bouts of depression, but usually, he comes out of it. Bethany tells us he still has nightmares sometimes, but not like in the early days. Once, right after he got back, while they were sleeping, and she pregnant with Lacy, Jude grabbed her, threw her on the carpet and covered her body with his to protect her against something that only he could see. Bethany says he wouldn't stop screaming, and she had a tough time waking him. It shook her up, but there haven't been many incidents like that since. He does get moody, withdrawn sometimes, but he seems mostly all right."

"That must be hard on your family."

"It was pretty difficult for me, at least initially. It was less hard on Russ, but right away I could see the change in Jude. Once the girls came along, he'd become more like his old self, though." Abigail stayed with Chaco while finished breakfast, then they climbed down to join the others.

"Any guesses as to when those men will be back?" Jude asked.

"We'll most likely have until dark, but of course, we have no way of knowing." Chaco shifted in his chair. "I predict they'll hit the empty houses first. We might want to check those out to see if there's anything we can scavenge before the looters get there. And we better keep a guard posted around the clock. We'll work in shifts."

"I'm not clear on something," Abigail said. "You mean to break into our neighbors' homes and steal their belongings? We can't do that."

"One of those houses has been sitting vacant for months, and the other…," Russell said.

"…the other belongs to good people who are on vacation." Abigail said.

"…and who won't be coming back." Russell sipped his coffee, put his mug down, stood and stretched. "Jude, let's find an empty cart and get across the road to that other house."

"I'll stand guard here and cover you," Chaco said.

Abigail looked stricken.

"Sweetie, if they happen to come home, we'll return all their belongings. Deal?" Russell said.

The back door of the house had been easy enough to break into. A couple of hours later, the men towed back a wagon loaded instant coffee, canned foods, clothing for Jude and Bethany, and some items small enough to fit the little girls.

"They won't like that these are boy's clothes," Jude said. "My girls are prissy little things."

"We'll promise to buy them pretty pink dresses when all this is over," Russell said.

Chaco helped unload the wagon, then grabbed a bottled water, his .38 and the binoculars. As he ascended the ladder to the roof, Rocky showed up with a loaded wheelbarrow.

"Who in the heck is that with him?" Abigail asked.

Russell craned his neck to take a better look. "I don't know. I've never seen him before."

Chaco stopped mid-way up the ladder to look. A slightly built man in loose-fitting jeans, work boots, a denim shirt, and a duck-billed cap followed close behind Rocky. He carried a backpack on his shoulders and pushed in front of him a second wheelbarrow piled high with goods making it difficult to see his face.

"Where's Margo?" asked Abigail.

The person with Rocky halted, dropped the handles of the wheelbarrow and spoke. "Fer gawdsake, Abby, ain't you never seen nobody without their makeup?"

CHAPTER 9

"We need to know what we've got in the way of food and supplies," Chaco said.

Always the accountant, Jude offered to log the inventory and keep a ledger. He located a yellow legal pad and a pen, and sat at the patio table. Bethany put on a second pot of coffee, and a pan with water for cocoa because, by that time, the little girls had awakened. They cuddled under a blanket, sleepy-eyed, on Abigail's lap. Lacy sucked her fingers. Rufus plopped down on the flagstones beside them and licked his paws.

Once Jude accounted for all the supplies from the shed, the vacationing neighbors, and the Walkers' pantry and garage, only the contents of the Pennymons' wheelbarrows remained. Rocky recited the items as he removed them one at a time and placed them on the flagstones. "One Remington rifle, two boxes of ammo and one partial box with…let's see." He opened the box. "Twelve rounds. A .22 pistol with four and one-half boxes of ammo, and look, a fine reproduction Winchester M1887 lever-action shotgun, and, four, make that five full boxes of ammo to go with that." He dug around the wheelbarrow. "There it is. Fishing tackle, two fishing poles, and three hunting knives. We also have ten pounds more or less of salted meat, and another ten of jerky. A four-person all-weather tent, a case of Spam, blankets, and pillows up the ass. Is that enough for you?"

"How many blankets and pillows, exactly?" Jude asked.

"Awwww, Jeez." Rocky made a frustrated huff. "Five cotton blankets, two down comforters, and five down pillows from Costco. Check this out. We bought one of those things from television that sucks all the air out of pillows and bedding so we could crunch them down to these little flat things." He held one of the packages aloft for everyone's inspection. "We also got a half gallon of olive oil and a loaded first-aid kit." He held up the white plastic container with a red cross on the cover, and shook it before putting it on the patio. "Eight bars of Ivory soap…". He stopped and grinned. "And will you look here! All the Wild Turkey and Jack Daniels we had in the bar.…and… what…the…royal…fuck?"

"Shush yer mouth, Rocky Pennymon," Margo said. "There's little girls right over there with their grandmaw. They kin *hear* you."

"Sorry. I meant, what the heck is this? Margo, why do we need two cases of 'White and Bright' toothpaste?"

"They had a sale over at the Wal-Mart. It's good…"

"Two cases? Really? We aren't lugging two damn cases of toothpaste around. This is ridiculous and…"

"I told ya…watch yer mouth."

"Sorry." Rocky nodded in Abigail's direction.

"You're right about the cursing, okay?" He said to Margo. "But, the fu…flipping toothpaste. Let's talk about that. Are you trying to tell me that you hicks couldn't get 'White and Bright' toothpaste on the ranch so you have to buy a goddamn twenty-year supply whenever it goes on sale at *that thar yonder Wal-Mart?*" Rocky hesitated. "I'll leave that out of the supplies, Margo. I'm sorry you need your teeth to be sparkling white, but…"

"Yer mouth! What's wrong with you? Now…what I'm tryin' ta' tell ya, that is if you'd shut yer trap fer a minute, is that particular kinda' toothpaste is great for keepin' away skeeters, and heals up chigger bites and bee stings in no time. Smear some on a sunburn and it takes the pain and redness clean away, too."

"You're kidding me."

"No, I ain't kiddin' you, smarty pants. Jist 'cause you went to community college for three semesters don't mean you know ever' thang."

"Okay. Two cases of 'White and Bright' toothpaste." Rocky rummaged around the wheelbarrow a little more. "What's this, your makeup? Minty lip-gloss? Are you kidding me? Next, it'll be…"

"Stop right there." Margo stood. "Everyone. I need y'all to hear me out." When no one paid attention, Margo put the first two fingers of her right hand between her lips and let out a piercing whistle. The atmosphere went silent, and Rufus's ears perked to attention.

"That's better." She nodded. "I know y'all think I'm a country bumpkin who dresses like a pricey tart, but I'm a lot more than that, a lot more. I wasn't always rich, ya know. I was raised on a little ranch. We was dirt poor, but we was happy and maybe I don't have book smarts like y'all, but I know plenty."

Rocky put a restraining hand on her forearm. She shook it off.

"I kin do thangs none of you spoilt city folks kin do. Fer instance, how many of you kin shoot, skin, and gut a rabbit, then cook it in a stew?" She looked around. "None of ya? How 'bout killin' and pluckin' a hen?" She hesitated to give time for a response "No? What a surprise that is." She smiled and pointed at herself. "Well, I kin do those thangs."

"We raised and butchered our own hogs, so I know how to do that, too. I know how to cure meat, grow vegetables from seeds and preserve 'em. By the way, I brought along a whole gob of vegetable seeds I saved myself, any of y'all think to do that?

"I kin hunt anything on four legs, throw a knife better than any man, fish usin' a line tied to a stick, and I can skin a deer in nothin' flat with jist an old dull huntin' knife."

"Okay, Margo," Rocky said, "That's…"

"I kin birth a calf, or a human baby, and I know which growin' thangs you can eat from out in the forest, and which are pure poison. How many of y'all kin do half that? C'mon, tell me. In fact, how many of you folks kin do *any* of that stuff a'tall?"

"Mrs. Pennymon, no doubt you'll prove to be the most useful person among us," Chaco said.

"Why, thank you, Chaco. I'm glad someone knows it." She gave her husband a dirty look. "And if you don't start callin' me Margo," she said to Chaco, "…even though you ain't much younger than me…well, I don't care if you're a big shot Ph.D., or not. You call me Margo. Ya hear me?"

"Yes, Margo, I hear you." Chaco did his best to conceal a smile for fear of offending her.

"By the way, Rocky Pennymon, I'll have you know that minty lipgloss you found is Mrs. Beasley's Beeswax Lip Butter."

"So?"

"So, it's the best thang in the world fer chapped lips and has a sunscreen of fifty. It can even be used on noses and ears, and it's gentle enough for them little girls. Won't irritate their skin, and that's the only so-called 'make up' I brought along. Those tubes of lip butter are gonna be damned useful to us."

"Look who's cussing now," Rocky said.

***

By dusk, the group had secured the supplies, boarded the windows, and reinforced the doors. After a simple meal of beans and rice, Russell and Jude kissed their families, then Abigail, Bethany, the girls, and Rufus made themselves comfortable in the wine cellar.

Rocky put his arm around Margo's waist. "Honey, I need you to go down into the cellar with the rest of the women and children."

"Heck, no. We need everyone who kin shoot a gun. I'm stayin' right here."

Rocky didn't argue.

Before they closed and barred the cellar door, Chaco handed Abigail his .38. "You hold it like this." He demonstrated. "And if anyone you don't know comes through that door, you can't hesitate even for one second. Aim for the chest and squeeze the trigger."

She shook her head. "I don't think I can do that."

"Yes, you can. If you don't, and those men get in, they will kill you, your daughter-in-law, and those little girls. They might rape all of you first, though. If you need to, you fire this gun, Mrs. Walker."

"You're right, of course. I'll do what I must. And, please, like Margo says, it's time we used first names. Call me Abby, won't you?"

"I'll think about it."

"Really, it's time to drop the formality."

"It's only that…you are much like…to me…"

"…your mother?"

"…not that you are old."

She lifted her chin and laughed. "It's okay, Chaco. Today, focus on taking care of yourself and my two boys."

He resisted an impulse to embrace the older woman. Instead, he smiled at her. "It will be all right. I'll keep your husband and son safe."

When Chaco emerged from the cellar, the three other men and Margo had taken their places in the living room with weapons and ammo at the ready. Jude's hands were steady. A focused calmness replaced the wild-animal look from the night before when they had driven up the hill from Green Lake. Chaco checked over the Winchester, laid it beside him and picked up the binoculars. He peered through a crack in the window boards they'd nailed on earlier, and adjusted the lenses of the glasses in time to see not one, not two, but three sets of vehicle headlamp beams bouncing up the hill.

CHAPTER 10

The houses built above Green Lake were well-spaced, each sitting on six to nine acres.

The properties were nestled deep into the trees so that many of the residents of the town didn't even know people lived on the hill, let alone in mega-million dollar estates.

A solitary road snaked between the houses on the rise and the town below, which meant only one viable way in or out, a single-lane dirt path through dense California oak, cedar, and Douglas fir. Hiking trails crisscrossed the area since the private land abutted the forest. Most of the paths ran along "the river," as the locals referred to it, although it could never have been much more than a wide, year-round stream.

Chaco considered the one serviceable road both a good thing and a bad thing—bad because, in emergencies, such as a forest fire, it would be more difficult for emergency vehicles to get through or to escape, but good because there existed only a single obvious way for the bad guys to get to them. A solitary road would be easier to defend.

As Chaco predicted, the looters hit the two vacant houses first. Chaco and Rocky watched through their glasses as the men lay waste to one of the houses.

"Those sonsabitches aren't so much interested in taking things as destroying property," Rocky said.

"You're right."

"They're probably the 'have nots' looking to get any kind of revenge they can on the 'haves.'"

"Right, again."

The men had left the doors open on the three old trucks they'd parked on the once well-manicured lawn of the first house. Without trying the doors, they smashed the plate glass windows with sledgehammers. Once inside, crashes, bangs, and pounding reverberated through the forest. From their whoops and yells, Chaco guessed the men were drunk or stoned out of their minds. *Good. The pendejos' reactions will be impaired.*

The men emerged from the house, piled their loot into the beds of the trucks, and fired their weapons into the air.

Rocky shook his head. "Those assholes have no idea where those bullets might land."

An hour passed before the men moved to the other vacant property. But before departing the first house, they set it ablaze.

"What's going on, Chaco?" Russell said. "Looks like flames. I hope the forest doesn't catch."

"Yes, Mr. Walker. They torched the first house."

"For Jesus' sake, why?"

"I don't know."

"Because they're a bunch of dicks, that's why," said Rocky, handing his binoculars to his friend.

Russell adjusted the viewfinder and focused on the inferno. "Shit!"

By then, the flames had engulfed the house, and black smoke billowed from the windows. The crazed men, passing a whiskey bottle, whooped it up like high school boys at a Friday night ball game. From where the looters were busy, a dog let out a pitiful yelp.

"I can't see a dog," Chaco said. "Can you, Mr. Pennymon?"

"Can't see any dog, but I heard it all right."

"It's not Rufus, is it?" Russell asked.

"He's safe in the cellar with everyone else," Margo said. "But that other one…poor thang. I think them looters hurt him bad for no reason at all. Maybe they even flat out kilt him."

"Probably a hungry stray hoping the men had food," Russell said.

"Men who would hurt an innocent, helpless, little hungry dog are gonna kill people, too. These guys need to be shot." Margo shouldered her rifle, and took aim.

Chaco stopped her. "Not yet, Margo. We have to save our ammo."

They watched in silence as the men looted and destroyed the second property, setting it ablaze, too.

Their trucks full, they climbed into their cabs, but one man stepped away from the others. Chaco thought the looter had to urinate, but the man stood still and stared toward the Walkers' residence. Chaco focused on him through the lenses of the glasses. There stood a young man, maybe in his early twenties with a stocky build, greasy dark hair and an unkempt beard. The man peered back through a set of binoculars with one hand, holding a flashlight in the other. For a moment, Chaco and Greasy stared at one another. The man set his binoculars on the dirt, directed the beam of his flashlight to illuminate his face and upper torso. Greasy raised his hand, stuck out his middle finger to Chaco, and mouthed the words, "Fuck you." Then, "You will die."

"Did that dude say what I think he said? That fucker said, 'you will die', I'm sure of it," Rocky said.

"Yes."

***

The men in their loaded trucks started back down the hill toward town. Chaco, Margo, Russell and Jude headed together toward the cellar. "It's us." Jude knocked against the door. "Open up."

Abigail poked her head out. "Are they gone for good?"

"No, sweetheart," Russell said. "I'm sure they'll be back as soon as they unload."

"We'll be ready for those sonsabitches." Margo patted her rifle.

"But, we aren't going to have much time to do what we need to first," Chaco said.

"What do you mean? What have you got in mind?" These

were the first words Jude had spoken to him since they'd taken their posts hours earlier.

"We can set up a barricade to make it easier to defend the front of the house. But we must get going now. Mr. Walker, you've got a chainsaw. What about you, Mr. Pennymon?"

"Sure do, Chaco. I'll go right now and get it." Rocky Pennymon had never addressed Chaco as anything but "boy," "wetback," or "Mexican" before. It startled Chaco to hear his name come from Rocky's mouth.

***

The girls and dog disappeared back into the cellar, and within minutes, Chaco and Rocky set to work felling trees. Jude and Russell hacked away at limbs with an ax, then dropped them and pulled them toward the front of the house. They blocked the driveway and most of the entrance. They'd set up oil lamps and set flashlights on rocks to light their way, but although they moved as fast as they could in the dimming light, creating the hazard took longer than they'd thought.

"We have to get back into the house or we won't make it before those murdering drunken idiots return." Chaco made a brisk departure through the dense foliage and pines in front of the house to the door.

Rocky took a deep breath, then doing his best to keep pace with Chaco, the two men ran to the house.

Once back, through a small opening in a front window, Chaco surveyed their handiwork. "Not bad. I wish had more time, though. I could have rigged a booby trap. I could have..."

"We did good," Rocky said, then clapped the Salvadoran on the shoulder.

Words froze in Chaco's mouth.

The "blockade construction duo," safe at the Walkers', with Russell close behind, checked on everyone in the cellar, and let

Rufus out for a second pee.

"Is it over? Are we safe?" Abigail asked Russell.

"Afraid not, honey. Go ahead and take a short break. You might want to empty the little porta-potty and put in some more snacks and extra water, but in a few minutes, we'll need you all to get back down into the cellar again and bolt the door."

"Aww," said Olivia. "Me and Lacy are bored, aren't we Lacy?" Chaco couldn't remember if he'd ever heard either of the little girls say much of anything.

The younger one nodded.

"It won't be long," Bethany said. "How 'bout when we go back to the cellar we play a game of Sugarland?"

Abigail, Bethany, the girls and the dog disappeared below, then latched the door behind them. Russell tried the door to ensure the bolt locked tight. No one wanted to eat, but Chaco and the others managed to get down a few handfuls of walnuts, some oranges, and sips from bottles of water. Chaco stirred some sugar into a cup of cold coffee and downed it.

We have to take our places," Russ said. "It'll be dark soon."

Everyone grabbed their weapons, took their positions, and watched for the looters' return. They didn't have to wait long.

CHAPTER 11

As a scientist, Chaco didn't put stock in astrology, but if any truth attached itself to the notion that "Mercury in Retrograde" caused problems, then Mercury certainly had gone retrograde now, wreaking extreme havoc. Everything that could go awry, did.

Rufus had scratched and whined at the cellar door with such urgency Abigail opened it, and Jude let him through the front. Mistake. The dog bolted into the forest on the chase, baying, and howling.

Chaco shook his head.

The little girls wailed. "Rufus! Come back! Daddy, get Rufus. Those bad men will hurt him like they did the other doggie."

Chaco looked at the girls. How do the kids know about the other dog?

Jude laid the AR-15 on a coffee table and started for the front door. "Girls, get back down with your mom. I'll get Rufus. Promise."

The girls disappeared back into the cellar.

"Dad, I've gotta' get that dog," Jude said. "Those girls have been through so much. They can't lose their pet. Not now."

"No, Jude. We don't know when those crazies are coming back, and if you're caught out there with them…the girls will lose their dog and their dad, too." Russell stood between his son and the set of risers leading to the front door.

"Sorry, Dad. I have to go." In a respectful, tender move, he pushed passed his father and picked up a flashlight. "I'll be back as soon as I can."

"You're unarmed. At least take a weapon."

"I'll move faster if I'm not lugging an AR-15 around with me. I'll remain well-concealed. I can do this, Dad."

"Calling for a dog? Every living thing in the forest will hear you. Take a weapon, at least." Russell put his arm out to his son. "Please."

"I've got an extra pistol," Rocky said. "It's not much more than a pea shooter, but it'll do the job at close range. Come on up and get it."

"Thanks." Jude had reached the last riser leading to the front door by then, and as he turned to ascend the stairs to take possession of the weapon he tripped and went down hard, twisting his ankle. He attempted to stand, cried out in pain, and collapsed. Jude tested his foot, tried to stand again, and fell backward onto his backside. "Damn! I can't put any weight on it."

There were only four steps to the set of stairs from the living room to the front door landing, but it might have well have been fifty. Jude like his dad had trouble fitting his frame comfortably into Mini Coopers, and when flying coach, he always requested seats behind the bulkhead or on the aisle. It took all three of the other men to him up the stairs. They put him on his back, stuck a couch cushion under his head, and Russell dropped down beside him. "Gotta get this boot off."

"No, don't," said Margo. "If ya do, and there's too much swellin', he won't be able to get his foot back into the boot. And, if his ankle is broke, you'll do more damage tryin' to remove the shoe. Leave it be."

Chaco pulled over a chair and attempted to elevate Jude's foot onto it. Jude cried out in pain, and Chaco, startled, nearly dropped the leg.

As though things weren't bad enough, Abigail burst through the doors from the wine cellar. "Where's Lacy's inhaler? She's so upset about Rufus running away it triggered an asthma attack!"

"Isn't it with you?" Russell said.

"No, I…my God! What happened to Jude's foot?" Abigail sprinted to her son.

"Don't worry about my foot. Just get the inhaler, Mom," Jude said. "It's in my coat pocket."

"Where's your jacket?"

"I don't know. I think it's outside in the back on the patio. Go. Hurry."

Abigail sprinted toward the patio.

"Rocky, follow her. Yer suppose' to be guardin' the back anyways," Margo said.

"She'll be right back. What'll you think is going to happen in the two seconds it'll take her to get the damned thing?"

"The little girl has asthma?" Chaco thought he'd spoken to himself, unaware anyone heard.

"Yeah, and a severe allergy to bees. We have to carry an inhaler and an epi-pen everywhere we go," Jude said.

Where will we get more of those when she needs them? She'll die. This time Chaco made sure to keep his words locked tight in his head.

As Abigail exited the patio door to the back, a loud crack reverberated through the living room. "They're back, and they're firing," Chaco said.

Margo shouldered her weapon, returned fire and a scream echoed back to them through the forest. "Got the bastard."

"Good shot, honey." Rocky patted his wife on the butt.

"Where's Abby?" Russell asked. "She's still outside looking for the inhaler?"

A man with a raspy voice, heavy with venom, said, "No she ain't. Now, drop your weapons." Chaco and the others swung around. A heavyset man in his late forties, with a shaved head and a lightning bolt tattoo on his forearm, stood at the living room entrance with Abigail. He held a hunting knife against her neck. "Do it now, or I'll slit her fucking throat."

Abigail registered no panic. She stared ahead, unmoving.

"Abby? No. Please, don't hurt her." Russell dropped his rifle.

Rocky and Margo followed suit, their firearms clattering against the hardwood floor.

"Mom!" Jude called out, distracting the man with the knife

for a slice of a second, enough time for Chaco to make his move.

In a single fluid motion, the Salvadoran raised the Remington and pulled the trigger. The man crumpled to the ground, the top of his head blown away. Blood mist and brain chunks splattered against the wall.

Abigail had been knocked over by the concussion of the gunshot but didn't stay down long. She scrambled to her feet, took her sleeve and wiped the intruder's blood spray from the side of her face.

Bethany emerged from the cellar and screamed, almost dropping the nearly unconscious Lacy who gasped for breath and turned blue.

***

Abigail pulled the inhaler from her shirt pocket and tossed it to her daughter-in-law. "Good thing I had time to get this before that bastard…before he…that…damned…bastard!"

As Russell and Jude dragged the invader's corpse onto the back patio, Bethany held the inhaler to her daughter's lips. "Take it in your mouth and breathe in, Lacy, sweetie. You're going to be okay."

The child struggled, wild-eyed, clawing at her mother. She made pitiful wheezing sounds.

Margo looked on with frantic worry. "Poor little thang. She's scared half to death."

"Lacy! Listen to Mommy. Breathe in deep. Stay calm. You can do this."

The little girl grabbed the inhaler in both hands, stuck it in her mouth and sucked on it. Gradually, her breath came in long, soft pulls and slow exhales. Color returned to her face. Abigail looked on, her face rigid with anger.

"That's my girl." Bethany grabbed her youngest child and held her tight. The little girl cried, "Mommy, I couldn't breathe."

"I know, honey, but it's all over now."

"Thank gawd." Margo said, and exhaled.

"She's all right?" Jude asked.

"That son of a bitch," Abigail said. "Because he slowed me down getting that inhaler, Lacy might have died. Son of a stinking bitch."

Gobsmacked, Chaco's mouth fell open. Not in nearly four years have I ever heard her use language like that.

"I think she's going to be fine," Bethany said. "We'll get her a drink of water, and…"

"Fuck! My house is on fire!" Rocky had been on "binocular duty," keeping a watchful eye on the looters.

The marauders had broken into the Pennymons' home. After three of the men loaded the stolen goods from the house into the bed of one of the trucks, another two torched the place. Although Rocky built his home with great expanses of glass and metal, plenty of fuel from the furnishings, carpets and wood frames fed the flames. Within fifteen minutes, fire engulfed the house. Glass shattered as the heat from the inferno exploded the plate windows and walls.

Rocky hopped from foot to foot like a beetle on a hotplate. "I need to get over there and douse those flames. God. Oh God. Oh God."

"Rocky, there ain't nuthin' we can do. Let it burn. It's only a house, fer gawdsake. We're alive, we're together, and nuthin' else matters." Margo rested her hand on her husband's shoulder. Her voice remained calm, soothing. Margo searched the faces of the others. "Y'all gotta understand. This house is special to Rocky. He built it with his own hands, near ever bit of it."

"Those bastards. I'll kill them all, every fucking one of them," Rocky's voice had broken into a high-pitched warble. He shouldered his rifle.

"Save your ammo," Chaco said. "We'll need every round once those men head back here."

***

From what Chaco could determine, there were seven men, maybe eight, remaining. Hard to tell. There would have been nine or ten if Margo had not killed or badly wounded one, and had he not blown the head off the guy who'd held Abigail hostage.

"We're good on ammo," Chaco said.

"Yup. Looks like we're fine for a while." Jude lifted the boxes on the coffee table one by one.

"Take your places, everyone. I think they're headed our way soon." Chaco waved his arm toward the back of the house. "Mrs. Walker, it's time you went to the cellar. They'll be here any second."

"Nope. I'm staying to fight."

Chaco snapped his head around to look at Russell. *Uh oh.*

"No," Russell said. "I need to know you're safe. Please, go back to the cellar."

"I said, I'm helping. Chaco showed me how to shoot this thing, and I'm not in the least bit afraid to use it. I know what I said before, but my granddaughter could have died because that jerk held me up from getting the inhaler. I felt exuberant when Chaco blew his damned head off."

"Don't argue with her, if you know what's good for you," Rocky snorted, then noticed his wife's expression. "Don't you give me the stink-eye, Margo."

"I'm going to guard the back," Margo said. "No one'll git by *me*. We already know if it's *you* coverin' the back, likely anyone kin get through." She stomped toward the patio.

"Abigail, please," Russell said. "I'll be worried about you if you're up here. I'll be distracted."

"Nope."

"Told you so," said Rocky.

"All right, then, Abby. Stay inside, away from the windows and doors. Position yourself near the cellar in case…"

"…why? You can't put yourself in danger and expect me to keep safe. I'm taking a post there." She pointed at a side window. "If one of those men gets near, I'll shoot him in the face."

"Mrs. Walker, your husband's right. We need someone inside to act as our second line of defense. If someone slips past us and gets into the house, who will protect Bethany and the girls since you have the .38? They're defenseless," Chaco said.

"Don't underestimate me. That man with his brains splattered on my wall pissed me off, and if anyone does anything to hurt my family…I'll…." She gritted her teeth.

Good for her. Chaco nodded. "I understand, Mrs. Walker. Hopefully, our blockade will at least make it a little more challenging for them to get to us from the front."

Rocky glared at Chaco. "Yeah, well that fucker got in through the back all right, undetected and unencumbered." Margo poked her head through the glass door to the patio. "Well, Rocky, since you was the one supposed to be guardin' the back, and I told you to go on out there with Abby, whose fault is it that someone got to her?" Margo said. "It ain't the fault of the blockade, and it ain't the fault of Chaco, neither. I'm goin' back out."

"Yeah, go out back, sure, since you think you can do a better job than me. You know? I don't get why you're always taking the side opposite of mine. You're my wife. You're supposed…"

While the Pennymons argued, Chaco kept his eye on the looters. He observed one man, who looked to be the leader, motioning for several men to head toward the back of the Walkers' property. Three men jumped into a truck and rammed the Walkers' back fence gate repeatedly, breaking through.

"Rocky, grab some ammo and help Margo in the back. We'll defend the front." Russell held up one hand as though to halt his wife. "Abby, please stay near the cellar door. Promise me."

Rocky laughed and slapped his thigh. "Yeah. We'll see where she stays."

***

For a moment, things were quiet. Through the binoculars, Chaco observed the looters moving into position. He became aware of the rhythm of his breathing, the sensation of his heart thumping against his ribs, the cool patches where sweat soaked through his shirt. He thought of Fiona, and went over his plans to get to her.

We can all make it to Moonforest Sanctuary, that is if we take back roads. Maybe we can travel part way via the Pacific Crest Trail, yes. The truck is four-wheel drive. It can make it, at least part way. No, no, too narrow and steep. We can…Crack! Rifle fire split the silence.

Rocky, the Walkers, and Chaco sprang into action, everyone hyper-alert. Another crack of rifle fire. Chaco swung his head with the binoculars pressed to his eyes with both hands. "There. I see him. He's kneeling beside the white pickup."

Jude leaned forward in his chair and fired the AR-15 through the window. It hit the shooter in the chest, then passed through his body and pierced the truck's wheel, deflating the truck's rear right tire. "Yeah, you motherfucker!" That insane look on Jude's face had returned in full force as though he'd been possessed. He trembled with excitement.

Chaco turned away from Jude. Can't worry about his state of mind right now.

More flashes, pops, and cracks of gunfire. Chaco discarded his binoculars and shouldered the Remington. Someone crept toward the house, hunched low among mature peonies and red tips lining the circular driveway, and made his way around and through the blockade.

"What's that in his hand? Shit! A bomb." Chaco aimed and pulled the trigger just as the man stood and raised his arm to lob the explosive. A single shot found its target in the man's chest. The looter buckled, clutched his midsection, and as he collapsed he dropped the explosive. A report so powerful it cracked one of the boarded front windows tore through the night. Pieces of rock from the cobblestone driveway, chunks of wood from the felled trees, and body parts flew in a bizarre pattern into the sky and back to Earth in a macabre hailstorm of blood, flesh, limbs, splinted wood, and rock shards.

Margo opened the slider and stuck her head in. "Everyone okay?"

"Yeah. Just stay put," Rocky said.

The man's arm and more than half his torso were gone, his body splayed across the ruined driveway like a bloody rag doll ripped in half, torn from shoulder to hip. The explosion blew off all his clothes except a single work boot.

Abigail did not stay near the wine cellar door as she'd promised Russell and Chaco. She had migrated to the side window. From outside, a man's head rose into view. Before his chin came into view, without even flinching, she shot him square in the face. Russell whipped around and stared at her, his expression registering astonishment.

"Four down. Where the fuck are the others?" Rocky said.

Chaco and Rocky put their binoculars to their eyes and scanned the property.

"I don't see anything or anyone out there, do you Chaco?"

"No, I don't."

"Maybe they're around back."

"Could be. Stand guard. I'm going out to the patio with Margo."

Jude had propped himself up, and with the pistol, fired through a crack in the door. Chaco tapped on Jude's shoulder and signaled for him to cease shooting.

A slight creaking came from above. Everyone looked to the ceiling. Chaco put his finger to his lips, and whispered, "They must have scaled the side of the house and broke in through an upstairs window. Everybody, stay quiet and cover me." Chaco tiptoed to the base of the stairs and raised his weapon.

The three men must have thought they had the element of surprise on their side. They charged down Rambo-style, firing wildly. Standing steady, unfazed, Chaco shot the one running point in the gut. As the first man dropped to his knees and tumbled down the stairs, in quick succession, he shot the other two, one through the Adam's apple. Clutching his throat, the man gurgled and fell, blood gushing through the wound in his neck. The other caught a bullet through the cheek slightly to the right of his nose. A spray of blood, bone, and brain burst through the back of his head.

"Jesus H. Christ. For a Mexican, you are one hell of a shot," Rocky said.

"I'm not Mexican. I'm Salvadoran."

Chaco checked the fallen men. The one who had taken a shot to the intestines cried out and writhed in pain. Chaco put a single bullet into the man's brain.

***

Mercury must have "gone direct," because at last, all turned right with the world. The Sun came up lighting the landscape in livid pinks and pale apricots, the call of a mockingbird the only sound. Chaco and the others dragged the bodies out and away from the house and concealed them under tarps.

Carrying a bucket filled with pool water, Margo entered from the patio. "We don't want them little girls seeing all this blood and guts." Using a rag she'd scavenged from the kitchen, she splashed water on the walls and floors, then got down on her hands and knees and scrubbed.

After Margo made things "presentable," Abigail knocked on the wine cellar door. A mussy-headed Bethany appeared. "The girls are still asleep. Is it over? Is it safe?"

"You slept through *everything*? You didn't hear *any* noise?"

"We heard plenty. I told the girls you were playing a grown-up game. After they'd fallen asleep, I heard an explosion of some kind outside. It frightened me, but the girls…they are so exhausted, I think if a bomb had gone off in the cellar they would have slept through it."

The group moved to the patio. Bethany lit the camp stove and poured water from a plastic bottle into a blue speckled enameled coffee pot. The little girls, with sleep still in their eyes, appeared together barefooted. They took their place on the grandmother's lap. Lacy stuck her fingers in her mouth and sucked, making little rhythmic sounds. Although the "defending army" had been awake all night, no one wanted to sleep.

Bethany suggested they get some rest. Jude responded, "We're all too wired." He sat with his wounded foot propped on a low table. "One heck of a night."

Lacy pulled her fingers out of her mouth and leaped off her grandmother's lap. "Rufus!" She pointed toward the forest. "Look, Olivia. Rufus is back." The girls ran toward their dog.

"He's got somethin', Daddy. Look," Olivia pointed.

"What is that?" Jude said.

"I don't know," said Bethany. "Looks like a thick twig or…I really don't know."

Rufus trotted to Jude. Wagging his tail, he spits his prize at the side of the chair. The dog, covered in mud, leaped onto the reclining man's lap as if to say, "See what I brought for you? What a good boy I am!"

Jude pushed the dog from his lap. "Jeez. You covered me in mud."

Margo, with the girls close behind, clamoring to get to their dog, halted to see what Rufus had dropped. "Y'all keep back!" In a sweeping motion with both arms, she pushed the girls behind her, restraining them. "Fer gawdsake," she whispered to Jude, "it's a big weenie."

Resting on the stones like a fat, meaty worm sporting a flesh helmet—a severed human penis.

"That boy was hung like a buck mule," Margo said.

CHAPTER 12

Following breakfast, Bethany set the girls up with a board game under an oak close to the patio where she could keep a protective eye on them. Rufus curled beside them and gnawed on a piece of wood.

Chaco called the group together. "We have to decide our next move. I've formulated a plan I'd like to present to everyone for consideration."

Rocky spit a mouthful of tepid coffee into the grass adjacent to the patio. "So, now *you're* the one deciding what we should do, is that it?"

I should have guessed his display of congeniality would be short lived. "I simply want to make a proposal. If you don't agree, or have a better idea…"

Margo glared at her husband. "Cain't you shush your mouth and listen for one single time in yer miserable life without interruptin'? Go right ahead, Chaco."

"Those men last night…I think we got them all, but we can't be certain, and even if we did, we don't know who is waiting for their return in Green Lake," Chaco said.

"Meaning, we may not have seen the last of their kind," Russell said.

"Exactly, Mr. Walker. Unless we know with certainty that we can fend them off for good, and find a way to block others from coming up the hill. If we stay here, we are in danger. My thought is…"

"You're proposing we leave? Where would we go, and how the hell would we get there, Mr. IQ?" Rocky tapped his forefinger against his temple.

Margo crossed her arms. "Yer ma didn't teach you even basic manners, did she?"

"Please, let Chaco present his plan," Russell said. "We'll have plenty of time for discussion after he's finished."

The hulk rolled his eyes like a typical emo adolescent.

Chaco took a swig of water from a plastic bottle. "My thought is that we could make our way to Moonforest Sanctuary."

"Yes!" Abigail clapped her hands. "I've been ripped up inside wondering what's been happening to Fiona and the boys. Yes. Please. Let's do go together."

"What the hell is *Moonforest Sanctuary*? Is that the hippie commune where your daughter lives? No way I'm going there. No fucking way." The veins on Rocky's neck protruded and turned purplish.

"Fer gawdsake, Rocky. Shut up. I mean it."

"Mr. Pennymon, Moonforest Sanctuary is a completely self-sufficient community, off-grid, and in a protected, remote area of a dense forest," Chaco said.

Jude nodded. "...and with multiple fresh water sources, abundant game, firewood, orchards, crops, livestock. Even though the winters can be rough, there are several well-insulated buildings on the property, too."

"But that's on Pine Mountain, almost 800 miles from here. We won't even have enough fuel to get us half the way. What do we do, walk?" Rocky chuckled and shook his head. "No way."

"Exactly." Chaco said. "We drive as far as we can make it, siphoning gas when we can, then, if need be, we walk."

"For how many miles? You see this?" He patted his gut. "I'm not exactly an Olympic athlete, and several of us aren't teenagers anymore, if you get my drift. And look at that." Rocky pointed to Jude. "He's got a badly injured ankle, and there's his two little girls who probably couldn't make it on foot half a block. Are you out of your fuckin' mind? And of course, there's the minor matter of men out there that'll shoot us all in the head for our beef jerky. Did you think of that, Mr. Intellect?"

"I've mapped a route that will circumvent the main highways, keep us somewhat hidden. And…I know where there are horses…"

"…if someone hasn't shot and eaten them."

"Well, we don't know that until we get to 'em, do we Rocky?" Margo glowered at her husband.

"Are we in agreement that early evening we pack, and before dawn, hit the road headed north?" Chaco said.

"I'm inclined to stay put and take my chances." Rocky implored Margo. "Will you stick here with me, honey?"

"What yer askin' is will I stick with you and die here rather than find a way to survive? What reason have we to stay? Our house is burnt up, there are killers down the hill that'll come up in groups with their rifles. With only you and me, we don't have a prayer of keepin' alive."

Rocky clenched his jaw and slammed his hand on a patio table. "Okay, okay, I'll go, dammit!"

***

The first time Chaco had visited Moonforest Sanctuary, he had never been to northern California. The mountains captivated him. Best of all, the trip had given him an opportunity to spend time with the love of his life, but the sanctuary itself made the biggest impression.

Acres of lavender fields in bloom stretched behind an archetypical red barn that, although well-maintained, had to be at least a hundred years old. Chickens and roosters ranged free. Sheep, goats, alpaca and a few milk cows fed on grasses in large fenced pastures.

A young man led a bay mare to the barn along a trail through a heritage apple orchard in bloom, abuzz with honey bees. Workers tended tomato, squash and cucumber seedlings in rows of wood-framed greenhouses. Burly men with sunburned arms tied grape vines. Canadian geese swam on Five Acre Lake with goslings trailing them. Connected by gravel paths, a series of yurts nestled beneath old growth cedar and blue spruce.

Chaco turned his head one way, then the other. "I can't believe what you have here," he'd said to Fiona.

Amid the 620-acre commune stood a 4,000-square foot one-story structure made of hand-hewn logs, some with blue stains indicating beetle kill. "We only harvested trees diseased or killed by pine beetles to construct The Common House," Fiona explained. "We don't touch the old growth trees. Cutting or injuring one of those is a big taboo here."

The hemp fields startled Chaco. "That's quite a grow plot."

"We're not a bunch of 'potheads,' if that's what you think." Fiona laughed. "Although some of us do smoke recreationally or to relieve stress. I'd be lying if I said I didn't take a hit once in a great while myself." She winked. "But the marijuana grown for recreational and medicinal use is much further away on the property in enclosed greenhouses to prevent cross-pollination. There is very little THC in hemp."

"Really?" said Chaco. "I thought hemp and marijuana were the same."

Fiona shook her head. "Same plant, different strains."

"What do you do with all this?" Chaco swept his arm toward the plot.

"When the bill passed legalizing marijuana a couple of years back, we cleared land and bought seed. We manufacture rope and fabric from the hemp. We are experimenting with paper-making, too. We even use the seeds."

"No kidding?"

"The seeds are useful for many things. They provide extraordinary nutrition, and produce great oil for cooking, skin care, and lamp fuel."

Brown and white-skinned children splashed in the cool stream under the watchful eye of women in long peasant skirts.

Men and women in work shirts and blue jeans kept busy with a variety of tasks, tending sheep, planting peas, weaving cloth. One man, an enormous African American with a shaved head, bent over his task of making sandals. A potter with twin gray braids and matching beard turned a bowl on a wheel that he used his foot to operate.

"We dig that clay right here on the property," Fiona said. "The soil here is filled with mica. Once they emerge from the Raku pit the pieces are gorgeous." The man at the wheel nodded to Fiona and Chaco. She picked up a fired red clay pot. The piece, embedded with gold like specks, glistened in the sunlight. She returned the pot to its shelf, thanked the potter, and they continued down the path.

A young Asian woman with bobbed hair and a dazzling smile waved a greeting as she walked past from the opposite direction. She carried a basket filled with reeds. Fiona waved in return. "Hello, Kiko."

"Pussy willows?" Chaco asked.

"No, cattails. The down makes a warm waterproof fill for quilts and jackets."

"How did you figure that out?"

"Research. People have been using cattail down for hundreds of years."

In a grassy clearing, little boys took turns on a tire swing.

"When will I meet your sons?"

"Not this weekend. They are with their dad." She looked at her feet and shook her head. "I did my best to persuade him that next weekend would be better, but…"

"Do you think he knows about us?"

"He might sense something. When he picked up the boys he said I looked happy and asked me why. I told him I looked forward to my parent's visit, but I don't know if he believed me."

A little girl with curly ginger hair and miles of freckles, cradled in her arms a Nubian kid goat not more than a few days old. "That is Marina," Fiona said. "Her grandfather is one of the founders of the commune. He's the unofficial mayor of Moonforest Sanctuary. You'll meet him later."

"I had no idea there were people who lived like this anywhere in the United States," he told her as she continued the tour. "None of you work outside the sanctuary?"

"There are some who have jobs in Pine Valley, but none of us *needs* to work outside. The property has three wells with hand pumps, solar arrays with generator back-ups, a spring-fed lake, and we've developed quite an industry."

"Industry?"

"Besides our hemp products and medicinal marijuana tinctures, we make lavender oil and soap. We dry our fruits and make delicious wines and apple cider. Our herbalists create tinctures from herbs wild-crafted right here on the property. A group of skilled craftspeople card, dye, and spin wool from our goats and alpacas. Our commune offers all manner of handcrafts and beeswax candles, as well as honey, ceramics, organic eggs, fresh produce."

"Who are your customers?"

"Our target market is affluent younger professionals to middle-aged people with an ecological mindset, and who prefer an organic lifestyle. Customers are local, national and Canadian. Our primary distribution and income channels include fairs, festivals, farmers' markets, natural food stores coast-to-coast, not considering our own co-op on the property, and we do robust on-line sales. This community, established in 1968, is a thriving independent, economic entity."

"On-line? I didn't think you had adequate electricity for internet connection."

"Our solar panels are efficient, but we could get along without electricity, or the dish network we use for connection. We simply would have to find other ways to sell or barter goods."

"Sounds perfect. Idyllic."

Fiona smiled and shook her head. "Far from it. We've had our problems, and not everyone who lives here is all about peace, love and sharing. But I suppose it's far better here than in congested, smoggy cities. Less stress, that's for sure."

"How do you handle food? With a short growing season, there can't possibly be enough to feed everyone year-round."

"Between the greenhouses, our food preservation operations, the fish in the lake, our abundant fields and orchards, and the livestock, we manage."

"What about social infrastructure?"

"We set up a school, a community center, and even our own medical facility directed by our retired medical doctor. We have three licensed nurses, and I practice herbology, so I help out, too."

"How many at the sanctuary are full-time residents?"

"Everyone who lives here is full-time."

Chaco raised his eyebrows. "There has to be two hundred people."

"Closer to three hundred."

"What about your boys' father...your ex...I mean...ah... does...he come around often? He doesn't live here, does he?"

Chaco looked around half expecting Fiona's vengeful husband to leap out from behind a tree, loaded rifle in-hand.

"My husband left Moonforest when we separated. He lives in San Francisco, and only shows up now and again to visit the boys." She smiled and rested a hand on Chaco's shoulder. "Don't worry. He stays in the Common House when he's here overnight. Usually, he picks up the boys and goes. I don't interact with him unless I have to, and even though it's sad for the boys to rarely see their dad, I'm happy his overnight stays are few and far between." She looked away then back at Chaco. "I don't mean to make him out to be a monster. He's a good guy. He does love his sons. We simply weren't...right for one another. He was over-the-top angry and hurt when I told him I wanted to separate, and he's still angry. But, really, he's not around much."

Chaco exhaled in relief. *I don't want to fight this man.* "These tents…"

She corrected him. "Yurts."

"Do the yurts provide adequate protection in snow?"

"They're strong, and warm. Although the Common House is made from logs, and we have the old wood barn, and one of our more eccentric residents built and lives in a tree house, almost everyone lives in a yurt. Even our medical facility, school, and library are housed in yurts."

"You have a library?" Chaco's smiled. "I'll be. A library."

"Yes. It's well-stocked, too, with everything from the classics to contemporary literature, and all manner of scientific and scholarly texts. C'mon. I'll show you."

As they rounded the corner on the path toward the library, they entered a canopy of blue spruce. He reached for her hand, wanting to feel her skin, to touch her for a brief moment.

She pulled away. "Not here," she whispered, although no one else appeared on the trail. "We need to keep this thing between us under wraps until the divorce is final and I know for a certainty my ex isn't going to harass me about custody. We'll have our time, I promise."

"You know, I'm absolutely and completely in love with you, Fiona MacDougal."

"I feel the same way about you, Chaco Rodriquez." She glanced one way, then the other. "Oh, what the hell." She turned and kissed him with such ardor that he couldn't help but lead her into the grove. On the soft forest loam, under the protection of dense, fragrant boughs, they stripped from the waist down and made urgent, reckless love.

That was months ago. Chaco missed Fiona so much he ached.

***

After a nap, while the others slept, or were otherwise occupied, Chaco stood guard. He alternated between scanning the surrounding forest and the road leading from town and observing the skies through the scopes he'd carted over from the guest cottage. The Takahashi Mewlong 300 was too large to haul up a ladder, but he had good binoculars, and the telescope he'd use today, the 25-pound SolarMax. He set himself up on flat space on the roof, a perch he could use as a lookout, and an observatory platform. Chaco mounted the telescope, removed the cap and focused on the Sun's surface. A fiery tube bolted and looped in on itself, like an angry dragon, part of it breaking away in a flash so violent and so large, it eclipsed the SolarMax's viewfinder. *Hijo de puta, another enormous solar prominence.*

***

Evening could not have come soon enough for Chaco. When Rocky relieved him for guard duty, Chaco thanked him. Abigail called him down from the roof for their meal. A hint of a breeze rustled the leaves in the oaks and the needles in the pines and cooled the Walkers' patio. The moon hung in the sky like a thin slice of honeydew melon, and relative calm had settled over the town below. Campfires lit the streets and sidewalks with a surrealistic glow, and as he looked through his binoculars, Chaco saw men and women huddled around the fires in tight knots even in the warmth of the summer evening. *Pobrecitos.*

After a dinner of lentil stew and dumplings, Chaco brought out maps and spread them over the patio table, smoothing the creases with the palms of his hands. The women packed cartons and plastic carryalls to load into the truck and trailer. As he traced what he thought would be the safest route between Green Lake and Pine Mountain, Rocky called out. "Someone's comin'!"

The sound of the approaching vehicle turned Chaco's blood to ice. He picked up the binoculars and looked through them. *Oh man.*

CHAPTER 13

"They're headed this way," Chaco told Russell. "We better get Bethany and the kids back into the wine cellar right now."

As though performing a well-rehearsed play, everyone took his or her place. Chaco, Remington at his side, stood at a small opening at a window nearest the front door. He trained the binoculars on the approaching truck, badly dinged fender and driver door, back window shattered, but painted an extraordinary metal flake blue.

The vehicle rolled to a stop in front of one of the burned houses across the road. A tall, slender man in his late twenties wearing a grey Stetson, along with a short, heavyset woman with waist-length platinum blonde hair that hung over her arms like a shawl, exited the truck. The man turned and lifted out a chunky, tow-headed boy, maybe five-years-old. The people stood still before the burned dwelling that had once been a multi-million-dollar showcase. The man held the boy's hand.

"Are those your neighbors, Mr. Walker?" Chaco said. "They don't look like the Jenkins family." He stretched his arm to Russell and handed him the binoculars.

Russell put the glasses to his eyes "Never seen them before." He handed the binoculars back to Chaco.

The woman put her face in her hands and hung her head. Her body shook. The little boy ran to the woman, his arms outstretched.

"Those people aren't hostile," Chaco said. "That woman is crying."

Abigail shouted toward the back of the house. "All clear. No danger."

Margo lifted the wine cellar door. "C'mon out, y'all. It's safe."

Tucking the .38 into her waistband, Abigail unlatched the heavy front door. "Jude, you, Bethany and the girls stay here with Margo and Rocky. We're going out to see if we can help those people."

"We'll cover you in case something goes wrong," Rocky said.

"Good call." Chaco set the binoculars on a table and placed the Remington on the floor.

"Once in a great while, I'm right, you know," Rocky said, "even though I don't have a doctorate in anything."

Chaco put his hand out to Abigail, and without being asked, she withdrew the .38 and handed it to him. He tucked it into his belt. "Thank you, Mrs. Walker."

The group exited the house and headed for the people. As they approached, the three turned toward them. The man wore an expression of wariness. His large round eyes resembled those of a frightened owl. The woman looked hollow and scared. She seemed less a woman and more a bewildered ghost caught in a hellish dimension looking to find her way to the light.

Without speaking, the man motioned for the woman and the boy to move nearer to him.

"Are you lost?" Russell asked the man.

"No, no. Not lost. It's that…. this is my brother's house…or it used to be. Are they around? The family, I mean. Where are they? What happened?"

"You must be Dave Jenkins. I've heard your brother, Jim, speak of you. I'm Russell Walker. This is my wife, Abigail, and this is our friend, Chaco."

"I'm Dave, yes, and this is my wife, Patty and our son, Jack. Where's my brother and his family? They were vacationing in the Bahamas, but they were supposed to be home days ago."

Patty Jenkins stepped to one side, wiping her eyes on a sleeve. "We've been working our way up here from the coast. You won't believe how horrible it is. People broke into our house. Our dog tried to chase them, but they stabbed him. They killed our Rusty."

"My doggie is in heaven," the little boy said.

Patty wiped her eyes again. "We ran out of the house with what we could grab. As we were driving away, they fired a gun. Someone shot directly into the truck. See?" She showed Abigail the shattered back window. "They could have killed my little boy."

"My God," Abigail said.

"We drove out of there as fast as we could. We went for a while without any problem other than having to dodge debris and get around stalled cars on the road. We thought we would be safe, then we lost everything, our food, clothes, camping stuff…"

"What do you mean, you 'lost' everything?" Abigail asked.

"Stolen. Somebody blocked the road with oil barrels. When we stopped to find a way around, a group of ugly, filthy men jumped out from nowhere, ran to our truck and pulled everything out of the bed. I yelled at them. Dave tried to get out to stop them, but they said if we made another move, they'd kill us. One had a rifle, a big one, and pointed it right at my face. I've never been so scared in my entire life." Patty stroked the head of her little boy who clung to her leg.

"Then we saw something…. something horrible and scary. Someone grabbed the man with the rifle. She lowered her voice so her child could not hear "and cutting the man's neck with something that resembled a saw, he tore the man's head off and flung it aside like a cantaloupe… awful…. blood everywhere. I can't think about it without getting sick to my stomach. And everything everywhere is on fire. Buildings, fields, cars. And we don't have food or water left, only the clothes we're wearing. We were thinking that if we came here…I mean, to Dave's brothers…Sweet Jesus. People are getting murdered in our neighborhood…right in the street, right in their own homes. We even saw dead animals, lots of them. We thought here… we thought…getting to Jim and his family…coming here… our best hope. Now, we don't know what to do, or even where they are." She turned her head both ways as though expecting her brother-in-law to materialize.

"We'll find Jim, Marion, and the kids, sweetheart. Don't worry, please," Dave said. He reached a hand toward his wife.

She pulled away. "But where could they have gone? What about Jim? For all we know, he could be dead! Maybe all of…"

"Mommy, is Uncle Jim dead?" The boy whimpered.

"No, no. Mommy didn't mean that." Patty dropped to her knees and clutched her son, holding him close to her. "They're fine, I'm sure. Mommy and Daddy will find Uncle Jim, Auntie Marion, Mikey and Sammy. Okay?"

"Okay, Mommy."

"Why don't you come into the house and get something to eat?" Abigail said. She put her arm around Patty, who carried her son. The six of them headed toward the Walkers'.

***

Olivia and Lacy hopped up and down, thrilled to have a boy their age to play with. Bethany mixed some powdered milk, water and cocoa for chocolate milk. She made peanut butter and honey sandwiches and found half a package of Fig Newtons. The children and the dog gathered under the oak with a picnic style lunch while Bethany and Margo rummaged through the supplies to put together a makeshift meal for the adults.

"Bethany can make a gourmet feast from an old tennis ball and a stale box of saltines," Jude said.

She created a decent stew with canned vegetables, kidney beans, dried onion and vegetable bouillon cubes.

"This is tasty, but I gotta ask two questions," Rocky said. "Number one. How in the hell can we afford to feed anyone but ourselves? We don't have unlimited supplies, certainly not enough for three extra mouths. We should conserve what we have. Shouldn't we vote on this before we give our food away?"

"Rocky Pennymon," Margo said. "What happened to yer

sense of Christian charity? These people are hungry and they got a little boy. Do you expect anyone here would let them starve?"

"The problem is, Margo, and I think everyone will agree, is that we're going to run into others who need food, too. Do we expect to have enough to feed the entire world?"

"We don't mean to cause any problems." Patty put down her bowl. "Let's go, Dave."

"Can the boy at least finish? I know he's hungry," Dave said.

"Of course," Abigail said. "You all eat, please. Pay no attention to Rocky. You are welcome to share a meal with us."

Russell glared at Rocky. "Absolutely. Stay right here and finish your meal. There's enough for everyone."

"You're an idiot," Rocky said to Russell.

"And you are welcome to leave if you don't like the way we do things."

"Gawd, Rocky. Jist shut yer mouth," Margo said. "We are feeding these folks and that's all there is to it. Didn't you say you had another question? Why don't you git on with that?"

"All right. Why don't we ever eat meat? We've got jerky, Spam, tuna, canned salmon, salted beef, and…"

"Bethany is a vegetarian," Jude said.

Margo shook her head. "Oh, no, that won't do. What'll happen if we run outta vegetables?"

"I'll figure something out," said Bethany. "But, I cannot in good consciousness support the suffering animals endure because we like the taste of their flesh."

"What the hell do you do for protein?" Rocky asked.

"I eat nuts and seeds, eggs, beans, and tofu."

"Tofu? Are you kidding me? You may have noticed that we don't have much in the way of nuts and seeds. We'll be running out of beans probably in two weeks, and, do you *see* any tofu or eggs around here?" Rocky asked.

"I've been a vegetarian all my life. Even the smell of cooking meat nauseates me," said Bethany. "Besides, no matter how hungry I am, I will never condone cruelty to animals. By the way, do you have any idea about how the beef and poultry industry impacts the environment, or how cruel we are to livestock? No one can say they love animals and care about the environment if they consume animal flesh."

"Yeah? Well, we'll see if when there's no nuts and tofu left, and you're starving, if you don't change your mind about that, Ms. Self-righteous."

Jude jumped to his feet. "You know, Rocky? You can be a real asshole."

"So, I've been told, but at least I'll be a living asshole, while your prissy, skinny little vegetarian wife shrivels up into buzzard food because she'd rather die than let animal flesh touch her dainty lips." Rocky dabbed at his mouth with his forefinger and thumb as though holding a lace handkerchief. "She's ignorant as hell and you better set her straight. That stupid little…"

Disregarding his wounded ankle, Jude stood on one foot and dove for Rocky, throwing the bigger man to the flagstones and pinning him. Chaco, Russell and Dave grabbed at Jude. He shook them off.

Bethany jumped up and down with both feet like a jack-in-the-box. "Jude, stop it! Stop!"

Margo and Patty sprinted to the children to keep them away from the fray. Rufus bolted toward the scrapping men, jumped around them barking, hackles raised.

Jude punched Rocky in the face, punched him again, and drew his hand back to deliver a third blow, when Chaco seized Jude's fist with both hands and pulled back hard.

Still sitting astride the older man who struggled to get out from beneath the younger and stronger man, Jude turned to Chaco and made piercing eye contact. In a controlled, even voice, he said: "Let go of my hand, you fuckin' hajji, you goddamned Iraqi scum. I'll take your balls home to my wife as trophies, you fuckin'…"

"…C'mon, son. Let go of Rocky," Russell said.

Jude's attention shifted to his father, his eyes blank. His expression softened and he relaxed his grip. Chaco released Jude's hand. Russell put his arm around his son and helped him to his feet, then Jude broke into tears. "Hey, Chaco, I'm sorry, man, really. I don't know what came over me…I mean…. I know you aren't an Iraqi, but for a minute there…"

"Don't worry about it, *hermano*. It's all good." Chaco patted the taller man's back.

Wobbling like a drunkard, Rocky struggled to his feet. He wiped his bloody mouth and cheek with the back of his hand. "I'm sorry, everybody."

Margo dabbed his face with a wet washcloth. "You did have that comin', you fat lug. Glad to see yer at least a bit ashamed of yerself. You should be."

CHAPTER 14

A slight breeze blew, reminding Chaco of the coming autumn. He pulled on his jacket and buttoned it. "Good thing we are getting on the road soon. With luck, we'll make it to the sanctuary before the first big snowfall."

"I couldn't agree more," said Russell.

Late afternoon the group had gathered in a circle on the patio. Rocky produced a Jack Daniels bottle, poured shots into Dixie Cups, and passed them around. "I'm sorry, folks, for the way I behaved earlier… my wife and I discussed it…and, well, I'm sorry."

"It's over. A cancelled check. We've other things to discuss now," Russell said, turning to David. "We'll be leaving for Pine Mountain early. You and your family come with us. I know you'll be welcomed at Moonforest Sanctuary. We can easily fit another few people in the truck bed, or you can follow us if you…."

"…you've got to be kidding," Rocky said. "This is bullshit. We won't make it halfway there with three more people. And how in the hell do you know we'll be welcomed? They'll probably shoot our asses before we even get to the gate." He spit out a mouthful of his precious whiskey, and stomped off the patio.

"What happened to 'sorry'?" Margo called after him. "You are sorry all right…go ahead and walk away you sorry bonehead."

Chaco nodded at David. "It would be safer for you and your family if you stayed with us."

"Thank you, but no. Patty and I talked it over. We are going to find my brother. He might be at our cousin's house east of San Diego. With the gas, food, and water you shared with us, we'll make it."

"Thanks for everything," Patty said. She hugged Margo,

Bethany, and Abigail. "I mean it. We are very appreciative."

"Well, we better hit the road before nightfall." David said, and stretched. "We don't know what we'll encounter after dark. If we leave now, we can be there before the moon rises."

Russell extended his hand. "Safe travels."

The men shook. "You, too," David said.

David, Patty, and Jack climbed into their bright blue pickup and started down the road.

"Bye bye, Jack," Olivia and Lacy called out to the little boy waving at them through the broken back window of the truck. He pulled the corners of his mouth into a clown smile with his chubby fingers, crossed his eyes, and stuck out his tongue. Both girls dissolved into giggling fits.

Vaya con Dios, Chaco said.

CHAPTER 15

The early morning rays had moments before crept over the mountain top when Chaco studied the Sun through his Coronado SolarMax Double Stack. It would probably be the last time he'd use either of his telescopes. Both were too large and unwieldy for the trip ahead. He'd spent the entire evening before alternating between guard duty, scoping out the road through his binoculars, and scanning the night sky through his Takahashi Mewlong 300 with a MS-5 Mount. Combined, the two telescopes and mounts had cost him a fortune. *They'll rust here, become broken things, useful only as homes for spiders and earwigs.*

In an hour or so, everyone but the children would be awake. The group would share a final meal together on the Walkers' patio, then they'd finish the job of sorting, packing, and preparing for the 800-mile trip from Green Valley to Pine Mountain, and Moonforest Sanctuary. Chaco's only consolation for leaving his telescopes behind was the thought of his future with Fiona.

Early morning had always been Chaco's favorite time of day. The apricot tinted dapples of sunlight sprinkled over the mountains brought promise, each new dawn filled with infinite possibilities. Although Chaco's family raised him Catholic, he'd never been particularly observant. After leaving home, much to the consternation of his mother and grandmother, he rarely attended mass. However, now and again, he felt the urge to call upon the God of his youth. Chaco felt most inclined to pray at sunrise when the morning light hit the hills turning them from black to purple, from purple to pink, from pink to green. This morning, he prayed their journey would be swift, uneventful, safe, and that in no time he'd be holding Fiona, stroking the warm skin of her neck, tracing her collar bone with his fingertips, and down the soft curve of her breasts. Fiona's skin. The purest spun silk. The finest satin. So soft he could melt into the warm pool of her body—Fiona his tumescent *reina*, his queen. He'd written poems for her, and one came to him in a sweet moment. He recited it aloud.

When you approach
All the seas and rivers of the world
Make a joyous noise.
Music of angels fill the skies
Rendering even the birds silent.
Every cell in my body resonates
With the song of you.
Listen.

"Good morning, Chaco. That's beautiful. Did you write it?" Abigail stood near him. She had walked out of the house in her bare feet, stealing across the flagstones soft as a kitten.

"I have no talent for poetry."

"Is it for someone? I don't intend to pry, but...if you are comfortable in sharing... do you have someone...special, Chaco?"

"Yes, I do. Someone very special."

"Back home?"

"She lives a long way from here."

***

By 9 a.m. everyone had finished breakfast, the children played fetch with Rufus, and the adults crowded around a map spread out on the patio table.

"I've worked out a route that avoids all the highways. We can go through Allessandro here and turn right at Redlands here." Chaco traced the route with his forefinger. "From San

Timoteo, we'll travel over sixty miles before we hit Waterman, then Crestline, then CA-173 to Arrowhead Lake where we get to 395 and cross into Nevada …."

"Won't that take us a hell of a distance out of our way?"

"Yes, Mr. Pennymon, but it's the only feasible northern route that keeps us off major freeways and highways."

"Let me see if I've got this right. We go at least 100 miles further than we would if we headed straight up Highway 5, with limited fuel, over mountainous terrain, then we cross into another state with no idea what we'll run into there, and you think that's the most 'feasible route' to Pine Mountain?"

"What direction would you recommend, Rocky?" Russell asked. "We decided together that avoiding the main highways and thoroughfares made the best sense, and Chaco has done a damned good job of detailing a course to keep us off them. We also need to avoid any areas with nuclear plants, and his plan accomplishes that nicely. If you have a better idea, let's hear it."

"Fer gawdsake, Rocky, why cain't you jist get on board with everyone else? You have to argue ever-little thang Chaco comes up with. So far, he's showin' us that he's smart, trustworthy, brave and a darn good leader, and you…"

"What did you say? You think he's a 'leader'? The only thing he's leading us to is our deaths if you ask me. What the hell qualifies him to head this expedition? He might be your leader, but as for me…"

"I mean it, Rocky. Shut yer trap. We don't have time for this nonsense. You should say sorry to Chaco."

"Yeah, okay, fine. I'm sorry for every damned thing!" Rocky threw his hands into the air, and yelled to the sky, "I fuckin' give up!"

***

Sorting and packing the truck and trailer proved a massive challenge. Abigail wept when it became clear to her there would not be room for her many volumes of family photos she'd put together over the decades. "This is my life, *our* life," she said to Russell.

"No. Our life is here and now. We have our memories. We don't need photos to remind us of what used to be."

Everyone had to leave something behind. Chaco left his telescopes, all but four of his books, and all but a few of his bottles of good German wine. He did, however, bring an abundance of writing pads, pens, and pencils, which were easy enough to stick in crevices and small spaces here and there. Russell and Rocky had to leave their fine automobiles. Rocky nearly had a fit when it became apparent that only three bottles from his case of Jack Daniels would fit into his allotted space. "Shit, we could use this booze for medicinal reasons, you know."

"Good try," Margo said.

"What about all that aluminum foil that Chaco's got? He gets to bring, what, twenty, thirty rolls of aluminum foil, but there's no room for my Jack? Are you kidding me?"

"Mr. Pennymon, there are over 102 uses for aluminum foil. We can even make a decent stove from foil. We aren't likely to find more." Chaco turned his back on Rocky and continued packing.

"What about all this damned salt? What're two cases of salt good for?"

Chaco gritted his teeth but kept his voice even. "Besides preserving meat, providing iodine and food seasoning, salt has many practical applications. And it's a valuable commodity."

"How so?"

"Since there will be no way to get salt, it will be worth its weight in gold when it comes to bartering."

"You said you know where there are horses we can get our hands on." Abigail directed the comment to Chaco.

"Yes, a few hundred miles toward our destination there's a horse rescue operation, but I don't know if they have any tack anywhere, so I'm not sure how it'll work for us to…"

"Surely, they do have tack, but anyways, with good sturdy rope, I kin make a harness and a lead," Margo said. "I kin help you catch 'em, too and calm 'em down if they're worked up. We'll tie blankets on 'em for saddles if we have to. I'm good with horses."

"Yeah, she's a regular horse whisperer," Rocky said, then quickly added, "I don't mean that sarcastically, folks. She really is good with them. I had planned on buying her a gelding, but…"

"It's fine without, darlin'." Margo stroked her husband's back.

***

Night fell before the women finished packing.

"So, when do we head out?" Rocky asked. "I thought we were leaving right away."

"Not for a few hours," Chaco said. "We want to encounter the least amount of resistance."

"We'd be safer if we leave after most people are asleep, two or three a.m.," Jude said.

The men took turns guarding so that everyone could get a little rest. Sometimes, Chaco heard Abigail crying. *She must feel like she's leaving behind her entire world.*

At 2:30 a.m., Chaco, who had taken the last watch, tapped on the Walkers' bedroom door.

"Is that you, Chaco?" Russell asked.

"Yes. It's time."

Everyone loaded into the cab or bed of the truck. The children tucked under a blanket in the back seat with their mother and fell asleep. Abigail rode in the front with Russell, who drove. Chaco and Jude took seats in the bed with Rufus, weapons at the ready, keeping a watchful eye on the terrain. Chaco had stretched layers of transparent plastic over the shattered windshield—a less than perfect solution, but adequate.

They had not even gotten as far as the town when Russell stopped the truck. Chaco jumped out.

"What's up?" Jude said. He had propped his wounded foot on a box. He reached down, rubbed his calf and touched his ankle, then winced. "Why did you stop?"

"Looks like someone's gone over the cliff," Russell said. "I can see what looks like skid marks in the dirt and it appears a car, or something, went into the ravine."

"I'll go down and look," Chaco said. He pulled a flashlight from the bed of the truck, put on his jacket and made his way down the steep incline, picking his way over rocks. When he neared the bottom of the cliff, he aimed the beam of his flashlight, and there in the beam—a blue truck turned on its side, with a crushed-in cab top and smashed windows. The truck had rolled. From the passenger side window, like satin in the moonlight, long platinum blonde hair fanned out over the dirt.

***

It took a while to recover the bodies. Little Jack had been thrown clear of the wreckage, his mangled doll-like figure smashed against a Ponderosa pine. Both adults were crushed in the cab.

Chaco shook his head and tisked. "Probably all died instantly. At least, hopefully, no one suffered."

***

Abigail insisted on burying them, but although accustomed to getting her way with her husband, who Chaco thought would give her the universe if it would make her happy, she would not win this argument.

"No, sweetheart, I'm sorry. If we take the time to bury them, we'll put ourselves in jeopardy," Russell said.

"We can't leave them there like that. Surely to God, we can at least put blankets over them, and someone might say a few words."

"We can't afford any more time, Mrs. Walker," Chaco said. "It'll be dawn soon. We need to get out of Green Lake under the cover of darkness."

The men searched the wreckage for food, water, blankets, anything of use. Russell pulled a small boy's jacket from the back seat, one they had given to the family earlier.

Abigail didn't say another word. She climbed into the truck and stared at nothing through the passenger window.

Bethany kept the girls away from the crash site with a game of Sugarland by the light of an oil lamp. Although late, the little girls were wide awake. One of the girls giggled.

Chaco smiled. *Perhaps this is all a big adventure for them.* The board game, some jacks, and two stuffed bunnies that their grandma had kept for them at her house were the only toys the little girls had. According to Abigail, at one time, they had so many toys there wasn't enough space in their bedrooms to hold them all. The days of dozens of toys spilling out of closets and drawers were over. *They will have to learn to live without toys… that is, if they survive.*

CHAPTER 16

There were so many abandoned vehicles and debris on the streets that by the time the group made it out of Green Lake late that morning. Other than a group of ragged men who failed in their attempt to chase them down on foot, there were no incidents. Mostly, Green Lake and the surrounding areas resembled a ghost town. Stray cats and dogs roamed the streets in large numbers. Chaco imagined that the animals would evolve, learn to walk on their hind legs, develop language and create sophisticated canine and feline societies. Cats and dogs would work together to plot a global takeover. They would capture and herd humans they would train to do their bidding, and force them to wear collars and tags. How else would these domesticated pets survive without anyone to care for them?

In a short while, when supplies and food ran low, they would no longer be pets for humans. Instead, for the humans who once loved them, they would become one more nutritional source.

Russell drove for hours until he, at last, pulled into an old apricot orchard. He parked the truck and trailer beneath trees which concealed them from possible marauders traveling the main road and provided shade against the heat of the day. "Might as well make camp here." Everyone climbed out of the truck.

No one objected to the stop. They planned to rest during the day, and travel back roads at night to avoid detection. After a breakfast of processed cheese and saltine crackers, Bethany put the girls down for a nap on a blanket in the shade.

The men helped Jude out of the truck, and Margo tended to his wounded ankle. She cradled his foot in her hand, and with tenderness and caution, removed his shoe. He winced, but the shoe slid off easily enough.

She examined his foot, prodding here and there. "Well, it ain't broke, that's fer sure. It's pretty bad, but looks like the swellin' has gone down a little. Sure wish we had some ice, though."

"It better be healed enough for him to walk a few hundred miles once we run out of gas," Rocky said. "We probably won't make it too far in the truck."

"With the fuel left in the tank, truck fully loaded, pulling a full trailer, I estimate we'll get no more than 15 miles to the gallon." Chaco jotted a calculation on the border of the map spread out on the dirt. "Depending on road conditions and weather, we'll make it about 420 miles, more or less."

"But we've got two five-gallon gas cans full, don't we?" Abigail said. "And, we have a siphoning hose, yes?"

"We aren't the only ones who have been siphoning gas over the past week or so. As for ten lousy gallons additional, big whoop. That'll get us another 100 miles or so if we're lucky. We would have had more if Mr. Brilliant hadn't given the other two full gas cans to that family, who obviously don't need it now, do they?" Rocky said. "On top of that, once we do run out of fuel, we have to figure out how to make it another 300 or 400 miles."

"Chaco did the charitable thang," Margo said. "Those folks needed our help, and I'm plain disgusted with you even bringin' up that poor family. Rest their souls. 'Sides, we might have horses soon."

"Only if they're still there, or still alive once we get to them," Rocky said.

"Ya know? We'd all be better off if you weren't so negative all the time. Cain't you jist envision a positive outcome for us all, or ain't you capable of nuthin' other than pissin' and moanin' about how awful thangs are gonna be, Mr. Doom and Gloom? We've made it this far, ain't we?"

***

The heat sweltered. Mosquitos and flies menaced the group, who had put up tents so sauna-like inside, no one could stay in them. Margo liberally applied her Mrs. Beasley's Bees Wax lipbalm to the girls' faces and exposed arms. The girls spread out on their blanket and slept. She and the others leaned their backs against tree trunks, fanned themselves with Chaco's writing tablets, and swatted at flies with rolled newspapers they'd found on a trash heap. They all dozed off and on, speaking seldom.

Before long, only the light buzzing of midges and mosquitos broke the silence. Once in a great while, a breeze rustled the leaves on the apricot trees. Chaco, who had taken the first watch, yawned and swatted away a June bug. He daydreamed of Fiona, about what it would be like to hold her again, to kiss her. He whispered the lines of another poem he'd written for her.

What I most remember
Is your slender fingers
Touching my skin like a
Butterfly wing against the petal
Of a rose
Then I become the butterfly
Seeking the nectar
Of your smile,
The sweetness of your skin.
Lovely one,
With your delicate…

"Fuck! Fuck!" Jude let out a chilling scream and threw punches like a crazed man in a bar brawl. Then he curled into a ball covering his head with his arms. "Get down! Incoming! Incoming!"

Bethany ran to his side. "It's okay, baby. Wake up. You're having a dream, a bad dream."

When she bent down to him and touched his shoulder, he twisted hard toward her, flashed open his eyes, and grabbed her by the neck. Despite his injured ankle, in a single violent move, he threw her to the ground, flat on her back. He straddled her and pressed his thumbs into her throat with both hands. She thrashed and squirmed, clawing at his hands.

Russell yanked at Jude's arms "Stop, Son. Stop! It's Bethany. You're killing her." It took the combined strength of the adults to pull him off.

Jude loosened his grip, released his fingers, and rolled off her. "Damn! I'm sorry, Bethany. Are you okay? Please tell me you are."

She coughed and sputtered, and clutched her neck, her face crimson. Abigail sat beside her. "Look at your neck."

"I'm…*cough*…fine. Jude does this now and again, but usually, he wakes up before it gets…he hasn't done this for a long time. We didn't have time to get his meds. Without them, he has terrible nightmares. It's not his fault."

Her voice came out in rasps, but natural color finally returned to her face. Abigail helped her to her feet. Although wobbly, Bethany could stand. She took a few deep breaths then crouched next to her husband. Jude got to his knees, put his arms around her, and rocked her from side-to-side. "I'm so sorry. I'm sorry. I'm sorry. I love you, baby. I didn't mean to…"

"I know you didn't mean it. Don't worry. I'm fine."

The girls, who had been startled awake, wailed. "What's wrong with mommy?" Olivia hopped from foot to foot trying to get a better view from behind Chaco, the Pennymons and her grandparents who stood between her and her mother.

"She's okay, sweetie. Your daddy had a bad dream, that's all," Abigail said.

"But he hurt mommy. Me and Lacy saw."

Bethany pulled away from Jude, whose arms hung limply at his side. Tears ran down both cheeks. Jude repeated, "I'm so sorry. I'm so sorry." The big man tried to get up, and in doing so, he reinjured his ankle and fell back hard onto the ground. "Damn, damn," he cried in pain.

"Jude. Look at what you've done to your ankle. It's worse… so much more swollen." Bethany bent to her daughters, taking them into her arms. "No, Daddy didn't hurt me. See? There's some little red spots on my neck. That's all. I'll be fine. He had a terrible nightmare, poor Daddy. He didn't mean it. It's all right. Now his sore ankle is hurt worse and you must help me take care of him. Will you?"

***

Once things had settled down and the girls were enjoying their snack of animal cookies and raisins, Chaco, Rocky, and Russell took a stroll through the orchard looking for fallen fruit or anything of use. They located water in an irrigation ditch. They filled several empty plastic milk cartons and dropped in purification tablets. Then they removed their shirts, splashed water onto their faces and hair, soaked their shirts, wrung them and put them back on.

"Hey, we found an irrigation ditch with water," Russell said as the men entered camp with the full containers.

Abigail stood and dusted herself off. "Is it difficult to get to?"

"No, not too bad. You might have to scoot on your rear down a steep part of a hill, but you'll manage."

"Well, I don't know about anyone else, but I could use a bath."

"Excellent idea," said Bethany. "I'll soak a towel and bring it up to you, sweetheart," she said to Jude. "You'll be okay here, won't you?" She turned her head. "Margo, are you coming with us?"

"You betcha, honey. I need to warsh these nasty panties of mine. I haven't changed 'em in three days and they're stickin' to me." She wiggled her butt as though shaking off ants.

"Ah, jeez," Rocky huffed in disgust. "Could you even be crasser?"

"Could you even shut yer mouth?"

Bethany and Abigail rummaged around the trailer and found a bar of Ivory soap, toothbrushes, and towels. The three women walked side-by-side to the ditch. Chaco followed close behind.

"You don't have to protect us none. I'll take care of everyone jist fine," Margo said and patted her weapon.

"I'm coming. I'll find a place on high ground to keep an eye on things so you can take your baths."

They picked their way down the rocky hill to the water. Bethany and Abigail stripped down to their underwear, laying their clothes on nearby rocks.

"Now, how y'all plannin' to warsh yerselves, ya know... down there," Margo whispered and pointed to the women's crotches, "...if you are wearin' yer panties? Chaco's no little boy. He's seen nekkid ladies before."

"I'm more comfortable in my underwear, if you don't mind," Abigail said.

"Me, too," said Bethany.

"Suit yourselves." Margo unhooked her red lace push-up bra, put it on a rock ledge, and stepped out of her black thong panties to join the other two. As she walked into the ditch, Chaco gulped and looked in the opposite direction. *¡Qué vista! What a view!*

The women stepped into the knee deep brackish water. They squealed and splashed each other like children, soaped one another's backs, and washed each other's hair. Out of respect, Chaco, who had perched himself on a nearby ledge, kept his eyes averted, but now and again, he couldn't help but see. He wasn't purposely voyeuristic, but he would do everything within his ability to protect them, which made it impossible not to look sometimes. "I'm sorry, ladies. But, I must scan all directions. I'm not trying to peek." He did his best not to look.

If he happened to glance toward the women cavorting in the shallow water, he'd catch a sight of Margo's bare breasts or buttocks. *Dios mio, I never thought of Margo as beautiful.* While washing herself, she bent over giving him a full view of her behind. His member stiffened. He willed himself to think of his *abuela* until, to his relief, his penis returned to a flaccid state.

Margo glanced back at him. She must have noticed his furtive glances in her direction. She stood and faced him full-on, unabashed, hands on her hips. When he cast his eyes downwards, she laughed.

"Don't you worry none, honey. Yer jist a normal man, and if you do happen to be lucky enough to see anythin' a mine, I promise you'll git the thrill of yer life."

"You're a character," Abigail said to her, laughing. "I've never known anyone quite like you."

"And, you won't never know anyone like me." Margo gave Abigail a playful one-handed push.

Embarrassed, Chaco kept his eyes on his feet until certain she no longer stared at him.

Bethany acted as if there had been no exchange between the other women and Chaco. She kept herself somewhat hidden behind a rock. "Would you scrub my scalp?" she asked Abigail. "I wish we had some conditioner," she said as Abigail lathered her head.

"You know Chaco's a good guy," Abigail said to Bethany.

"I'm sure he is, but I don't know him well, and I'm not used to bathing in my underwear in front of…well, you know."

"In front of men, or in front of Latino men?"

"I'm not prejudiced. It's not that. I've have just never known…I guess I'm shyer than some women, especially in front of…" She stared at Margo who stared at Chaco who quickly looked in the opposite direction.

"Are you telling me that my son is the only man you've ever been with?" Abigail asked.

Bethany blushed.

"You really are a sweet girl, Bethany. And I'm sorry. I didn't mean to embarrass you. It's really none of my business. Let's rinse your hair." Abigail cupped some water in her palm and poured it over Bethany's head.

Margo snatched her underwear off the dirt. Abigail tossed the soap to her so she could scrub them. "Oh fer gawdsake. I completely forgot to get a dry pair. I'll have to wear 'em wet like you girls, I suppose. At least since I'm wearing my Victoria Secret thong, I won't have to go around with a wet butt all day."

The women climbed out of the water and dried themselves. Bethany and Abigail kept their backs turned to Chaco. Bethany, a towel wrapped around her, tip-toed over the dirt to her clothes. She got dressed and put on one shoe, but when she reached for the other, she knocked it off the rock and it rolled down the steep incline, landing under a low overhang. "Crap," she said. She partially trotted and partially skidded down the hill, bent over and reached beneath the overhang to retrieve the other shoe.

"No! Don't put yer hand under that rock!" Margo shouted. "There might be…"

The snake must have been too startled to give adequate warning. The viper sunk its fangs into the fleshy part between Bethany's thumb and forefinger.

Bethany screamed, jerked her hand from under the rock and leapt back, falling on her rear. "It'll bite me again." She scooted herself backward hard up the hill with both feet, holding her bitten hand, and screaming. Chaco jumped off the rocks and sprinted to the ledge. Abigail and Margo ran to Bethany, who struggled to her feet.

"Stay down. Don't move," Margo said. "You'll make the poison go through yer body faster. Jist breathe nice and easy through yer nose."

Bethany forced ragged breathes through her flared nostrils, her eyes glazed with pain and panic, but she laid still.

"Thatta girl."

Chaco found the rattler still under the overhang and shot

it. It writhed, knotting and unknotting itself, then he retrieved Bethany's other shoe.

Margo had pulled her t-shirt off over her head, bit a hole in a corner so she could tear it into strips. She made a bandage and tied it around Bethany's injured hand.

"Shouldn't we cut open the wound and suck the venom out? Or, can we make a tourniquet or something?" Abigail asked.

"No, honey. That don't work," Margo said. "What we need is a good hospital and a dose of anti-venom, but since we cain't get that, we'll have to jist keep her quiet, let her rest, and pray to Jesus." She looked up at Abigail and Chaco. "We don't want her movin' much, or the poison will git to her heart. Gotta keep her real still."

Bethany moaned in pain. "It hurts so much." She rocked back and forth cradling her bandaged hand against her chest.

"It'll be all right, sweetie. Let's get you on back to camp," Abigail said.

Chaco handed the Remington to Abigail, put Bethany's other shoe on her foot and laced it up. He picked her up in his arms, and carefully made his way toward camp, the women on his heels, Margo in her cut-off jeans, shoes and red lace bra trailing behind.

"Go on ahead without me, okay?" Margo said, catching up to Abigail.

"Sure, but why?"

"Gotta go back and fetch something I forgot. Y'all go on ahead. I'll catch up right away."

Margo raced back to the ditch. As the others crested the hill to camp, they ran into a panicked Rocky and Russell coming from the opposite direction.

"We heard screams and a shot. What the hell happened?" Rocky whipped his head around, searching. "Where's Margo? Where is she, goddammit!"

"She's okay," Abigail said. "She left something behind. She'll catch up."

"What's wrong with Bethany?" Russell asked. "What happened to her hand?"

"A snake bit me," Bethany said. "It hurts so bad." Her hand, now purple, had swollen to the size of a ripe melon. Her breath came in rasps.

"If you take Bethany back to camp, Rocky, I'll go back and find Margo," Chaco said.

Upon hearing his first name issue from Chaco's mouth, Rocky flinched as though someone had thrown ice in his face. "I'll find my wife if you don't mind. *You* take Bethany to camp."

"I know the exact way. It'll be faster if I go. I'll bring her back safe."

"I don't give a rat's ass if you…"

"Oh, fer gawdsake," No one had noticed that Margo had returned. "Quit your damn squabblin' and get Bethany to where she kin rest. And…what's wrong with y'all?" In one hand dangled the lifeless three-foot long rattler. "Quit yer gapin'. Y'all ain't seen a woman in a bra before?"

"It's not your bra we're looking at," Rocky said.

"You mean this little ole' snake?" She studied the rattler for a second, held it out from her body and gave it a single shake. "Chaco shot it way dead, didn't ya?" She called out after Chaco as he scrambled up a ledge, carrying Bethany in his arms. "It ain't gonna do no harm now, and these days we cain't let nuthin' go to waste. These things is real good eatin'."

CHAPTER 17

The afternoon passed in a haze. On a rumpled blanket, Bethany passed out in a fitful tangle of limbs. The little girls remained by her side, sniffling. The group decided to stay put until Bethany healed enough to travel. Margo and Abigail took turns tending the injured woman.

"I'd prefer we left now," said Rocky. "The longer the delay, the more chance we have of running into dangerous weather."

"Bethany is far too injured to travel," said Russell.

"Whatever," said Rocky, throwing up his hands in resignation. "I think it's too risky for us to stay here, but I suppose my opinion doesn't matter."

"There's water, shade, and we are well off the main road. As long as we stay low and remain quiet, no one traveling this way will even know we're here. We can take turns on guard duty. There's a protected ledge over the ridge there," Chaco said, "and from top, we can get a clear view in all directions."

Margo took a short walk to relieve herself behind the bushes. A few minutes later, she reappeared, her face flushed with excitement. "I hate to tell y'all this, but as unlikely as it may be in these parts, I jist saw a bear. We better not keep the food too close to where we're campin' because a hungry bear kin hurt a person if it's tryin' to git food."

"We better move the truck and trailer," Russell said. "Let's park it over the ridge. It's out of site from the road, but not so close to where we're going to be resting. Looks like with Bethany—the way she is, we might be here for a few days, or longer. Chaco, would you mind moving the truck?"

"Put Bethany near me." Jude rubbed his re-injured ankle. "I'll take care of her."

"She might get restless," Margo said. "It would be better if she had…some room." She glanced at Chaco.

He nodded. Yes, we are all concerned that Jude might experience another loco nightmare, and this time choke Bethany to death in front of her little girls.

"I'll tell you what, Jude," Chaco said. "We'll put her right under that tree nearest you where you can keep a closer eye on her. Does that make you feel better?"

"I'd prefer to have her next to me…so I can guard her while…where's my AR-15?" He patted the soil around him.

After Jude's earlier "episode," Russell had handed the weapon to Chaco. "Keep this," he'd whispered.

"I understand Mr. Walker."

"I've got it, Jude," Chaco said. "I'll clean it and bring it back to you later. Better get some rest so you can heal that ankle. I need to get the food moved to a safer place." He secured the food and water and drove the truck over the ridge.

***

In El Salvador, there are many varieties of poisonous snakes, some so deadly that within a few minutes of a bite, if envenomed, the victim dies. While fighting for the resistance, Chaco spent many weeks in the mountains and uninhabited areas where toxic snakes frequented. He, along with the other revolutionaries, had to learn about serpents, how to identify the poisonous ones and avoid them, and how to treat their bites.

Their medics carried with them anti-venom for the most common, such as the K'anti, or "cantil de aqua," a particularly vicious and aggressive viper that strikes repeatedly, the "Cantil Sapo" a jumping pit viper, and the Sheta, a type of serpent that injects venom that is rarely fatal but nonetheless so painful that Chaco heard from his men that its victims beg for death.

And of course, in Central America, there are several varieties of Cascabel, the rattlesnake. There were other toxic serpents, too, so many, in fact, that Chaco had nightmares about them. He watched a soldier die who had been bitten by K'anti. Even though the field medic injected the man with anti-venom, he must have administered the medicine too little or too late. Chaco witnessed the soldier die a gruesome and agonizing death—his tongue swollen, protruded from his mouth, his eyes rolled back into his head. Spittle like foamy soap bubbles issued in bursts from his nose and mouth. His body seized, then went rigid like a corpse with advanced rigor mortis. The man moaned with a voice so loud and pitiful it sounded like a house cat being burned alive, or a chupacabra wailing in the night. He cried out in one long howl, then died. That sound and the accompanying vision haunted him for years. Nothing he had witnessed or studied about snake bites, however, prepared Chaco for what happened to Bethany.

Chaco read that in the United States, only five or six people die each year from rattlesnake bites. The rattler envenomation is a hemotoxic, affecting the circulatory system, but generally less deadly than the neurotoxin venom of some snakes that damage the nervous system and brain. Her chances of survival were fair, even without anti-venom, unless she had an allergy to the toxin.

"I know something about snakes," said Chaco. "We don't have access to anti-venom, and that's not good, but although there is a chance that Bethany might lose her hand, she could survive."

"Do you know that for certain? I mean, that she'll live?" Russell asked.

"Unfortunately, there is no way to predict what might happen once someone is bitten. There are many variables to take into consideration that factor into a snake bite victim's survival and recovery."

"Such as?" Russell asked.

"General health and body weight, possible allergy, the quantity of envenomation…"

"What the hell is 'enven-o-mashun'?" Rocky asked.

"It's the amount of venom a snake injects into a bite."

"Why in the hell don't you just say that? Do you have to show us every single day you've got a PhD?"

"Jist because our vocabulary ain't is good as his doesn't mean Chaco should dumb it down to make yer sore ego feel better, Rocky. Let him talk, for gawdsake," said Margo. "Go on ahead, Chaco." She nodded for him to continue.

"The specific variety of rattlesnake matters, too. Some rattlers' venom is more toxic than others. A Mojave Green bit Bethany, and they are nasty."

Abigail gasped.

"I'm sorry, Mrs. Walker. I don't mean to alarm you, but I won't sugarcoat the situation either. Rattlesnake bites are serious. Without proper medical care and anti-venom—I'm afraid her survival is out of our hands."

"Can we at least give her some aspirin to ease the pain?" Russell asked.

"Nope. Aspirin is a real bad thang for rattler bites. It's a blood thinner, and given' it to her will make it worse," Margo said.

Bethany, mercifully unconscious, let out a cry. Margo pressed a damp cloth to the injured woman's forehead. "There, there, darlin'."

Russell and Rocky stood guard duty, and Abigail kept herself busy putting together a meal. While Margo tended Bethany to the best of her ability, Jude leaned against a tree and moaned, uttering incomprehensible sentences, calling Bethany's name. He pointed at Chaco. "You did this to her. You! If she dies… she better be okay."

Russell tasked Chaco with keeping the children away from their mother. It was a rough afternoon and evening for everyone.

Within two days, Bethany's arm had swollen to three times its normal size, and her hand turned black. The skin around the bite had split open and oozed blood and watery pus. Her arm from the fleshy part between her thumb and forefinger where the viper had sunk its fangs to the elbow looked as though it had dissolved into a gelatinous black mess. Muscle and tendons were exposed in sections, and the bones of her wrist protruded through the ruined flesh. When Chaco saw Bethany's arm, he knew he'd have to keep the little girls from seeing their mother, or they'd be horrified, scarred, maybe affected for life. "We have to amputate," he said to Margo.

"She ain't never been strong enough for us to do that. She'd be in way more agony if we'd go sawin' off her hand without anesthesia or proper care. We gotta pray real hard and hope fer the best." Margo motioned for Chaco to keep the little girls away. She shook her head and mouthed, "She's dyin'."

"I know," Chaco mouthed back.

Bethany moaned again.

"All right, girls. Let's go to the water and cool off." Chaco gathered the squirming children into his arms and carried one on each hip.

Olivia strained to see her mother over Chaco's shoulder. "But is Mommy okay? Isn't she gonna be all better soon? Why did she cry?"

"Margo is taking care of her. Let's go and let your mommy rest for a little while."

Bethany cried out again, this time louder.

"Mommy!" Olivia said. She kicked.

Lacy pushed away from Chaco. "I want Mommy. Lemme down!" she shrieked.

Jude, who had been dozing off and on, popped open his eyes. He struggled to stand but fell back into the dirt. "Dammit! What's going on? Why are Olivia and Lacy screaming? Won't someone tell me what the hell is happening with my wife?" He propped himself on an elbow and again attempted to stand.

"Please." Margo ran to help Jude back onto his blanket. "Jist rest right there. We're doin' the best we can, I promise you, but if you hurt yerself worse, we'll have two people to care for. I mean it."

"Can we amputate or something? Anything to keep her alive. Please."

"We ain't got anesthesia. Without it, the shock will be too much on her." She lingered for a moment longer to check his ankle. "Yer foot is all swollen up bad again. You cain't be jumpin' up on it." She gave Jude a sip of water from a red Solo cup.

With both girls clutched in his arms, Chaco turned so they could no longer see their mother's face.

By the time Margo returned to Bethany's side, the little girls' mommy had passed. Flies had already landed on the dead woman's opened eyes. Margo swatted them away and covered Bethany's face with the damp cloth she'd used moments before to cool the dying woman's forehead.

"No!" Jude screamed. "God no! God no! God no!" He crawled on all fours to his wife's corpse.

The little girls screeched, flailed, and kicked at Chaco harder in an effort to twist around to see their mother, or to make him let them go so they could run to her, but he held them all the tighter and carried them away.

***

As they dug Bethany's grave, Chaco and Rocky worked together to chip away at the hard clay. Even with a sharp pickaxe and heavy shovel, it seemed to Chaco as though there were a million granite chunks embedded in the dried soil, and every other strike with his pick knocked against a rock so hard that it sent a shock through Chaco's arm and neck like an electrical jolt. Both men sweated profusely, allowing drops to fall into the hole, each splash creating a dark spot that spread into a nearly perfect circle. There were so many droplets against the red clay the spots looked like blood splatters. Neither of the men spoke. They kept at their task, both knowing that in the heat, and with the fly swarms, the corpse would rot quickly, making a horrible situation even more so. They didn't have much time.

Attended by his mother and father, Jude nearly comatose, did not, or could not, acknowledge his inconsolable little girls who tried to clamor onto his lap as he sat, slumped with his arms limp against his sides.

Jude's fingers curled and uncurled on hands that, otherwise, hung slack in the dirt. He shed no tears as he stared transfixed at the lifeless body of his beloved wife. He blinked his eyes now and again, as if by force, but for the most part, his face remained still, cold and silent as granite.

Abigail and Russell did their best to comfort Jude, to soothe his pain. Abigail cried silent tears she rubbed away with her dust-coated sleeve, leaving broad dirt smudges on her cheeks. Russell remained stoic. He rested his hand with great tenderness on his son's shoulder.

After pulling both the anguished little girls off their daddy, Margo sat on the bare ground and held them, allowing them to sob against her, leaving round wet patches that appeared to Chaco like the milk leaking through a new mother's nipples, dampening her cotton blouse. He'd once seen that very thing in the public square of Soyapango, and the lovely image of a young mother with her fuzzy-headed newborn in a sling, her blouse damp at her breasts with her own milk. The memory came back to him in a rush.

As he took a moment to rest, leaning against his pick, he focused on Margo with her lap full of grief-stricken little girls. She rocked Olivia and Lacy in a relaxing rhythm, cradling them close to her, and cooing to them in a soft sing-song voice as though they were tiny, injured birds. 'It's gonna' be jist fine, little ones. It's gonna' be all okay."

Chaco, Russell, and Rocky dug a grave, rolled Bethany into

a blanket, carried her to the hole, and lowered her. She felt light, too light for a grown woman. The weight of her was that of cotton candy, as though when she'd died, she'd taken the substance of her body with her and left behind only a fragile shell. Chaco could have easily done the job himself.

After covering her with dirt, the men piled rocks on the soil. With a pocket knife, Chaco scratched into a broad, flat piece of rock, "Bethany Walker." He hesitated. "What is her birthdate?" he asked Russell.

"Honestly, I don't know. She's younger than Jude, but I can't recall off-hand how much, or when her actual birthdate is. I think it's in September…I don't know. You'll have to ask Jude."

"No need, Mr. Walker." Chaco scratched into the rock the date of her death, dusted off the face of the makeshift plaque with his shirt to remove loose particles, then placed the marker at the head of the grave, and secured it with a deliberate push into the dirt.

Jude never moved from his seated position. His mother remained at his side, stroking his forehead. He stared at the empty space where his wife had lain, as though she were still there, the last place he'd seen her alive, and the whole while, he murmured incomprehensible words.

Margo brought the girls to the grave of their mother. She'd picked a few wilted yellow flowers, nothing more than weeds, really, but she divided them into two small bundles. The girls clutched them in their hands as though they were prize roses. She lifted first Olivia, who placed her bundle on the rocks as she sniffed back tears. "Goodbye, Mommy." Then, Margo lifted Lacy who set her flowers on the grave, patting them into place with both of her chubby little hands, the entire time wailing, hiccupping, and sputtering, unable to form words.

The Sun's rays had begun to sink behind the mountains, which had turned from light brown to a dark purple. The sky started a clear pink and faded into a pale, blue heaven. Chaco, looking into the sunset, whispered, *¿Quién será próxima?* Who will be next?

CHAPTER 18

Early the following morning, the group prepared to break camp and continue their travels. Hours before dawn, Rufus trotted off by himself. Since the beginning of their journey, and while everyone slept, the dog often wandered off into the night alone to return hungry later in the morning. If he didn't return by the time they were ready to depart, Russell or Jude would whistle for him, and he'd come bounding back, tail akimbo, paws often muddied, his big pink tongue hanging from his slobbery jowls. Chaco had developed a fondness for Rufus, always glad to see the dog running back into camp. "That dog has more personality than some people," he'd said to Russell once, "and more compassion and intelligence, too," he said glancing in Rocky's direction.

Russell laughed. "You're certainly right about that."

Except for the sounds of the women rustling about the camp gathering clothes and blankets together, all went silent. The dawn air had taken on a new chill.

"Getting closer to autumn. I kin smell it in the air," Margo said, as she bundled the little girls until they resembled teddy bears. Nonetheless, the children shivered against the cold, their eyes red from crying. Neither said much and they fell back asleep resting against one another.

From a fallen branch, Russell and Chaco fashioned a crutch for Jude and helped him to his feet. During the night, Jude had snapped out of his catatonia, but somber—the look in his eyes more angry than grief-stricken. He had yet to shed a tear for his dead wife, at least not that Chaco could tell. Jude moved mechanically as he tried the crutch, and stepped forward exerting a bit of pressure on his injured ankle. He winced, then tried again, this time with more success. "This'll work," he said, tipping the crutch toward his father. "Thanks, Dad."

"Chaco did the lion's share of the work in making that crutch for you," Russell said.

"Yeah, I'm sure he did."

"How about a thank you to him as well?"

"Oh yeah, I almost forgot. Thank you for getting my wife killed. Oops, I mean, for making this fine crutch."

Chaco recoiled but said nothing.

"I know you're hurting, son. We hurt, too. We all loved Bethany, but Chaco had nothing to do with her getting bitten. How can you even say that?"

"Chaco went with the women to protect them, right?" He snapped his head toward Chaco, looking at him for the first time since his wife's death. "Where the fuck were you when she stuck her hand under that goddamn rock? Why did you let her do that?" He chuckled. "You *are* to blame, yes, you are."

Chaco gestured with palms turned up, "I sat on a hill more than forty feet away. I couldn't…"

"You couldn't what? You couldn't shout to warn her not to do that?"

"Hold on right there," Margo said. "We done our level best to keep her from stickin' her hand under there. She jist did it so fast. Nuthin' we could do. We honestly tried to…"

Jude leaned on his crutch and clapped both hands in mock applause. "Well, then, good job Margo and Chaco." He clenched his teeth. "And, Margo, I don't even want to know how you think you tried to help my wife. You aren't fit to carry her lunch. You dress and act like a cheap whore, and I doubt you even have a fourth-grade education, you ignorant…"

"Stop right there," said Rocky. "That's my wife you're talking to."

"Don't bother with it, Rocky. He's grievin,' that's all. He's lashin' out at me, but not on purpose. He's jist hurtin' real bad," Margo said.

"No, I'm not 'jist hurtin real bad'," Jude said. "My wife is dead, and you and Chaco are to blame. Neither of you wants to take any responsibility for your failure to protect Bethany. But I'm going to goddamn make you take responsibility." He pointed at each in turn. "Both of you."

"Jude, please," Abigail said. "Losing Bethany is terrible for everyone, but we all know this is hardest on you and the girls. Every one of us understands how you must be feeling right now. I know you want to blame someone, but..."

"Mom, you don't know shit about how I feel."

"That's enough, son. You need time to process this, to grieve, but you have no right to blame anyone or to be disrespectful to Margo or to your mother. You know, we are trying to help," Russell said.

Jude did not reply, instead, he practiced walking using his crutch a few more steps.

"In the meantime, you still have two precious little girls who need their daddy," Abigail said.

Jude stopped short and turned his head to her. "No."

"What do you mean, 'no'?" said Abigail. "They lost their mother in a horrible way, and they need you now more than ever."

"Can't do it."

"Of course you can 'do it'. You have to."

"Daddy?" Said Olivia. "Don't you love us?" Tears brimmed her eyes.

"My gosh. I thought you two was nappin'," Margo said. "What y'all doing here? Of course, he loves ya both a whole big bunch. Yer daddy is sad right now, jist like you. Let's me, you, and Lacy go see if we cain't find some cocoa somewheres around here, and I'll make y'all a big mug." Margo took both girls by the hand, and the three walked over the rise toward the truck and trailer.

"Mom, I can't do it," Jude whispered. "They remind me too much of Bethany. I can't even look at either of them right now.

I don't want to even be around them."

"How can you say that?"

"Sorry, Mom. This is how I feel."

"Oh, Jude. I know you don't mean that."

He allowed his mother to embrace him, and as she murmured kindnesses, he turned to Chaco and his pursed lips broke into a tight smile. His eyes went steely and dark, as though nothing lived behind them. During the resistance, Chaco had often seen this. Soldiers, after having witnessed or participated in one too many horrible atrocities, literally overnight lost their sense of humanity, and with it, any shred of compassion. Their eyes went vacant, no light, no soul left in them, exactly like Jude's. Chaco shuddered.

"M'gawd! Come quick, Rocky. Ever'one. Oh, m'gawd," Margo shouted.

The Walkers, Chaco and Rocky sprinted toward the truck, and there they found nothing. The lock on the trailer had been broken off, and all the food, water and most of the supplies were missing. The remaining gas had been siphoned from the gas tank, as well.

"There's no food. Nuthin left," said Margo.

"Jesus. How could they have done this without our knowing?" said Russell. "I stayed on guard, and I didn't hear a peep, not from anyone. Where's Rufus? That dog didn't make a sound. He would have barked his head off if he'd seen or smelled anything near the camp or the truck. I wonder why he didn't even…"

"That's because he's way over there," said Margo, letting go of the girls' hands and pointing. "They kilt him. He probably didn't even see those men before they put that arrow in him. Damn their souls, they kilt the dog."

A short distance away, partially concealed beneath trees, Rufus's body splayed across the ground, an arrow sunk deep into his ribs. His thick tongue lolled from his mouth into the dirt.

Free from Margo's grasp, the girls sprinted to their dead pet. Chaco grabbed for them, but they ducked away, and within a few seconds were at Rufus' side.

Lacy stroked the dog's head, and let out a wail. Her face contorted in agony.

"Rufus," cried out Olivia, burying her head into the fur of dog's haunch.

"No," said Abigail. "No." She collapsed onto her knees and moaned.

CHAPTER 19

The group gathered around a fire. Jude, who had become confident with his crutch, took the girls to relieve themselves in the orchard. "How 'bout we play a game before bed."

"Need help?" Margo called after him.

"No. Got it handled. Thanks."

Abigail rose from her seat as well. "Jude? Are you certain? I can take the girls, if you'd prefer."

"Mom, I'm all right. It's fine."

Margo rose from her seat and dusted off her rear. "Rocky, let's me and you take a little stroll. We ain't spent time together jist talkin' in ages."

The couple walked together into the orchard.

When Abigail, Russell, and Chaco were left to themselves, the older man opened up to Chaco. "I don't know you. You lived in our guest house for years, but I…don't… know… you."

"What do you mean?" Chaco said.

"What I mean is, that I never took the time to really talk to you, to understand who you are."

"What reason would you have had to get to know me? You hired me to caretake your property. If you were satisfied with my work, we wouldn't have needed to talk."

"I see that as a problem."

"How so?"

"Year in and year out people rush about their daily business, interacting with their peers, their neighbors, the merchants at the stores where they shop, but no one ever takes the time to know one another. I about fell off my chair when you told us you were a Ph.D. in physics and a university professor." Russell shook his head and smiled. "I made some unfair judgments about you, I'm afraid. I'm truly sorry for that."

"I probably did the same about you. It's what people do sometimes."

Russell shifted in his seat. "I know a lot more about you now than I did, and I have to thank you for all you're doing for us, and have done. I don't know if we'd made it this far without you."

"You're welcome, but you would have probably been fine without me."

"I doubt it."

Abigail nodded. "I agree with Russ, Chaco. We owe you our gratitude at the very least. "But—" She looked at him and bit down on her bottom lip. "There is so much about you that we still don't know. Won't you share a little bit more about yourself with us?"

"What would you like to know? I have nothing to hide now."

"Nothing to hide, now? What would you have to hide? Tell us more about your life in El Salvador. What prompted you to come to the United States? What were your last memories of Soyapango?"

"Wow. That's a load of questions." Chaco smiled, cleared his throat, and began. He told them about the resistance, his parents, the torture death of his *abuela*, his Mirabella, and what had happened when he ordered the car bomb, and about the price on his head.

Once Chaco started talking, he couldn't stop. The words poured out of his mouth until he'd told them everything he'd shared with Fiona. "I am a killer. I cannot forgive myself for those innocent lives I ended."

Chaco had not noticed that fat tears like glycerin drops rolled down Abigail's face. He had not noticed that Russell had risen from his seat, had walked to him and put his hand on his shoulder. He had not noticed Rocky and Margo had returned and heard everything. He kept talking. He thought it best to omit the detail of his relationship with Fiona. He prayed they would not ask about his love life, because he would have certainly told them, and maybe they would not approve, maybe they would be angry. Chaco wanted so much for them not to be angry.

Once finished with his confession, he felt spent, empty. He wanted only to lie down and sleep for days. Chaco raised his head to Russell. "Do you know me well enough, now?"

Russell pulled the younger, smaller man up from his seat and into an embrace. Chaco couldn't recall the last time another man had hugged him. Had it been his good friend and mentor, Javier? Had it been Alberto? His father? He buried his head in the older man's chest and wept.

CHAPTER 20

The rising sun took the chill off the morning. The group would stay one more night and one more day, maybe bag some game, pack and prepare, then depart at the first light of the following day.

"I'm not a bad shot," Jude said. "Why not give me a gun and I'll hunt for deer."

Russell shook his head. "Not with that ankle."

"We aren't travelling by night?" Rocky asked.

"No need to," Russell said. "We're headed into an unpopulated forested area, so not much danger of running into anyone."

"Besides," said Chaco, "with the rough trails, wildlife, and rattlesnakes…" Chaco cast a sideways glance in Jude's direction, then turned back to Rocky, "…we need sunlight to see what's around us."

The little girls were a short distance away under Margo's watchful eye, quiet. Now and again, one of the girls would tear up, snuffle.

"I'll be glad when we're out of here. Two graves in two days," Abigail said, putting up two fingers to Chaco.

Jude snapped his head around to face his mother. "How in the hell can you compare Bethany to a dog?"

"No, Jude. I didn't mean it that way at all. What I meant…"

"What way *did* you mean it, Mom?" He sneered at his mother. His face angry and tight. "You never liked Bethany, did you?"

"Of course, I did. We always thought of her as a lovely girl, and not only as your wife, but the mother of my…"

"The fuck you liked her! Don't give me that bullshit. How can you disrespect her memory like that when she's only one day in the ground?"

"Son, that's enough." Russell jerked his head toward Jude. "You lost Bethany, you're in pain from that ankle, and you're off your meds, so I'm cutting you some slack, but you do not talk to your mother like that, not ever. We both loved Bethany, and her loss is hard on us, too, damn it."

"I'm sorry, Dad, but I don't want to hear about the two graves, one being my wife's and other a dog's. I hope you understand why that might upset me."

"Your mother only meant there has been so much death and loss, too much for your little girls to endure, too much for all of us. She certainly wasn't comparing Bethany to Rufus. You know that." Russell laid his hand on Jude's forearm.

"Your dad is right. I did…I mean, both of us…did love Bethany, very much," said Abigail.

"You have to get it together, Jude," Rocky said. "We've got enough to worry about for those of us still alive, now that Mr. Ph.D. over there drove our supplies to a place where it ended up easy pickings for thieves."

"I asked Chaco to drive the truck away from the camp," said Russell. "You don't recall that your wife saw a bear?"

"No matter, we have to travel how far now? 350 miles? 500?" He held up his hand and counted fingers, "with no food except a few crappy protein bars that won't last a day, not enough water for a week, a man with a twisted ankle who can't walk on his own, two little girls who won't last…"

Margo had returned to get the girls a drink of water. "Fer gawdsake, Rocky. Shut up, will ya? There are ways to make it if we all put our heads together and figure thangs out. Why cain't you use yer good brains and help?" Margo stood taller, her back rigid as a cement plank. You are the best thang that ever did happen to me, but sometimes the way you act…. it's like you ain't no good, Rocky Pennymon, 'cept fer makin' thangs worse."

Chaco had never seen Rocky hurt, but when the hulking man took a step back from his wife, and raised his head, he saw a film of tears in Rocky's eyes.

Rocky turned away from the group and walked toward the irrigation ditch.

"Aw, c'mon, Rocky. Git back here, honey. I didn't mean it thata way, not really," Margo said.

Rocky continued toward the ditch.

"Rocky is right," said Chaco. "We've got a good many challenges ahead of us. And Margo is right, too, we can make it if we intelligently use the resources at hand, and stick together as a unit. I've been studying the map, by the way. I think I've worked out a shorter route. And, besides, we aren't out of food and supplies."

"You'll get us through this," Abigail said.

"I don't know if I'm the one to 'get us through,' Mrs. Walker."

"Of course you are. You know more about what's going on than any of us. We defer to your knowledge, and depend on you to use it."

"I hope I can live up to your expectations."

"Wait. Back up." Russell lifted one eyebrow, and smiled. "What do you mean we aren't out of food and supplies?"

"Come with me. I've got something to show you." Chaco started toward the stripped truck.

"I'll stay with the girls," Margo said.

"I'll keep an eye on them," Jude said. "Olivia, Lacy, come over here."

"Really, Jude, are you sure?" Abigail asked.

"Mom, it's fine. I'll take care of them."

"I'm glad you've come around, son, but you said yesterday…"

"I wasn't myself…It'll be all right."

The little girls, with their stuffed toys in their hands, ran to their father. Lacy leaped onto his lap.

"Hey watch it, there, Skeeter. I still have a hurt ankle, you know." He cuddled both girls in his arms and kissed them. "I love you," he said to them. "We all miss Mommy very much, but everything is going to be fine."

Abigail smiled before joining the others, and followed Chaco into the orchard.

***

By the time they'd untied the sacks from the tree branches, hauled them back to camp and opened them, Rocky had returned in full form. "How far away are these horses supposed to be?" he asked Chaco. "That is, unless you were bullshitting us so you can keep on playing the big man." He gaped at the provisions laid out on the ground. "Where did all this come from?"

"I didn't get everything out," said Chaco, but I managed to retrieve a bit more than half before the looters got to the truck."

Russell scratched his scalp. "How did you know…?"

"I didn't," said Chaco. "To tell you the truth, I've been concerned that we've been keeping all of our food and other supplies in one place. Too easy for bears or people to take. After I drove the truck over the hill, I removed some and stashed it in the orchard, and left the rest."

"You didn't say anything when we found the truck looted. Why?"

"I wasn't certain if the food and other things were still safe in the orchard. I didn't want to get anyone's hopes up until I'd checked."

"Why did you leave anything in the truck at all?" Rocky said. "Jude said we had enough to last us at least nine weeks when we started out, so what's left? Maybe there is only, what, three or four weeks' worth? Not too bright."

"I left some in hopes if someone, like those thieves, showed up they may be under the impression they'd taken it all—a little trick I learned while fighting for the resistance. We'll be all right for a while. I got quite a bit of the food, and some of the salt. I retrieved all but a half box of ammo, and I got most of the fishing gear, batteries, med supplies, tarps, clothing…"

"…. what ain't so bright, Rocky, is yer thinkin' that Chaco savin' more than half our food and stuff ain't a great thang for all of us. I swear, sometimes I thank you wouldn't know a good idea if it nipped ya on the head a yer pecker, would ya? You outta be thankin' Chaco for what he did for us." This time, Margo stomped off to the ditch.

***

After Margo's return, Chaco spread the map on the ground, and with his forefinger, traced a route. "Going this way will shave nearly 120 miles off our trip, but we'll have steeper mountains to contend with, and maybe no roads in some places. We will connect with some hiking trails through here, too, that we can follow at least part way to our destination, and there are natural springs, rivers and alpine lakes for water." He pointed to a series of lines on the map and bodies of water. He shifted position and traced an alternate course. "This is the way we are currently headed. If we continue, we will have better roads, and we'll get to the horse rescue here. I worked there one summer, and I know the area." He pointed to a spot on the map fifty or so miles further from the orchard.

"That's fairly close. Why didn't we simply drive there where the horses are instead of stopping here?" Abigail asked.

"If we had, maybe Bethany would be alive right now," Jude spit on the dirt.

"We can't do anything about that now, son. Let's stay focused here." Then Russell turned to his wife. "It was getting light, hon. It would have been far too dangerous if we'd stayed on the main road."

"Will there be horses along the shorter route?" Abigail asked Chaco.

"I don't know. Maybe."

"If we stick to the route we're on, we'll certainly find the horses, right?" Russell said.

Rocky, stood with his back rigid, rocked back onto his

heels. "I keep telling everyone, there's no way of knowing if horses are still there. They could have died from starvation by now, or maybe someone else took them. Someone might have killed them and eaten them for all we know. Isn't that so, Señor Revolutionary Commander?"

Chaco tensed, then clenched his jaw. "That is correct. We take a chance either way."

"And that's been the truth all along, hasn't it? You don't know Jack shit. You have no idea of what we'll run into, or how we're going to survive, do you?"

"No, I don't, but I'm sure we'd all be overjoyed to hear your better plan."

The bigger man strode to Chaco and leaned into his face. "Don't you get smart with me." The tendons in his neck pulsed. "You have no damned idea who you're messing with. I know you're a big resistance fighter and all, but I'll kick your skinny little Mexican ass from here back to Tijuana."

Chaco stood his ground. "I'm Salvadoran."

"Rocky, jist stop, right now. Stop. We got a lot a plannin' to do, and you better git on board with all of us now. If you spend all yer time tryin' to knock down Chaco, instead of cooperatin', we ain't gonna make it."

"What about snow?" Russell asked. "Which way would we least likely run into weather?"

"I don't know, Mr. Walker. I wish I did."

Rocky snorted. "Well, what a surprise. He doesn't know."

Russell wheeled around and faced Rocky. "We're all getting tired of your attitude. I'm going to have to ask you to either come up with helpful solutions or stay quiet while we figure this out."

"Obviously, what I want doesn't matter anyway."

"You never say what you want," Margo said. "You jist gripe, and make ever-one upset. I'm gittin' sick a you, too."

"You seem to be pretty interested in protecting Chaco. So far, you've taken his side at every turn. Tell me, is there something between you two I should know about?" Rocky looked from Margo to Chaco, then back to Margo.

"Oh fer gawdsake, Rocky."

***

The group voted to risk the shorter route. While Rocky leaned against a tree pouting like a child, Chaco and Russell worked together to find enough fallen branches, tree limbs, and material to make sled-type contraptions to pull Jude and the supplies. When they located a heavy branch difficult to manage, Rocky stepped in.

"Thanks," said Russell. "We appreciate the help."

Rocky mumbled a weak, "You're welcome," and pulled the heavy branch into camp. By the time the three men had lashed together enough branches with a torn blanket, and covered them with tarps, they had made two sturdy carriers, one travois for Jude, and another to haul their remaining supplies and personal belongings.

It grew late in the afternoon, nearly dark when Lacy whined for the fourth time about being hungry. Chaco distributed protein bars, and no one objected.

Rocky called to Margo to give her a bar, but she didn't respond. "Where the heck is Margo?"

"I don't know," said Abigail. "She took off, leaving Jude and me with the girls. Said she'd be back."

"When did she leave?" Rocky asked.

"A couple of hours ago."

"You're kidding me," said Rocky. "Did she take anything with her?"

"Her rifle, her jacket, and a half bottle of water."

Another hour and a half passed. Rocky paced. "Which way did she go? I'm going to look for her."

"Not now. It's dark, and we should conserve the flashlight batteries. Your wife is resourceful. She'll be back," said Chaco.

"I have to agree," said Russell. "If she's not back soon, Chaco and I will help you find her, but right now, none of us wants to have to worry about you as well as her. Sit tight."

The sound of two rifle shots in quick succession split the silence. Rocky jumped to his feet and started off in the direction where Margo had gone. He put his hands to his mouth creating a megaphone from his palms and fingers. "Margo! Where are you, honey? Jesus, are you okay? Answer me!" By then, Chaco and Russell had joined him. Russell flipped on the flashlight and aimed the beam in the direction where they had heard the shots. Rocky whistled between his teeth, then called out again. "Margo!"

"Didn't I hear Chaco and Russ both tell you to stay put? Whaddaya think I was doin', runnin' off with a male stripper?" Margo appeared over a rise holding two dead jackrabbits by their ears. "We cain't jist eat them dried up protein bars. They'll probably constipate the hell outta us all."

In short order, she skinned and gutted the rabbits, put them in a pot of water on the camp stove, threw in a handful of wild mustard and a bit of sorrel she'd harvested from the hills on her way back to camp. "This stew ain't gonna be tasty, and Jackrabbit is tougher than tennis shoes, but plenty nourishin', and other than salt, we don't have to unpack any of that food Chaco saved fer us."

The stew tasted far better than Margo told them it would. Even the little girls ate their fill without complaint. In a short while, sated, they fell asleep. Overcome with exhaustion, the men didn't even try to keep guard.

"We sleep with our weapons within arm's reach, and the food is safe for now," said Russell. "We all might as well get a little rest before we leave."

The only people awake were Chaco and Jude. Chaco, pretending sleep, rolled over in his bag, concealing most of his face to observe Jude clumping along with his crutch for hours, pacing back and forth like an anxious animal, first one way across the campground, then the other. Back and forth. Back and forth. All the while he paced, Jude muttered under his breath.

CHAPTER 21

Chaco found one peaceful spot, a seven-foot-tall rock with a level surface. The rock jutted from the otherwise flat plain less than a hundred yards from camp, far enough. When he'd had enough of everyone's chatter and drama, he would say, "I'm going to my rock," and disappear for an hour or more.

Sitting on the rock gave Chaco quiet time to process, to think, to plan. At least once daily, he could be found there staring steeped in his musings. At this moment, his thoughts turned to his friendships. He'd never had many male friends. He'd loved his father, his uncle and his grandfather, but otherwise, he stayed to himself. He never grew too intimate with the boys he played baseball with, or any of his classmates, who sometimes taunted him because Chaco had long before earned a reputation as a loner. Some of the kids thought him snobbish.

Over the course of his life, he allowed himself to become close to maybe four or five other men, including his mentor, Javier, his buddy, Alberto, the one colleague who he trusted to keep him informed of matters in El Salvador after Chaco had fled his country, and now, Russell Walker.

He never much liked Americans with their imperious attitudes, their national consciousness of bigotry and ignorant xenophobic attitudes. He shifted his position on the rock. He'd learned well to use that American ignorance to his advantage… he knew once he entered the country, his brown skin would be a perfect way to hide in the U.S. because not one of these *gringos* would ever question a Latino with a leaf blower and a set of hedge clippers. But, despite himself, he had developed a profound affection for this particular group of privileged white people. Of course, he loved Fiona with every cell of his body and every ounce of his soul, but some of....

A scraping and rustling came from behind. Chaco put his hand on his rifle and turned his head toward the source of the sound. Margo. She clambered up the rock toward him. He removed his hand from the weapon.

"Sorry to disturb ya," she said. "I have somethin' I need to talk over with ya in private."

He scooted over to make room. "What's this about?"

"Well, frankly, it's about Jude. Me and Rocky was talkin' after we heard what you was sayin' to Russ and Abby about yer life in El Salvador and all what happened to you there."

"Yes?"

"The way we see it, you've been through an awful lot."

Chaco shrugged his shoulders. "What does that have to do with Jude?"

"He's got that PTSD thang, right?"

Chaco shrugged again. "Yes?"

"We don't git how you could go through so much, and see all that death and not have it, too."

"Everyone responds to stress and trauma differently, Margo. Besides, what makes you think I don't have it?"

"That may well be. But our thankin' is that mebe..."

"I do have problems, many of them. I didn't come out of El Salvador unscathed." He told her about the Pipil Indian village that burned to the ground in front of him as a child and related the horrors of war he'd experienced as a freedom fighter. "No one sees what I've seen and is okay after. I have PTSD. But, I handle my differently than Jude. That's the only difference between us."

"But you ain't crazy. I mean, Jude seems not quite right in the head. He's jist plain unstable and we are a bit worried about it. Seems like you went through a whole bunch more than he did, and if anyone was goin' to have problems, it would be you, not him."

"None of us knows for certain what Jude went through, or what atrocities he actually witnessed or participated in. What he chooses to share with others is only the tip of an iceberg. We can't judge."

Margo shook her head. "That's not what I mean. We ain't judging' at all. What me and Rocky is worried about is you."

Chaco shrugged his shoulders and shook his head. "You are concerned about me? Why?"

"What Jude did back before we left Green Lake, you know, when he thought you was an Iraqi and threatened you? 'Member that? Then, we've seen him look bat-shit crazy when he was shootin' at those folks while defending the properties. I know you saw it, too. We all did."

"I'm certain it's only the PTSD."

"Precisely my meanin'." She looked at Chaco as though the Salvadoran were a Sasquatch. "I swear to gawd, Chaco. Sometimes you are as much of a bonehead as Rocky. Cain't you see what's right in front a' ya?"

Chaco laughed. "Of course. What you are saying is that you think because of his PTSD, Jude is going to try to harm me. Is that it?"

"BINGO. You got it. Halleluiah!" She raised her eyes to the sky and clapped her hands. "First, Jude goes thinkin' yer an Iraqi, then he shows his crazy side when he's firin' a gun, now he's convinced that me and you had somethin' to do with Bethany gittin' bit and dyin', and says he's gonna make us take responsibility. He don't think I'm nuthin'. He don't give a flea-infested rat's ass about me, but it makes good sense that he's gonna come after you, don't ya think?"

"I appreciate your concern, but I can take care of myself. You and Rocky can rest assured…"

"Rocky acts like an ass towards ya sometimes. Between me and you, I think he's a little bit jealous because ya got so much goin' fer yerself. But I really need ya to listen." She modulated her tone to a slow and even pace. "Even though he's Russ and Abigail's son, this guy is different from Rocky in not a good way. Rocky's keepin' an eye on him, jist so ya know. He's thinkin' that Bethany's dyin' might have put Jude over the edge, and y'all might need his help if Jude tries any-thang."

Chaco raised an eyebrow in surprise. "That's truly nice of Rocky. I would not have expected that from him. But, I'm good, and…."

In the distance, a coyote pack yipped and howled.

"They probably caught a rabbit." Chaco turned toward the coyote sound. "Listen. I hope they don't come close. I'm really afraid of…"

"Don't be changin' the subject. We ain't' talking about coyotes and rabbits jist now. Look at me." Chaco turned his head to Margo. "You don't know Rocky. He ain't so bad. Basically, he's got a good heart. His biggest problem is he jist cain't keep his trap shut. He don't have much manners, but he ain't evil or nuthin." She rested a hand on Chaco's shoulder. "I don't want ya to hate him. You gotta know, in spite of how he acts, Rocky really and truly is worried about ya."

"Once again, I appreciate Rocky's concern, but I am perfectly capable…."

"Mebbe you kin take care of yerself, but Rocky is lookin' in Jude's direction now and again anyways, and so am I, even if you don't much like it."

***

The last dawn in the orchard proved one of the most extraordinary. He remembered a similar morning after he and Mirabella had camped out under the stars. Chaco awoke before her to build a fire and put on a pot of coffee. While waiting for her to emerge from their tent, he sat on the stump of an ancient tree and wrote in his journal. He could not recall what he wrote, but he remembered how he could almost taste the crisp air, and the fragrance of the morning itself, as though it were rosewater flan rather than a time of day.

In haste, the group consumed a cold breakfast, and once the dishes were rinsed clean, Margo and Abigail finished loading one of the two travoises with the supplies, piling the goods high, but balanced. It would be easy to later secure everything with tarp and rope. Chaco circled the travois and smiled in appreciation for these *chele* women. "Excellent job, ladies."

The two women beamed.

While Rocky meandered off to take one of his epic thirty-minute bowel movements, Jude took the girls to Bethany's grave site to say goodbye. Russell and Chaco surveyed the camp perimeter to ensure nothing had been left behind. They walked the rows of apricot trees to check one last time for anything they might use later, and they took time to bury any remaining garbage.

"Why are we bothering to do this?" Russell said. "There is no one coming around here that would be offended that we littered."

One look at Chaco gave him the answer.

"I know. It's the right thing to do." Russell clapped Chaco on the shoulder.

On the way back to the camp, Chaco picked up a sturdy limb.

"That'll make a fine axe handle if the one we have breaks," Russell said.

"Or, a hefty cudgel." Chaco smiled while balancing the limb in his hand.

The moment Chaco and Russell returned, Rocky marched up to the two men with a satisfied grin on his face. "I swear. The older I get, the better that feels. These days, I'd rather have a good crap than a blow job."

Russell took a step back and raised both eyebrows. Chaco shook his head, suppressing a guffaw.

Jude and the girls had returned a few minutes earlier, and as everyone else completed the last of the loading, and prepared the second sled for Jude, the father and his girls played one last game of Sugarland before hitting the trail.

"Yay! I got an eleven," Olivia said after her turn rolling the dice. "Look, Daddy, an eleven. Just what I needed. Woot! Woot! Gimme five," she said and raised her hand to Lacy.

"Goddammit! Goddammit all too goddamn fuckin' hell!" Jude shouted and upended the board onto the clay, scattering the game pieces. He jutted his jaw and glared at his girls, who jumped to their feet and scampered to their grandmother.

"What happened?" Abigail asked. "Jude? Did an ant or something bite you?"

Jude, his eyes lowered, picked up the game pieces and the board in slow, deliberate motions, and put them back into the box, closing the lid with care. The girls clung to their grandmother's waist.

"Jude?" Abigail said. "What in Hell happened?"

Jude turned away from her.

"Daddy got mad at us because he was losing, and I was about to win," Olivia said, snuffling.

CHAPTER 22

The travelers struggled over the steep mountains. One on each handle, the women pulled the supply travois. Now and again, they'd come across a smooth spot, and would practically sail over the ground, but most of the time, they found themselves straining to get over, or around, rocks and sharp edges, bouncing the travois so hard that sometimes they'd have to stop to pick up goods that had shaken loose from the tarps and ties.

Chaco, Rocky, and Russell took turns pulling Jude because. The ankle might have been damaged far worse than anyone could know, and no one wanted to take any chance of further injuring it. The men alternated guard duty, one behind the group with a rifle, another taking point. Olivia and Lacy steered clear of their father, opting to stay close to Margo and Abigail instead. Because of the little girls, the group had to make frequent stops. Olivia stubbed her toe and they halted for a band aid. Lacy cried when she received a deep thistle scrape. She needed a band-aid, too. One had to go the bathroom as the other whined, "I'm hungry," or "I'm tired."

The stops were too many for Rocky, who became increasingly exasperated with each delay. "C'mon! At this rate, we aren't going to make two miles a day. It'll take years to get to Pine Mountain. I told you these little girls were not going to be able to…."

"Please, shut yer mouth," Margo said.

They trudged up and over hills and mountains, making camp at dusk. Now and again, to ensure they were headed in the right direction, Chaco looked at his compass, cross-checking it against the position of the Sun or night stars.

Jude, who had not said much the entire trip, grew nervous and antsy. "Look. I can manage well enough to do some hunting. Toss me a rifle, Dad, and I'll see if I can't get a buck. I'm going crazy here with you pulling me all day every day without a damned useful thing for me to do."

"Let me check on his ankle," Margo said. She squatted and pulled off his boot. "Swellin's gone down. Kin you move yer toes any?"

Jude flexed his foot and wiggled his toes. "Really. I'm fine. I've got my crutch if I need it."

"We cain't risk you hurtin' it worse," Margo said. "I think you outta give yerself longer to heal up before you try walking these hills and goin' over these rocks. It ain't easy for us who don't have twisted ankles."

"Son, you injured yourself pretty badly." Russell said. "You might have a damaged a tendon, and you could do permanent harm. Badly twisted ankles can take months to heal. Please, do as Margo says."

Jude folded his arms tightly across his chest. "At least let me have a weapon so I can help out on guard duty." When his father failed to respond, Jude raised his voice, "Why in hell don't you want to give me a rifle, or maybe a handgun? If we run against something, or someone, I'd like to be able to protect myself, if you don't mind." He threw up his hands. "Hey! Is anyone listening to me?"

"We can hear you, son."

"Are you denying me the right to a firearm because of the way I acted back in the orchard? I was upset over Bethany, that's all. Really."

Russell and Chaco exchanged glances. Chaco shook his head.

"Why the hell are you looking at Chaco?" Jude said. "This isn't his decision to make. Can I have a gun or not? And, if not, why? You at least owe me an explanation."

Russell sighed. "Here's the deal. I'll give you the .38, but only for emergencies. I want you to stow the gun under your bedroll, and keep the bullets separate. And, you have to promise me that you'll stay off that ankle until Margo says it's good enough for you to walk on."

Russell pulled a gun from his pack and emptied the bullets, prepared to hand them over to Jude.

"Dad. These conditions are bullshit, and you know it."

"So you'd rather not have the .38 and the bullets, then?" He withdrew his hand with the bullets and dropped a couple into his pocket.

"Okay. Just give me the damned gun and ammo." He extended his open hand. Russell looked into his son's eyes. "You will do as I ask?"

Jude nodded.

Russell placed gun and bullets in his son's palm. All the while, Rocky, and Chaco kept their eyes locked onto one another. Margo looked from Chaco to Rocky. "Bad idea," Rocky mouthed.

***

Many weeks passed. The group made progress one challenging step at a time, but the difficulty of the journey paled in importance to their dwindling food supplies. During these days in the California mountains, Chaco had learned more about subsistence living than he'd ever known while fighting in the resistance.

One dusk, as the group prepared to stop for the night, Chaco announced, "I saw a few deer while guarding the back. I'm going to return and see if I can't shoot a buck for us."

"It's getting dark. Are you sure you want to venture out there on your own? I'll come with you, if you want," Russell said.

"I can take Dad's place as guard." Jude said.

"No. I'm faster on my own. Your dad and Rocky have guard duty covered."

"You know, I'm a pretty decent shot. I don't know why

everyone thinks I can't handle a gun because my ankle is injured." Jude smiled. "But, I could be of help if you'd only let me do…"

A two-pronged buck leaped over a low grouping of bushes and bounded in front of the group. Chaco, swung his rifle around, pulled the trigger, and the mortally wounded buck dropped to its knees then fell onto its side.

"Whee hoo!" Rocky said. "Damn good shot. You got him right below the shoulder, boy. That sucker is dead. Venison steaks tonight! Hot damn!" He snapped his fingers against his jeans. "Hey, baby, you're going to have to make some of that good jerky of yours," he said to Margo.

"Then it was a good thang Chaco saved all that salt," Margo said. "And you ain't even thanked him once for that."

Jude hoisted himself off the travois and stood with his crutch, glaring at Chaco. "Yeah, damned good shot." His face tightened into a mass of angry knots. "I have to take a piss." He limped off toward the woods, the .38 tucked into his belt.

***

Chaco looked on in respect as Margo gutted and skinned the buck, removed the antlers and, with Rocky's help, buried the offal. She butchered the deer, cutting pieces from the muscle meat. "Even though Chaco shot this buck before the poor thang knew what hit him, it was runnin' when he got it, so this meat might be a bit gamey, but it'll make a good supper anyways."

"Looks fine to me," Chaco said. "It's been a long while since any of us has had fresh venison. We're all getting tired of rabbits, squirrels, and birds."

She ordered Rocky to start a fire, and she salted the steaks and laid them on a tarp. As the fire grew to a sizable blaze she cut the meat into thin strips. "Tomorrow, if we kin afford to stay a few hours, I'll make a lot of jerky fer us to take along, and Rocky, yer gonna have 'ta hang the rest of this meat somewheres so wild cats and bears cain't get to it."

"What about the hide?" Abigail asked. "Can we do something with that?"

"Depends on how much salt Chaco is willin' to let go of, and how much cookin' oil we got. The oil we got ain't exactly the right kind, but it'll do. I kin flesh the hideout tonight, and we kin tan it tomorrow. Ain't hard, jist takes a little time and some patience. Y'all kin help, if ya want."

"I'd be delighted," Abigail said.

"I'll help, too," Chaco said.

"Shore. Anyone who wants to pitch in, I'll be happy to show ya what ya need to do."

Within minutes, under Margo's keen supervision, Chaco and Abigail got busy scraping flesh from the hide. "Git ever' bit of that meat and gristle off that hide with them knives and use whatever else you might need to scrape, and once yer done with that, you gotta rub salt in real good to keep down bacteria."

"Is that all there is to it?" asked Abigail.

"Nope. Then you gotta use yer bare hands to work oil into the skin side." She stood and looked around for her husband. "Hey, Rocky, I'm gonna need ya to build a scaffold to hold the jerky, and a smoke ring in time fer me to hang them meat strips first thang tomorrow, hon."

Rocky, who had been whittling a bit of wood, nodded. "You bet."

"How long do you think it will take the jerky to be completed?" Russell threw the venison steaks on the fire, salting them again. "I had hoped to get an early start. Looks like weather coming in." He turned his head skyward at a cloud bank rolling in from the east.

"If Rocky gits a move on with the scaffold, and we git a nice smoke goin', mebe two or three hours after that. I'll soak the strips in vinegar and salt overnight. That gives good flavor, and helps preserve the meat, too. We'll have us some fine protein fer awhile. We're gonna need it."

"Yes, indeed we are," said Abigail.

Chaco thought Abigail, her clothes covered in bits of blood and flesh, on her hands and knees scraping bits of deer meat from the hide, seemed happier than she'd been in a long while. Serene.

Jude returned to camp, sat with his back against a tree, and gazed off into the trees. He'd been gone a couple of hours, but no one seemed to notice his absence. Since the incident with the board game, his little girls kept their distance from him, rarely even looking in his direction. They played on the other side of the camp with their stuffed bunnies and carved kittens, keeping their voices low.

Once in a while, one of the girls would giggle, or the bigger and bossier Olivia would scold her little sister. "I didn't say your pink bunny could be the mommy. She's supposed to be the baby. My blue bunny is the mommy."

"But who is going to be the daddy rabbit?" Lacy said.

"No one. There is no more daddy."

Jude looked in their direction, cocked his head, and turned his attention back to his mindless staring.

"For someone who says he wants to be of use, Jude's not doing much to help, is he?" Rocky said to Chaco.

The sky darkened, and Margo put her hands out palms up as though to catch a rain drop. "Jeez, I hope we don't git rain right away," she said. "I kin feel the damp in the air, and if it rains or snows before the jerky's set, it could ruin all this deer meat."

CHAPTER 23

On July 23, 2012, the Sun's surface exploded in a swarm of solar storms, each equal in ferocity to the Carrington Event. The resulting CMEs spewed giant magnetic filaments of solar material and super-heated wind that would have slammed into Earth directly had the storms only happened nine days earlier. In the following few years, the Sun neared the end of its eleven-year cycle, and even larger, potentially deadlier solar storms than those of 2012 rocked its surface. Chaco had spent hours on the phone with Javier discussing the close calls, speculating over the resulting catastrophic damage had Earth taken a direct hit.

These days, Chaco often wondered what his life would be like had those giant CMEs crashed into Earth while he lived in El Salvador. Things might have been different. Very different. Maybe the solar storms would have disrupted or even ended the hostilities before that car bomb exploded killing the General's wife, children, and nanny. Maybe he would be with his family and Mirabella. Those times of the massive Sun storms, the ones that *didn't* hit the planet, Chaco fought in the hills, entrenched with the Resistance as a freedom fighter. Only Mirabella, his friend, Javier, and one trusted colleague at the Universidad Tecnológica de El Salvador knew.

To the resistance fighters, Chaco stood out as a powerful commander who could shoot the eye out of a beetle from 100 yards away. To everyone else, he was a young, brilliant physics professor about to be married to a beautiful woman. He struggled to keep his two worlds apart, hiding from his family and life-long friends the reality of his nocturnal and weekend activities. "I am speaking on a panel at a physics conference in San Salvador this weekend," he'd say to his grandmother when she questioned why he would not be attending mass with the family, and sitting afterward at her table.

On Sunday afternoons, Abuela Erhard set her heavy mahogany dining table with antique Dresden china, imported linens from Spain, and real silver. With assistance from one or two of her maids, she created for her family a "Cena Tipica Salvadoran" (typical Salvadoran meal) with *caldo pescado* (fish stew), *pupusas* stuffed with *loroca* flowers, *platanos fritos* or *yuca frita* with *crema fresca*, thick slices of fresh avocado, refried beans, and *curtido* (pickled cabbage). Besides the platanos, Chaco most of all looked forward to the *pacalla*, batter fried palm flowers with *salsa roja,* a savory tomato sauce, accompanied by mugs of cold *tamarindo*, a sweet drink made of sugar and tamarind, and home brewed *chichi*, fermented corn and pineapple beer.

"Don't drink too much of that chichi," Abuela Erhard warned Chaco. "If you do, you will dream you can fly like a condor, and you might jump off a rooftop and break one of your boney legs."

But the Sun decided to throw a tantrum, and fling its deadly CMEs at Earth while Chaco hid like a criminal in Green Lake, California, U.S.A., an alien land populated by big, coarse, white people who didn't speak his language, and dismissed him because of the color of his skin, people who didn't give a damn about his culture, or his sacred family traditions.

He wondered if he would ever see El Salvador again. His parents, his *abuela,* and his sweet Mirabella were with the angels, and who knows where Javier and his colleague from the University were now. Instead of dining on *platanos* with sour cream, and *pacalla*, he chewed on tough deer jerky under an ominous sky in this unwelcoming world. The only upside to being here now is that he would see his beloved Fiona. But this Sunday, even with ethereal, beautiful visions of Fiona in his head, foremost in Chaco's mind was El Salvador, he thought himself so homesick his heart would shrivel into an empty, leathery casing within his chest, as if sucked dry by a chupacabra.

***

The rain and snow held off and allowed the venison the time required to properly smoke, a blessing given that over the many weeks of their journey, food supplies had dwindled to barely enough to sate a pair of goldfinches.

Since Jude, in his morose, self-absorbed state of mind, had become essentially useless, Rocky and Margo assumed the accounting duties. Before packing the food, as Russell, Abigail, Olivia, and Lacy took a short walk by the stream, and Jude sat alone in his ennui, back against a dead tree, the Pennymons inventoried the stores. Rocky counted, and Margo, with a chewed No. 2 pencil and a yellow-lined pad, recorded each item in neat columns.

Bent over the plastic bins of food, Rocky pointed and counted, occasionally pulling out an item and inspecting it. "We've got lots of salt. I see fifteen boxes. Five onions starting to get a little mushy. We better cook those up soon. Two good sized jugs of cooking oil…" and so on until he thought he'd counted everything. "Wait. There's more under these kitchen towels, a half jar of peanut butter, and a near empty box of crackers." He dug around the plastic bin, held up the saltines, and gave them a shake.

"That ain't much. Them little girls are gonna need some variety in their protein." Margo grabbed a rifle. "I'll go see if I cain't git us another rabbit or a squirrel before we head out."

"We should leave now. Maybe we can make it over that highest mountain pass before the weather comes in." Chaco pointed toward the range. "We can hunt once we crest the ridge and set up camp."

"If you say so. I kin at least forage while we're walkin'. Y'all kin help. You'd be surprised at what's good to eat that you kin find right near the creeks and along mountainsides. You kin even make tea from pine needles. It'll knock a flu bug outta ya."

Rocky stood upright and put his hands on his hips. "Where did you get your Ph.D.?" he asked Chaco, busy breaking down tents and folding bedding.

"Bonn, Germany."

"Germany, eh? Why not Mexico or wherever the hell you came from?"

"My grandfather lived in Bonn near the university."

"Your grandpa is German, then? Maybe that's why you're so damned smart…. because you're part, Kraut. Is that it?"

Chaco shook his head and turned back to his duties.

"Hey, listen. I'm trying to make a point."

"And your point is?" The muscles in Chaco's neck seized as he turned to Rocky.

"Well, let's see. You have this Ph.D. You were, what, a general or something in your war, or whatever you…"

"Commander."

"What?"

"Commander."

"Let me be clear. I don't give a shit if you were president of Guatemala, or wherever the fuck you came from. You taught at some college, a professor or something, right?"

"Yes. Professor of Physics, in El Salvador."

"Fine. That's just fine. And you think you are a darn good shot."

Chaco sat on a Douglas fir stump. He'd much rather be thinking of Fiona, or writing a poem, or dreaming of his life on the sanctuary grounds, anything but talking to Rocky. "I am," he said.

"Do you suppose you're any better than Margo?"

Margo whipped her head toward Rocky. "Cain't you leave Chaco alone for one solitary minute?" She put up her index finger up to indicate "one."

Rocky waved his hand to shush her, then dropped his arm. "Let me make my point, will you?"

"Git on with it, then."

The big man rocked back onto his heels. "Let me see if I've all this right. I'll go over it again. You're a Ph.D., a professor, a big commander, but you can't even tan a deer hide?"

Chaco nodded. "I can now…"

"Yeah, because of Margo, right?"

"That is correct."

"So, other than shoot a gun, which all of us can do, and some maybe as good as you, how exactly are you planning to keep us alive while we try to make it over those steep mountains," he pointed to the northern peaks, "all the way to Pine?"

Russell, Abbey and the girls returned in time to catch Rocky's last comment. Russell took a step toward the corpulent man. "What's this about?"

Margo tisked and rolled her eyes. "Rocky is jist about to make a big 'ole important point. This has *got* to be *real* good."

"This is my point," Rocky said. "My wife, a little gal from Texas with no more than a 7th-grade education, has more survival skills in her little finger than our big Ph.D. here has in his whole nut brown body." He held up the little finger of his right hand and pointed to the nail with the forefinger of his other hand. "Maybe, she even has more skills in her little fingernail. Why in hell isn't she leading this expedition to the hippie farm?"

Russell shook his head. "Rocky, Chaco has been to the commune. He knows the way. And, you have no idea what Chaco can do, or what his guerrilla warfare skills are. May God help us if he has to use them."

Chaco stood and dusted his pants. "The sky looks bad. Weather rolling in fast. We need to get going now."

As they loaded the last of the supplies onto the second travois and bundled the little girls into their coats, the first of many fat raindrops fell onto Chaco's "nut brown" arm, and slid onto the ground. Then snowflakes the size of quarters floated from the sky, beautiful death angels.

***

As the snow accumulated into a sizable pack, Chaco stopped the group and set to the task of making snowshoes.

"Where'd you learn to do that? Much snow where you come from, boy?" Rocky said to Chaco.

"I read in a book about how to make snowshoes." *The fat pendejo has probably never opened a book in his life.*

"You read it in a book, did you? You didn't learn it at that fancy German college you went to? Ha! Well, at least you have one useful talent, even though unlike Margo who comes by her talents from experience, you had to get yours from a book."

"What do y'all need for us to do, Chaco?" Margo ignored Rocky and looked to Chaco.

Chaco instructed Russell, Abigail, Margo and Rocky to break or cut off evergreen boughs. He didn't bother to ask Jude, who stood to one side away from the group, staring at him with eyes colder than metal. "The greener the better. Find thin ones you can bend without trouble."

Even the little girls pitched in, finding branches within reach, and asking their grandparents or the Pennymons for help when they needed it. "Grandma, I can't get this one off the tree," Olivia said, tugging at the slender bough with both hands.

Once they'd amassed a good pile of pliable boughs, Chaco stood and brushed snow off his jeans. "That's more than enough. Everyone, move in closer, and I'll show you how to do this." The group crowded around as he squatted back into the snow, and showed them how to strip the boughs and bend the larger sticks into the shape of a snowshoe. He used double fishing line to tie the ends together. Then he used the thinner branches, stripping them and bending them into shape and forming them around the frame. "This will reinforce the shoes, making them strong enough to hold up."

He cut bigger branches to the approximate width of the snowshoe frames as cross braces, tied them and cinched them tight, one at a time. He continued to add cross braces until there were enough to go around both the front of the shoe and behind. "This is to better support your weight." He repeated the process for the other shoe, then aligned both so that any remaining needles or brush stuck out behind the shoes. "Hopefully, when you lift your feet, the shoes won't catch in the snow and break, or stick and slow you down."

Once satisfied he had constructed them the way he wanted, Chaco removed his boots, one at a time, and secured each to a snowshoe. He put them back on, and walked on the snow, causing great delight for the little girls, who broke into giggles. "Uncle Chaco has big feet like a rabbit," said Olivia.

Each person set about making their own pair. Rocky made small ones for the little girls. Russell made a pair for Jude who never took his eyes off Chaco, and never spoke a word.

***

There are more dangers in the California high country than most people can conceive. Years earlier, right after he ended up working for the Walkers, he had read a book he'd borrowed from Russ' bookshelf called *Death in the High Sierras*. The same book that taught him how to construct snowshoes, surprised him with information that avalanches, as much as starvation, wild animals or hypothermia, rank high in threats to life. He learned the four kinds of avalanches and now found the information invaluable. Chaco rehearsed in his mind while the snow continued to fall.

Slab avalanches occur when plates of snow break off a mountain face and slide down in one cohesive piece that is often many feet thick. Slabs like these are the most dangerous of all. *If you see one coming at you, you're in big trouble.*

Hard slab avalanches happen when a snow plate rushes down in a single hunk, but because the snow is hard-packed, it often breaks into pieces as it tumbles downwards.

A *Soft slab* is an avalanche sharing characteristics with a hard slab, but because it is made from softer and dryer snow, it tends to readily break into smaller chunks.

A *loose snow avalanche*, also known as a "point release," or "wet slide," is triggered when snow accumulates developing into a slide. All avalanches have within them the potential to take life within seconds. Chaco thought to be caught beneath a snow slide suffocating to death in cold and darkness might be worse than being torn apart by a hungry mountain lion. A wild cat would likely tear out your throat before pulling out your intestines. Death would come quick enough, where an avalanche could suffocate a man slowly.

To lessen the chances of "death by avalanche" Chaco led the group away from long open 30-45-degree barrier-free slopes that snowboarders and skiers might find delightful, but meant danger to anyone on foot. He knew their combined weight, their footsteps, their sledded provisions, even their voices could trigger a massive snow slide. He cautioned everyone to step in slow measured steps, and to keep their voices down. "Shhhhh," Abigail said to the little girls when they grew too boisterous. "You have to be very, very quiet on this mountain."

"Why, Grandma?" said Lacy.

"So, we don't wake the little hibernating animal babies. They need their sleep."

Then there are the rock slides, falling ice, crevasses that can swallow a full grown adult whole, and altitude sickness. Chaco, navigating mostly by the stars, did his best to follow the most promising and safe forest service roads leading to Pine Mountain, always keeping near streams where game might be more plentiful. Some of the way seemed impassable, but they trudged forward, one step at a time.

Margo had done a splendid job of foraging. She dug a variety of roots and uncovered half frozen, but still edible, herbs and foliage from the snow, including cresses, mustard, wild onion, wild rose hips. She knew where to dig to find roots of thistle, burdock and wild carrot, and she peeled the bark from white willow trees to make a brew. "This is better than store-bought Bayer aspirin fer a headache." She showed the others how to pry seeds from pine cones, and she made pots of pine needle tea, adding a pinch of their precious sugar supply to the little girls' mugs. Lacy and Olivia, who initially made faces when trying the brew, learned to like "forest tea," and sometimes asked for it.

As the weeks progressed, Margo taught the others to become proficient in acquiring more varieties of food. The little girls and Abigail became expert foragers. The adults hunted game mostly at night when easier to bag deer, squirrels, rabbits, and occasionally, birds, that when cooked and served on plates, Abby told her granddaughters were "little chickens." Fishing in the near-frozen streams proved a challenge, but Margo, Rocky, and Chaco broke through the ice and piled rocks in the streams to funnel fish into "traps" making it easier to catch them.

In early spring, forever away, Margo said there would be mule ears, a healthful food that could be cooked and eaten raw, as well as a known remedy for lung and bronchial disorders. "I'll make a fine Mule Ear tincture fer Lacy's asthma. It'll clear it right up." In the meantime, the pine needle tea kept the little girl's bronchial passages clear. "We gotta keep our fingers crossed tight that little girl don't have another attack."

Margo talked about the foods besides Mule's Ear that would be available come spring. "There'll be lots of wild onions, and in some fields, maybe dandelions, nuts, berries, fresh wild mustard, and other greens. Fer now, we kin dig under the snow fer roots. I'll show y'all how to git the best. Some ain't bad when boiled into a soup, and there is always pine nuts and some game."

Although there wasn't much variety, and the girls were dismayed once their peanut butter and crackers were gone, no one lacked for nourishment. "When the time is right, we'll git white acorns from them native oaks jist like that one." Margo pointed at an oak for the girls. "Ya pick 'em right off the ground, but ya don't want the ones with holes in 'em. That means worms got in."

"Ewwww, worms." Olivia said.

When they pitched their tents at dusk, the group built walls by packing snow around the flimsier structures for further insulation, and to keep the winds from rattling and flapping the sides of the tents quite so much. For warmth, instead of pitching separate tents, several huddled together in one. The Pennymons shared their tent with the little girls, while Chaco, Russell, and Abigail shared another.

Only Jude remained apart from the rest, refusing to share his space with anyone. He pitched his own tent a distance from the others. These days, Jude rarely spoke. He rebuffed his parents' attempts to comfort him. And since the time he'd lost the board game, he all but ignored his daughters, who returned the favor. When they cried for their mother and needed comfort, the little girls turned to their grandparents, the Pennymons, or Chaco. Abigail tried to smooth things between the children and their father. But neither side would budge.

"Let it go," Russell said to her. "He'll either come around, or he won't. It'll be his loss if he destroys the love and trust of his daughters."

"They lost their mother. They need their daddy," she said. "It's not his fault that he has PTSD and can't get his meds, but his little daughters...."

"I know, hon. I feel for our son, but the girls have all of us as their family." Russell embraced his wife with one arm and waved his other arm to indicate Chaco and the Pennymons. "Olivia and Lacy have plenty of good people right here who love them. And when he finally comes around, Jude will also see there are lots of people who love him, too."

Chaco sometimes caught sight of Jude pacing alone in the darkest hours of the night, nervous and fitful. Of all the dangers facing them in these frightening peaks, Jude made Chaco the most nervous.

CHAPTER 24

From the position of the stars, Chaco determined it had to be close to Christmas. "Mrs. Walker, I don't know how we can celebrate but is there a little something we can do for the girls?"

"Oh, my. Yes. I'll figure out some way to make the occasion special. Let me talk to Russ and Margo."

When Chaco found the girls sobbing on a blanket under a tree, he thought it might be because they knew it was Christmas, and there would be no Santa this year, but that wasn't it.

"I want my mommy," said Lacy. "Is she in heaven?"

"It's okay," said Olivia. "We'll see her again, and Rufus, too. Won't we, Chaco?" With the back of her hand, Olivia wiped tears from her cheeks.

There would be no Christmas dinner or wrapped gifts, but Margo and Rocky found a small blue spruce and made snowflake ornaments from scraps of ledger paper, and everyone but Jude pitched in to decorated the tree best they could. Rocky carved two small cats out of white pine and hid them under the tree for the girls to find.

On Christmas Eve, Abigail cuddled with her granddaughters by the "Christmas Tree" and told them the story of Joseph and Mary. "Even though we aren't home, and there's no chimney, I think Santa managed to get a little something for you. It's not big, and it's not a lot, but go on under the tree and see what might be there."

The girls raced to the tree and hunted beneath its branches. Lacy discovered the tiny wooden kittens and squealed. "Look what Santa gave us, Olivia. We got kitties to play with!"

"Bring your kittens over here and I'll tell you a Pipil Indian story my grandmother used to tell me when I was little," Chaco said.

The girls sat cross-legged on a deer hide next to Chaco, their toy kittens in their hands.

"Thousands and thousands of years ago, a beautiful goddess, Sihute, gave birth to an illegitimate boy…"

"What does 'illegitimate' mean?" Olivia asked.

"It means Sihute was not married when she had her baby. That's not a bad thing, but back then, and even sometimes now, when a woman has a baby, and she's not married to the father, some people say the child is illegitimate. Do you understand?"

Olivia nodded and scooted into Chaco's lap.

"The beautiful goddess named her son, El Cipitio, which means 'the child' in the Pipil language. Sihute had been married a long time before to the god, Tlaloc, a very jealous and mean man who was angry her baby was not his. He put a terrible curse on her and her little boy.

Tlaloc condemned poor Sihute to roam the dark and scary fields of La Siguanaba alone forever, and he sentenced poor little Cipitio to a lifetime of being a boy. He would never grow up."

"But then Cipitio could play forever and not have to work. That's not a bad punishment," Olivia said.

"Would you never like to grow up, maybe go to college, or find a nice husband and have children of your own?" Chaco asked

"I'm not getting married. I want to wear silver sparkly grown-up shoes, and I am going to be a doctor."

"You can't do that if you stay a little girl forever. Think about Cipitio. He'll never, ever, get old enough to be a doctor. He will never grow older than ten years."

"That's really sad. He won't even get to go to high school." Olivia shuffled in Chaco's lap.

"And even though Cipitio is the son of a goddess, instead of wearing beautiful clothes, he always has to dress in old, thin rags."

"Wouldn't he get cold? What if it snows?" Lacy asked.

"The good thing is, there is no snow where Cipitio lives. It's always warm there. But he does have a big straw hat and a little blanket." Chaco paused and gave Olivia a little squeeze. "Okay, so the mean god, Tlaloc, put Cipitio's feet on backward so that if villagers try to follow him, they will walk in the opposite direction and never find him. Cipitio does have one power. He can magically transport himself anywhere he wants to go."

"Transport?" Lacy ask

"That means Cipitio can go anywhere he wants in a second. He just has to think of a place and like magic, he will be there."

"I wish I could do that," Olivia said. "Then I could go back home and be with Mommy and Rufus again."

Chaco put both arms around the little girl. "I know you miss Rufus and your mommy. I do, too. Cipitio must also miss his mommy. He must be very lonely."

Chaco glanced up to see Russell and Abigail standing together, listening to the story. He smiled at them. *Family. This is my family now.*

"If I met Cipitio, me and Lacy would be his friend so he won't be alone."

"He likes girls. In fact, if he finds a pretty girl all by herself washing clothes by a river, he'll throw flowers at her and whistle at her. Sometimes a girl doesn't like that, and if Cipitio really bothers a girl, guess what she does?"

"What?"

"She'll go to the bathroom right there to make him not like her."

"Yucky. Me and Lacy don't go to the bathroom in front of anyone."

"You might if you wanted someone not to bother you. But, some girls like when Cipitio whistles and throws flowers because. Guess why?"

"Why, Uncle Chaco?"

"Because he only throws flowers and whistles at the prettiest girls, like you and Lacy."

The girls beamed.

"Cipitio is a trouble maker, though. He likes to make jokes

and play tricks on grownups. He eats bananas and throws the peels on the floor for adults to slip on. And, he spreads ashes around to mess up their houses. Even today, if a woman wakes up to find a messy kitchen, she'll say 'That El Cipitio is at it again!'"

"Where's El Cipitio now?"

"He could be anywhere. If you wash clothes at a river by yourself, and a boy in a straw hat throws flowers at you and whistles, it could be El Cipitio. Do you like that story?"

"Yes. We do like it, don't we, Lacy? Do you have more Indian stories for us?"

"I'll tell you more another time."

He folded both girls into an embrace.

***

Christmas day, as they walked through the snow, the group sang carols and children's songs. "Rudolph the Red Nosed Reindeer" turned out a big hit with the Olivia and Lacy, and they sang it dozens of times, never quite getting the words right.

Chaco counted the days until what could have been New Year's Eve. Over after-dinner pine needle tea, into which Margo splashed a bit of her medicinal brandy for the adults, they made a toast and wished one another a better year. Then on the following day, the clouds rolled in, dark and thick.

***

The blizzard hit without warning. The wind screamed like a female mountain lion in heat, and sheets of snow pounded the ragtag band. Even with heavy coats, gloves, and boots, bones ached with cold and teeth chattered. No one could see well, let alone walk well. Each labored step took forever. The travelers leaned hard against the wall of ice, sleet, and snow that pummeled them head on.

"Everyone, stay close. Otherwise, we'll lose someone." Chaco shouted hoping they could hear him above the squall. Squinting and feeling his way for what seemed hours, Chaco discovered a granite wall, a cliff, and he called out. "Here! Over here! Quick!" He continued to shout until he could see the dark shapes of the others one at a time making their way to him. Chaco pulled the little girls along with him. By this time, they were sobbing. He had sought a safer place to provide protection against the blistering winds and heavy snow, and he'd found it. At one point, as Chaco felt along the wall, he let go of the younger one's hand for just for a second to adjust his parka. He wished he hadn't. She'd never kept her laces tied, and in this storm, he'd not been able to stop and ensure her snowshoes were secure. With two soft plops, the snow sucked both of Lacy's snowshoes from her feet, she sank to her chest in the snow and wailed. One handed, Chaco tugged her out of the snow and carried her in one arm, still pulling Olivia along with his free hand, getting each girl beneath what turned out to be a good overhang that inhibited the riot of snow threatening to bury them alive. He called out again.

"Thank sweet Jesus, you have them little girls," Margo said to Chaco when she reached him. "I's worried sick they'd got lost in this storm."

One by one, the others appeared like shadowy wraiths emerging from the whiteout. Rocky struggled to pull one travois through the wet, heavy slush, and Russell and Abigail dragged the other. Jude appeared with his hands shoved into his pockets, trailing behind.

Fighting against the elements, Chaco, Russell, and Rocky managed to build a decent snow shelter beneath the overhand while Margo and Abigail snuggled against the little girls to keep them warm. The group huddled into a human ball within the relative safety and warmth of the snow hut, staying put through the late afternoon, the night, until the morning sun broke over the horizon.

Overnight, the blizzard dumped at least three feet of white over the already snow-packed landscape. Eight-foot snow drifts piled against trees, obscured boulders, and almost completely covered the shelter. Chaco, Rocky, and Russell dug through the bank that had blocked their exit. Chaco took inventory. Everyone, cold, hungry, had to pee, but they were all alive, and they were together. He shaded his eyes against the brilliant Sun. All traces of the forestry road and stream were gone.

***

After dining on a breakfast of jerky and pine nuts, Chaco, Rocky and Russell set out to locate the creek and logging road they'd followed prior to the blizzard. It took hours with Chaco checked the Sun's position against land markers to find the creek. From there, pinpointing the road would be a simple matter of fixing direction with the compass.

By the time the men had returned to the shelter to fetch the others, Margo had made a pair of new snowshoes for Lacy. She found enough pliable twigs and branches, and Chaco had taught her well. The women cleared the snow from the supplies and set to their task of loading the second travois. The little girls rested on a tarp in the Sun.

"Where's Jude?" Russell asked Abigail.

She shook her head. "I don't know what to do, Russ. He's miserable and won't let anyone in. I'm worried. Without his meds, and with what happened to Beth, he's…it's no good."

Margo rested her hand on Abigail's shoulder. "Hon, you've done everthang you know to do. That boy is a hot mess, but yer his mama, and if he won't even let you help him, nuthin' or nobody kin help him. Jist let him be."

"But where is he?" Russell asked again.

Abigail sighed and shrugged. "He said he was going after game."

"With what? You didn't let him take a gun, did you? How could you let him have another loaded weapon?"

Margo stood. "Russ, don't be mad at Abby. Jude jist grabbed that rifle, and when she tried to talk him out of it, he cussed her right in front of his little girls. He went runnin' off and there weren't nuthin' me or Abby could do."

That loco man has a loaded weapon. Chaco froze. For the first time, Chaco feared Rocky and Margo were right about how dangerous Jude might be to him.

"When did he leave, and what direction did he go?" Rocky said, as grabbed his gun and checked for ammunition. "I'll find him."

"I'd prefer that you don't look for him," Abigail said. "Margo's right. It's best we leave him alone for now. He's been gone for about two hours, but he'll be back when he's ready."

Two shots in the distance reverberated through the forest, echoing through the canyon below.

"Doesn't he know he could trigger an avalanche?" Rocky said. "That's the last damned thing we need."

"Shush." Margo said. "Don't be takin' the Lord's name in vain in front of them little girls."

"I only pray that with his state of mind," Abigail whispered to Margo, "that he hasn't taken his own life. I couldn't bear it if he did."

"Don't even think that way, Abby." Margo rubbed Abigail's back with affection.

Chaco stood by and watched in admiration of Margo's tenderness and her capacity for kindness.

Margo kneaded Abby's shoulders with both hands, "He's jist fine. Maybe he shot a rabbit fer us."

"Let's go," Chaco said. He and Russell started toward the sound of the shots, tracking Jude's footsteps, and Rocky ran to catch up.

Some time later, all four men returned. Slung around Jude's shoulders, a young doe hung lifeless, already gutted. Her plum-colored blood stained the back of his jacket.

He dropped the doe at his mother's feet. "I told you I could help. Why you and Dad think I can't handle a gun anymore is beyond me. But I don't give a shit if you all like it or not. I'm keeping this rifle, and Dad, no rules. I'm not keeping the bullets separate. I'm not using it only when you tell me I can. Got that?"

"Son, there is no reason for you…"

"Dad, I'm keeping the fucking gun."

Abigail moved toward her son and put her hand on his shoulder. "Please, you can keep the gun, but don't talk like that in front of your little girls."

"*My* little girls? They haven't had crap to do with me since Chaco showed up." Jude jerked away from his mother's touch, then glared at Chaco. "First you kill my wife, then you turn my own daughters, and my mother and father, against me, is that it? I thought you were my friend. What in the hell did I ever do to you?"

"Stop right there, son," Russell said. "Chaco tried to help Bethany. And your mother and I are on your side. As for your little girls, you've done an excellent job of alienating them all on your own." Russell's voice softened. "Look, we know you've been through a great deal, and we love you, but right now, you aren't rational."

Jude swung the rifle around and aimed the barrel at his father. Russell threw his hands up and stepped back. Chaco went for his weapon, and in a fraction of a second, had Jude in his sites. Jude lowered the barrel. "Just leave me alone. And Chaco, stay the fuck out of my way." He turned and walked back into the forest. Hours later, Jude returned, dour as ever, taking a place away from the others, but this time, with a loaded rifle in his hands.

***

By early afternoon, Margo and Rocky had skinned the deer, butchered it, shoved them in plastic lawn bags, and loaded them onto a travois. The group continued, trudging through the new powder toward their destination. The intense sunlight had already begun to melt the snow, the sky turned a brilliant azure. Other than the crunch of snow beneath the travelers' feet, the scraping of the travois, and a lone crow cawing, there were no other sounds.

"I wonder how far we are from Moonforest Sanctuary. Any idea, Chaco?" Abigail asked.

"I'd say we have another 170 or more miles." Chaco wished he'd had a pedometer.

"I can't wait to see Fiona and boys," Abigail said.

Me, too. Oh, my love, Fiona. Me, too.

***

They hadn't been on the trail for more than a couple of hours when Chaco held his hand high, signaling the others to stop. "Shhhhh," he said. "I think I heard voices."

Everyone stopped and quieted. The sound of people chatting echoed through the forest behind them.

"Get off the road into those trees." Chaco pointed to a copse of blue spruce. "Go, now. Run."

The others bolted for the trees while Chaco followed behind attempting to smooth their footsteps and the travois tracks with a conifer bough. The tracks were deep, too deep to conceal. They all crouched behind the trees. About five minutes passed before a trio of young people on snowshoes, bearing heavy backpacks came trudging along the trail. One, a girl of maybe 19 or 20 with copper-penny colored hair bore a Day-Glo pink backpack. The other two were young men maybe a little older, one with a ruddy complexion and light brown shoulder-length hair, the other, an African American with waist length dreadlocks tied back into a rubber band. All three were slender, fit, and tall. The kids laughed and talked as though on a casual day hike. The African American stopped. "Hey, look! I think someone is around here. Check out those tracks." He pointed at the snow to the tracks leading to the trees.

"Hard to tell…they're kinda messed up. Could be animal tracks," the brown-haired kid said. He put his hands to his mouth creating a megaphone with his palms and fingers. "Anyone there? Hello!"

Chaco rose to his feet, slapped snow from his jeans, and grabbed the Remington.

Rocky yanked on Chaco's arm and whispered, "Are you out of your ever-living mind? Those kids might be armed, and they could kill us all, little hombre."

"They're aren't going to hurt us," Chaco said. "Stay here with everyone else, and cover me just in case. I'm going to check them out." He motioned with his hands for everyone to stay put, then stepped out from the forest's protection.

"Wow," said the girl. "There *is* someone here. Hi! I'm Mindy. This is Nick," she said, pointing at the red-faced boy, "and this is Abdul. What are you doing out here, and where are you headed?"

"I was about to ask you the same thing," Chaco said.

"That was a monster blizzard, wasn't it?" Mindy said. "We had to dig a big ice cave. Tell me how you got through it, and I'll tell you where we're headed. Deal?"

"Wait a second." Chaco whistled for the others to come out.

"You're with a lot of people," Nick said, as the group approached.

Mindy clapped her gloved hands together and grinned. "Those two little girls are *so* adorable."

Chaco introduced the young backpackers to the group, then addressed Mindy. "You were about to tell me where you were headed?"

"First, you were going to tell me how you all survived that blizzard, and…."

Abdul interrupted. "We heard a hundred miles or more from here on Pine Mountain is a self-sustaining commune. Moon something. We don't know what's up with the electricity, but it doesn't look like it's going to come back anytime soon. Word's going around, too, that the San Onofre Nuclear Plant is melting down. Everyone is fleeing the coast in a panic. This whole thing is so surrealistic, man. It all just sort of happened while we were in the college library with our study group. We were in the middle of a discussion about string theory, then, boom." He waved his hands in the air to simulate an explosion. "Lights out, then everything went to hell. No one knows how long all this is going to last, but it's serious, and we were hoping they'd let us in at that compound, or whatever it is."

"The Sun," Chaco said.

"What you mean?" Nick asked.

"We were hit by a series of X-class solar storms."

"How do you know?" Nick shook his head and shifted from one foot to the other. "I mean, who would know if something like that happened if there's no way to communicate?"

"Chaco is an astrophysicist and saw it happen through his solar telescope," Russ said.

"Cool," Nick said, nodding.

"We were slammed by some badass CMEs?" Abdul said. "I'd been reading about those. Heard one hit Macedonia. Totally overloaded the sensors at the Solar Dynamic Observatory back in 2011. Shut down the grid for a long time. There were a few near misses in 2012 and 2013, too. If they'd hit, they could have really fucked us up." He glanced down at Olivia and Lacy. "Ooops. Sorry. I meant *messed* us up."

"How do you know all that?" Chaco asked.

"They don't call me 'Abdul, The Science Dude' for nothing."

"More like 'Abdul, The Science Geek,'" Nick said. "I thought he might actually cry when we had to leave his physics texts behind."

"Maybe later we can get together," Chaco said to Abdul. "It's been a long while since I've had a chance to talk science with anyone."

"That'd be cool." Abdul smiled showing a row of even white teeth, apart from one gold incisor.

"I don't mean to interrupt you scientists," Abigail said. "But what did I hear you say about a compound?"

"Yeah, Moon Trees, or something like that," Abdul said.

"Moonforest Sanctuary?"

"Yeah, that's it." Abdul snapped his fingers.

"Really? My daughter and grandsons live there. That's where we're headed."

"No kidding?" said Mindy. "That's great."

"You know, we could travel together. Safety in numbers and all that," Abigail said. "Besides, my granddaughters would probably love to have someone around besides us old fogies. And Chaco and Abdul can talk about science until they're blue in the face. It would be wonderful."

"Uh. Can I talk to everybody for a second?" Rocky whispered. "Abby and Jude, can you stay here with the girls?" In a louder voice, he said to Mindy et al, "We'll be right back."

Chaco, Russell, and Margo followed Rocky about 200 feet away. They turned their backs to the others, and Rocky grabbed the sides of his head as though holding in his brains. "Are you all goddamn nuts?" When he let go of his head, Chaco marveled that no brain matter leaked from the man's ears. "You don't know these kids, or what they're up to, or what they might do. First Mr. IQ here," he pointed a thumb at Chaco, "endangers us all by letting these happy campers know we're here, and she," he said, stabbing a finger at Abigail in the distance, "invites them to come along with us? How in hell does she know those wholesome little hikers won't slit our throats while we sleep, and steal everything we have? Is she nuts?"

"Don't talk about my wife like that," Russell said. "I mean it."

"Well, I'm sorry, but I think I have a right to be worried a little bit. I'm goddamned tired of Chaco and the rest of you making goddamned decisions that affect my goddamned life without even consulting me."

"Settle down," Russell said. "We're well-armed, and we outnumber them by nearly two to one. What are you scared of?"

"I'm not scared of…" Rocky threw his hands into the air. "What the hell."

"Yer jist bein' plain ridiculous," Margo said and walked back toward the others. Russell, Chaco, and Rocky followed.

"We were thinking," Russell said to Mindy. "Maybe we can find a place to share a little repast and talk over a plan for us all to go to Pine Mountain together. My wife is right. There is safety in numbers. What do you say?"

Mindy looked at Nick, who looked at Abdul, who looked back at Mindy. "It's like this. I mean, we like all of you, but we are pretty fast, you know?" She said.

"You think we'd slow you down," said Russell.

"No offense, but, yeah. I mean, we're all seasoned backpackers. Nick hiked the entire Pacific Trail on his own. We're athletic. We climb rocks, we extreme ski, Abdul competes on our college track team. He's breaking so many records the Olympic committee looked at him…well, before the electricity blew. But…you know what I'm trying to say, right?"

Russell smiled. "I understand."

"How about we do this," Nick said. "We'll get there a few days before you and let everyone know you're coming. I'll tell your daughter we saw you. We'll let her know you're safe, and you're on your way."

"That would be splendid," Abigail said. "Her name is Fiona, and she has two sweet little boys."

"All right, then." Mindy clapped her hands once. "We're on our way. See you at Moonforest Sanctuary."

The three started down the path at a brisk pace.

"Maybe now that Jude's ankle is healed, and Chaco is young and in good shape, they could keep up, but I'm afraid Mindy is right. The rest of us would slow them down," Russell said.

"One thing fer sure," Margo said. "With that bright pink pack thang that girl's got, they don't need no flashlight at night, do they?" She laughed.

***

The group trudged onward keeping the creek to their left. The winter moved into a wet spring, some days of rain, others of snow, some days warmer than others.

They made excellent time because they had crested the mountain and were on a somewhat level plateau. Abigail bounced around giddy as a child. She talked on and on about how those kids were going to find Fiona and let them know they'd be together again soon. The general mood among the group was buoyant. Even Jude seemed less morose.

The numbers of warm days with sunshine were on the increase, and for the time being, no rain or snow. The nights were frigid, but they managed to keep warm enough, and with the deer Jude had shot, and with all the foraged goods, food was plentiful.

Sometime after their encounter with the young backpackers, Russell sidled up to Chaco and leaned in. "Do you smell wood smoke?"

"I do, Mr. Walker. I'm a bit concerned."

"Do you think it's a forest fire?"

"Could be. I thought I might get to higher ground, or climb a tree, and look around with the binoculars."

"Abigail and I would appreciate it, Chaco. I heard Rocky grumbling about it to Margo, too. We all smell it."

Chaco hiked a steep hill and pulled out his field glasses. With his naked eye, he saw a thin column of smoke rising into the air. Not a forest fire, *gracias a Dios*. He put the glasses to his eyes, adjusted them. A camp. Hanging on a sturdy line, the skinned game hung, limbs trussed. In a rock-lined pit, the remains of a fire smoldered. The hunters had created a makeshift structure, a wooden lean-to. There were men, four of them, no, five, maybe more. They left camp and headed toward the creek. One wore a bright orange bulky jacket and green camo pants. Another, in overalls, wore an oversized bright green hat that tied under the chin. Another sported a long black beard and hair to match. He walked with a distinct limp, and dragging one foot. Even though it was a brisk morning, and all the men wore jackets and boots, the bearded one wore only dirty jeans, athletic shoes, and a short-sleeved t-shirt with dark stains. Chaco had no way of knowing how many of the men he might have missed, but there were others. He took in as many details as possible. One dressed in all camo, hat included. Chaco thought the bright orange peace sign embroidered on the hat rather incongruous. Another in bright red, an odd color to wear in the forest, stood tall and lanky as a scarecrow. The scarecrow laughed in a high pitch that sounded like an injured blue jay squawking. The other man, further away and harder to make out, wore all black. Other than his bushy blonde hair, the hunter in black, with a long, oiled coat, reminded Chaco of a young Johnny Cash, or an actor in a spaghetti western, right down to his impractical cowboy boots. The men moved further away from their camp. Although Chaco could no longer see them, he heard one man squawk, and squawk again, until his squawking grew faint. Chaco sprinted back to the group.

"Looks like hunters set up camp and bagged a few deer," he said to Russell.

"What a relief. I'll tell you, a forest fire around here, even in winter, could be devastating. Do you think we ought to introduce ourselves?"

"I'm not sure," Chaco said. "I don't want them to think we

intend to steal their game, but I don't want to surprise them if we end up too near their campsite later. They aren't far off the trail."

"Maybe we can take a casual stroll to the campsite and just let them know who we are." Rocky said.

"Okay. Let's do it," Chaco said.

Russell asked Jude to stay behind to guard, which seemed to almost flatter Jude, who held tight to his rifle. The other three men set out to introduce themselves to the hunters. When they entered the encampment, they found it empty. Russell called out. "Hey, anyone around?" No response.

While Russell and Rocky checked out the lean-to, Chaco decided to inspect the carcasses. When he got close to them, his throat shut. He meant to shout, but his words came out in croaks. "Christ!"

"What's going on?" said Russell. The men trotted to Chaco's side. One look and Rocky made a sound like a wounded calf, bent over, and with his hands on his waist, he vomited into the snow. There, on a heavy rope strewn tight between two old grown conifers, three skinned human figures hung by hooks, headless, one with a leg gone. The remains of a femur and a foot, with chunks of meat still clinging to the charred bone, along with three burned-to-a-black-crisp human heads, one with a gold incisor, nestled in the ashes of the still-hot fire pit. A blue and white speckled camp plate sat on a flat rock, loaded with half-eaten pinkish meat covered in flies. One identifiable human toe, gnawed to the bone with the blackened nail still attached, perched on the rim. Adjacent to the pit, like oversized deflated balloons, a pile of dirty, empty backpacks, the one on top…Day-Glo pink.

CHAPTER 25

The men moved a safe distance away behind a tree line from the hunters' camp and stood in a close knot.

Rocky spit a glob of mucous into a patch of snow. "What do we tell the others?" He whispered.

"Nothing. I'll take care of it," Chaco said.

"There you go again, making decisions for the rest of us, little compadre. There's fuckin' cannibals runnin' loose, and you don't think it's a good idea to warn anybody?" Rocky contorted his face into a malicious grimace that, from a distance, might have been mistaken for a friendly grin. "That's plain stupid."

"Settle down, Rocky. Chaco's right," Russell said. "What good would it do to upset everyone? Abigail would be horrified to know what happened to those kids. It's…there's no need to frighten her or the others." He looked over his shoulder as though expecting the cannibals to return. "Let's agree to keep this under our hats, and stay more vigilant. We can take turns on additional guard duty."

"You agree with Chaco, then?" Rocky shook his head. "What a surprise that you'd take his side. Why do I even bother trying to talk to…oh never mind." He made his grin-face again, pulling back his lips to expose his teeth like a dog. Rocky turned away from the others and stomped toward the path leading back to camp.

***

"What did y'all find out about that fire?" Margo asked as the guys entered camp.

"Oh, I don't know, Margo." With an exaggerated bow,

Rocky gestured with his hand to Chaco. "You have to ask him, since he seems to have all the answers, and everyone seems to think anything he says is right and good."

"Fer gawdsake, Rocky, jist tell us what's goin' on," Margo said.

"If it goes out of control, a fire here could be devastating," Abigail said. "Will one of you please answer Margo's question?"

"It's nothing," said Russell.

"Small brush fire near the river…no problem. We kicked dirt over it," Chaco said.

"As long as there is no danger of it spreading…," Abigail said.

Margo stepped closer to the men and looked into their eyes. "Why do I git the feelin' there's more to this? Y'all ain't keepin anythin' from us, are ya?" She looked from man to man. "The way Rocky is actin', I have half a mind to go there myself and check thangs out."

"It's fine, Margo. Let it go," Rocky said.

"Sumpin' got your panties in a wad over Chaco agin. I'm askin' ya one more time, what's…goin'…on?" Rocky and Russell averted their eyes. Only Chaco maintained eye contact.

"Nothing. Let it go," Rocky said. "We took care of it, all right?"

"I know when yer lyin' to me, Rocky Pennymon."

"I told you we dealt with it. Are you saying you don't believe me? Is that it?"

"You're in a pissy mood, ain't ya?" Margo turned heel. "I'm gonna check on the girls and see if Jude's around. Y'all can stay here all day in a wad talkin' nonsense if ya want to. I got thangs to do."

"One thing we can all be happy about…" said Abigail, "… those kids who have gone ahead to let Fiona know to expect us. How serendipitous they, too, are headed for Moonforest Sanctuary. I mean, what are the chances of those young hikers even running into us on the trail to begin with? Lucky for us and for them, right?" She beamed as she searched Russell and Chaco's faces. Both men turned their gaze to the ground.

***

The eventful midday settled into a peaceful afternoon. The breeze through the pines made the loudest of any sound. The men took turns walking the perimeter. They all managed to maintain a stoic demeanor. One man would look at another, and when they'd made eye contact, they'd nod, bonded now by their conspiracy.

"What y'all nervous about?" Margo asked as Chaco picked the Remington to take his turn.

"Russell thought he saw a mountain lion when we were kicking out that fire. Taking extra precautions for a day or two is prudent."

After his turn at guard duty, Rocky sat cross-legged on the blanket with Lacy and Olivia

They played a game of tic-tac-toe in the dirt. Abigail sat nearby scrubbing a pan with creek water and a piece of wadded aluminum foil.

***

The band moved on, but although the weather improved, there were still bad days, snow, ice, bitter cold nights. When food supplies ran low, they decided to find a good spot for hunting and gathering early spring greens. Chaco found a bucolic meadow on the edge of a conifer stand near a fresh pond. "Good place to hunt and maybe fish, too."

They erected their tents and made plans to store food. Rocky spent his free time whittling little things. He'd prop his back against a tree, take out a pen knife, and work away. He'd never showed his projects to anyone.

One day, Lacy held one of the sticks in front of her face and wiggled it. "Look, Grandma. Uncle Rocky made these for us with his knife."

Abigail smiled. "Well, that's very nice. What is that?"

"Pick-up-stick. He made a lot more of them, and he's teaching us how to play."

"Did you remember to say thank you?"

"They certainly did," Rocky said.

Olivia leapt to her feet and flung her arms around Rocky. "Thank you anyways, a million times." She planted a kiss on his cheek, and Rocky blushed.

"I would have never believed this if I'd not seen it myself," Chaco said to Margo.

"What? You mean Rocky playin' with them little girls? He loves kids. My only real sorrow is that I couldn't never give him any of his own. He'd make a real good daddy."

Chaco shook his head and clicked his tongue. "It's so bloody incongruous."

"I don't know what that *congruwhatever* is, but I kin guess you mean him playin' with them children is not what you expect?"

"Something like that."

"Has anyone seen my son?" Russell asked as he approached. "It's getting late, and the girls will be hungry. Jude said he'd come with me to get firewood. Can't find him."

"I seen him wander off by himself somewhere with his gun earlier when y'all were gallivanting' in the forest lookin' after that mystery fire. Maybe he's gone huntin'." Margo lowered her voice. "Ya know, I don't mean to make anyone feel bad or nothin', but I've noticed he seems worse lately."

"I've noticed, too," Abigail said. "I want so much to help him, but …. I don't know what to do."

Russell put his arm around his wife. "He's still grieving, and you have to let him work things out in his own time." He kissed her cheek. "He'll get through this, sweetheart." He pulled back and dusted his hands off onto his pants' legs. "I'm going to gather some wood before it gets any later. Chaco, wanna come along?"

"My turn at duty," Chaco said and patted his rifle.

"You boys go ahead," Margo said. "Abby and me will wash all

these greens we dug up this mornin'." Margo gestured toward a messy pile of roots. "C'mon, we best git to it. By the time we clean off all that mud and I fix a stew, it'll be midnight." She turned to Chaco. "I'll find ya and bring you a bowl, Chaco. And, Russ, why not take Rocky to git wood with you?"

"He's entertaining the girls. That's the best thing he could do for us right now."

Chaco checked his weapon and headed for the perimeter.

"Wait," Russell said. "I need to talk to you for a minute." He took several broad steps to catch up to the younger man.

"Yes, Mr. Walker?" Chaco said.

"Let's wait until we are further away from camp."

Once out of earshot, the two men stopped beneath a ponderosa pine, and Russell turned to Chaco. "It's Jude. I didn't want to alarm Abby, but I'm more concerned than I let on back there. I'm afraid he's rounded the bend."

"What do you mean, Mr. Walker?"

"He doesn't sleep. He hardly eats. He either sits trancelike staring into space for hours or else he paces like a nervous wildcat. Jude keeps his distance from everyone, even his daughters." The older man's shoulders slumped. "It's his PTSD. It's gotten much worse. Don't tell me you haven't noticed."

"Yes, I have, actually."

"Yet you haven't said a thing about him. Why?"

"I figured that you and Mrs. Walker have been troubled enough as it is. Besides…it's none of my business."

Russell stiffened. "Wait right there. You are no longer my hired hand. We're in this together. What happens to any of us affects all of us. If you know something about my son or have noticed anything out of the ordinary with him, it is most certainly your business. At least I *hope* you'll tell me about it."

The rocking and cawing of a lone raven circling overhead caught the men's attention, just as the explosion of a rifle shot split the afternoon's peace. A bullet lodged in the pine trunk, and pieces of wood splintered inches from Chaco's head.

Both men dropped to their knees. Chaco motioned for Russell to move behind the tree before shouldering his weapon.

"Jesus Christ," Russell whispered. "The cannibals. They found us."

"*Hijo de madre*. Jude," Chaco muttered.

"What did you say? Did you get a look at who it was?"

"No. Stay put. I'm going to check it out." Chaco crawled on his belly to the safety of a fallen tree. As he peered through the branches, he saw a lone man leap over a boulder and run through the forest toward the river bank.

When the men returned to camp, they found Jude squatted a distance from the others, skinning a jack rabbit.

"We heard a shot," Abigail said. "What's going on?"

Russell and Chaco looked at one another. Rocky stood and walked to Russell and Chaco. He whispered, "Those cannibalistic bastards?"

"Don't know," Russell said. "Couldn't tell."

"What y'all whisperin' about?" Margo said.

"I saw a buck, and thought we could have venison for dinner," Chaco said. "I missed. I guess your husband thinks it's funny."

"Yeah. Damned funny that Mr. Sharpshooter here can't get a buck now, even when it's right in front of him." Rocky grabbed his rifle. "Hon, I'll be walking around the outside of camp for a while. I'm giving our little *compadre* a break. He needs a rest after that trauma of missing his shot, don't you, boy?" He winked at Chaco then turned his attention back to his wife. "Bring me some of those root things when they're cooked, will you, darlin'?" Rocky leaned over to Margo and planted a noisy kiss on her mouth.

***

They'd stocked up on dried fish, venison, and rabbit. After dinner, they set to the task of breaking camp and packing for their continuing journey. Russell took his turn at guard duty. Rocky loaded his and Margo's gear, then sat near the fire and whittled on a small piece of pine. After tucking the little girls in for the night, the women washed and stowed the remaining pots and pans. Certain that no one followed, Chaco retrieved a bottle of his precious Spätburgunder and retreated to a spot near the river. He pulled his jacket close around him. Although early spring, the evening air chilled him to the marrow, so brisk and icy. The snow glistened in the light of the waning gibbous moon.

This time of year in Soyapango, El Salvador, the weather would be warm and sultry. Red and yellow hibiscus, vainglorious in their full bloom, would wave in unison motivated by the breeze, and the pretty *chicas* would wear summer dresses the color of orchids. In better times, tonight he'd be dancing the *merenga* with Mirabella on his abuela's veranda to a live band, under the light of dozens of torches because there would have been a grand fiesta. In addition to *platanos, yuca, tamales* and *pupusas*, his abuela would have served *sopa de pescado*, rice and *curtido*, maybe *chicharones*. All his favorites. The adults would sip *cervesa* and *Tick Táck* until they were silly-drunk, and the children would drink ice cold *tamarindo*. For dessert, Abuela Erhard would bring out *Tres Leches* cake topped by lit sparklers. Friends, colleagues, and family would applaud, press in around him, and lift their glasses in a toast.

Chaco opened the wine that he'd placed in a patch of snow to chill and drank straight from the bottle. He wiped his mouth with the sleeve of his coat and looked into the sky. "*Feliz cumpleaños* to me," then took a second draft from the bottle of wine, spilling a little down his chin. He wiped it from his skin with his forefinger and licked it. After a third swallow, he held the bottle to the moon in a mock cheer. "I am honored that the stars and the moon celebrate this most auspicious occasion with me." He lowered the bottle and closed his eyes. "Happy Birthday, Chaco Erhard Rodriguez."

CHAPTER 26

The next morning, a hangover gripped Chaco. At one time, he could drink three bottles of wine with no ill effects. Not now. His head throbbed, and each movement hurt as though he'd swallowed needles and they'd worked their way into every artery and muscle, stabbing into his joints, his neck and gut. He sat on a stump, pulled a blanket around himself, and rubbed his temples one-handed.

Margo walked to him and squeezed his shoulder. "Me and Rocky have been watchin' you. You don't look so good, and yer up so late this mornin' you missed breakfast."

"Sorry, I…"

"That ain't like you in the least." She shook her head. "Yer either sick, or you drank too much of somethin'. Yer head hurt? Want some food?"

Chaco shook his head.

She leaned over to examine his face. "What's that supposed to mean? You don't want nothin' to eat, or yer head ain't hurtin'? Jist tell me. Which is it?"

Chaco's mouth felt as though someone had stuffed it with grit. He didn't know if he could speak another word, or if nothing but puffs of sand would come out if he tried. "My head hurts, and I don't want anything to eat, but thanks."

Margo padded away, returning in a few minutes with a mug clutched in both hands. She handed the cup, filled with steaming liquid, to Chaco, careful not to spill. "Drink this."

"Oh, God. No coffee." He waved her away.

"It ain't coffee. It's white willow bark tea. It's what aspirin is made of, I told ya. Sip it down, and it'll help yer sore head."

He took the mug and held it to his nose. He inhaled the musky, sharp fragrance.

Margo stood by as he put the mug to his lips. "Kin I sit with you while you drink that?"

"Sure." Chaco took a sip of the bitter tea and another. It felt good going down. "I gather you need to talk to me about something?"

"Me and Rocky have been thinking a lot about Jude and the way he is with you."

"You're concerned again? Why? I know he doesn't like me much, but I...."

"He don't like me neither. He cain't git it through his hard head that me and you didn't cause his wife to die. He blames us still. That's not what worries us, though."

"What is it?"

"He's got a special kinda hate fer you, and it's gettin' worse."

"I appreciate your ongoing concern, and Rocky's, but I am acutely aware of Jude's actions and reactions. I keep a close eye on him."

"That's comfortin' to hear, but it's jist that me an' Rocky don't think yer takin' this stuff with Jude serious enough."

"I'm not sure what you expect me to do."

"Jist watch yer back a little better. Probably not a good idea for you to go traipsin' off in the woods by yerself like you did last night." She patted his knee.

"I need alone time, Margo."

"That's fine and dandy, but kin you wait fer yer alone time until we get to the sanctuary where there's more people? We are jist worried, that's all. Jude and that PTSD stuff...it's not good, ya know?"

"I'm more worried Jude might hurt himself than I'm concerned he'd hurt me."

"What are you talkin' about?" Margo took the now empty mug from Chaco's hand. She peered into the cup and smiled. "Good. You drank it up. You'll feel better soon."

"The suicide rate among veterans with PTSD is an epidemic.

I read that one of five suicides in the U.S. is veterans suffering from the disorder, not counting thousands more homeless vets without good records on file who kill themselves or those who drink themselves to death. Some commit suicide via 'death by cop,' or…"

"Meanin' what, exactly?"

"Meaning some people intentionally put themselves in the way of a cop's bullet."

"I don't git it. Why would anyone do a stupid thang like that? They don't jist kill themselves, but they hurt the poor cop that did it."

"When people are in that much emotional pain, they aren't rational. In that moment when they've lost that delicate balance between coping with pain and barely managing to get out of bed, and when they reach the tipping point where they can no longer live with the agony, they aren't capable of thinking about anyone or anything. They simply must rid themselves of the pain. In some cases, a person can't bring themselves to hold a gun to their temple and pull the trigger. That's why sometimes when someone wants to die, they'll commit a crime, and when the police respond, the perpetrator pulls a knife or a gun and charges the officers, forcing one or more cops to fire."

"That's jist plain tragic. I ain't never heard of such a thang."

"It happens. But no matter the method, every hour of every day in the U.S., a veteran with PTSD commits suicide."

"Holy cow." Margo shook her head. "Awful."

"We…*they* have been subjected to horrors beyond imagining, and when the fighting is over and they come back home, they live with paranoia, nightmares, and guilt forever. Of course, meds and counseling help, but Jude doesn't have any support like that now. And with the love of his life gone…"

"You think that boy might off hisself instead of tryin' to kill you?"

"I don't know."

***

The ice in the swelling creek broke off into heavy chunks and swirled downstream, making noisy splashes as they cascaded over rocks into the fast-moving water. The weather had not thawed the snow entirely, but patches of bare ground spotted the landscape, a welcome sign of spring. After the willow bark tea and a good long nap, Chaco stretched and yawned. He felt better, but his head still hurt. He squinted his eyes at the late day Sun.

Margo muddled pine seeds with a pestle in a metal bowl, but the sound punched holes in Chaco's brain. He grimaced. "Sorry 'bout the noise. I'm makin' a sort of pesto for the fish Rocky caught. Ya still feelin' bad?"

"A little bit, yes. Better than this morning."

The tease of spring put everyone in a happy mood. Chaco even caught Jude smiling, the first he'd seen on Jude's face in a long while. Jude looked relaxed, almost contented.

The cannibals had apparently moved on. There were no more distant campfire smoke plumes, no stray shots from the dark, no camp invasions. For the time being, all was soft and peaceful. Safe.

Margo said she'd seen a robin. "It's early yet, but spring's nearly here. The robin comin' 'round says so." She jumped up and down and clapped her hands like a little girl. "It's all gonna be easier fer us now. Jist wait and see."

Abigail laughed in delight. "For the first time in a long while, I feel like everything is right with the world."

March. But what date? Chaco wondered. They could be in for more brutal snowstorms, icy grey rain, the wind like knives, but not today. With any luck, if this weather held up, they'd reach Moonforest Sanctuary in a few weeks, maybe by early April, or before. Chaco would grasp Fiona in his arms so hard she'd have to struggle for air. He held the memory of her in his thighs, his belly, and his groin. He closed his eyes and remembered the feel of her hair, soft and fine like a baby's. Mostly, he remembered the smell of her, like blooming hyacinth, a flower of spring. Everything about her was spring. The way she moved, her Caribbean green eyes, her laugh. The last time they'd made love had been a few weeks before the blackout. While visiting her parents, like a thief she'd snuck to Chaco's cabin, stripped and climbed into his bed. She straddled him. When she leaned into him pressing her bare hardened nipples against his chest, then licked the side of his neck like a cat, he thought he'd explode before he entered her. They made insane love, then again, and after a glass of wine, they made love a third time. They fell asleep against one another, sweaty, and spent. Chaco awoke in the latest hour of the night and let his hand rest on her breast, brushing her soft skin with his fingertips. His penis stiffened against her. But peaceful in her sleep, Chaco decided to let Fiona be. He counted her breaths until drowsiness took over, but before allowing himself to fall into a light slumber, he whispered, "I could stay here all night and every night for a hundred years"

As the Sun crested the hills, Chaco nudged her. "Wake up, *mi amor.*"

Her eyes flew open and she jumped to her feet. "Shit! What time is it?" Leaving her panties on the floor, she yanked on her jeans, pulled her t-shirt on inside out, and kissed Chaco on the lips so fast, he almost didn't feel it. Carrying her shoes in one hand, she grabbed her jacket, then scuttled barefooted to her parent's home. *When was that? Late August? Such a bloody long time ago.* He crawled into his tent.

***

When Chaco emerged, Abigail and Margo were busy with dinner. The children played with their pick-up-sticks on a blanket near the fire, and Rocky had gone to gather kindling. Russell stood guard duty. And, Jude? Jude had disappeared… somewhere. No one knew where. His unannounced disappearances had become so routine, no one thought much about them. Chaco wondered if they wouldn't find him dead one day, perhaps drowned in the creek, or hanging by his belt from a tree limb.

Earlier, when the others wondered where Chaco had gone to, Margo covered for him. "He's not feelin' so good. Y'all can git along without him fer a little bit. Let the poor guy have some sleep."

For the first time, Chaco had missed his turn at guard duty. He apologized to Russell, who had taken his shift.

"Chaco, you needed the rest. If you're up to it, you can take late duty tonight. Rocky is on the next shift. I think we're fine for now, let's get something to eat, shall we?"

"You go ahead. I'll be there in a minute." Chaco walked a short way into the forest to relieve himself. As he finished up, about to return to camp, a rustling in a nearby bush startled him. He dropped to one knee and shouldered his rifle. "Who the hell is there? Come out now or I'll blast the shit out of you!" Whatever hid in the brush moved again. It seemed like a big something, a bear, a man. "I'm warning you, if you don't show yourself, I'm going to shoot." Chaco took aim about to pull the trigger when a fat raccoon poked his head through the brush. Chaco laughed.

After dinner, Chaco helped clean and stow the cooking supplies. He'd taken a pail of dirty dishwater to the side of camp to dump it, and as he tipped the pail at the base of a blue spruce, Jude screeched. "You fuckin' Iraqi scum. Say your prayers to Allah, you rag-headed hajib prick!"

As he swung around to face Jude, Chaco dropped the pail, and the contents splattered the ground soaking his feet. In that infinitesimal space in the mind between darkness and light, he heard the discharge and witnessed the muzzle flash from a single shot of gunfire, and in quick succession, a second blast. Chaco's knees buckled and his world went black. *No, I can't die like this.* Blood trickled down his forehead and filled his eyes. "Fiona. *Mi amor.* My love. *Te amo mucho.* I love you so much."

CHAPTER 27

What is that sound? Screaming? Far away. Under the ocean? In the sky? A raptor? A puma? A howler monkey in South America. Am I in Brazil? It's a woman. Screaming. Under water. How can I hear a woman screaming under water? Not under water. Why is she screaming? My ears are filled with something. Cotton? Water? Yes. No. Blood. My blood. Blood. How can this be? I can't hear. Hurts. It hurts. Who is screaming? Stop. Stop screaming. By all that is holy, stop.

***

"Wake up, Chaco. Wake up." Someone shook him by the shoulders. Hard. The shaking hurt his head. He opened his eyes but could see only a monster, the fuzzy image of a monster. A giant, no, an ant, a big ant on the bridge of his nose peering into his half-opened eyes. Chaco reached with one hand to swat it from his face, but didn't, couldn't, move. Then an involuntary shudder. No. Someone still shaking him. *Why is that woman screaming? Yes, the woman. Still screaming. Who is it? I'm alive? No. I am dead. How can this be? I'm to die at the hands of a madman while I empty dishwater? Here in the dirt like a dog among dung beetles and ants? Quit shaking me. Stop.*

"Oh fer gawdsake. Cain't you hear me? Wake up, you lazy peckerwood."

Chaco opened his eyes a little more and regained focus. Margo. He wanted to speak to her, but his mouth felt dry as stale crackers. His head. *It hurts. Can't hear.*

"Talk. Say somethin'. Let me know you kin hear me. C'mon, now."

Chaco bolted to a sitting position. Water and blood

everywhere. Blood on his face. He reached one hand to his hair. Touched his scalp. Sticky with blood.

"There ya are," Margo mopped his face with a rag. "You got yer head grazed good, and a bit of yer ear is missin'. You ain't so handsome now, are ya?" She laughed. "I suspect you got a big concussion and might have a hell of a headache fer awhile. But, you'll live." With a handkerchief, she dabbed at the wound on his scalp.

Chaco winced. "What happened? Jude shot me? Who has been screaming?"

"I don't know how he missed. He was jist four or five feet from ya."

Chaco attempted to clear his thoughts. When he tried to stand, Margo pushed him back onto the dirt. "You stay right there. You need to get yer bearings before you start walkin', 'sides, I gotta tell ya how this all happened. Are ya gonna listen?"

"I'm listening."

"Jude was gonna kill you. He fired, and somehow didn't git ya, but was fixin' to fire again when Rocky kilt him."

"What?"

"I said Rocky saved yer life, that's what. He blew half of Jude's head right off before that boy could squeeze off another round."

"What?"

"Ya heard me. And that woman who was screamin' is Abby. She's a mess, and so is them little girls. Rocky kilt Jude right in front of Abby, jist a yard or two away from where she was standin'. And in front of Russ and them little girls, too. Olivia and Lacy were hollerin' so loud. They might be in shock. Rocky is tendin' to them, which ain't easy 'cause they saw him kill their daddy. Them little girls are gonna need lots of counselin' with a professional after what they've been through. I can't imagine… it was plain awful, but Rocky had to do it. Had to. Jude was yellin' and sayin' you was an Iraqi. He was completely out of his head and, gawd, he wanted you dead in the worst way."

"I remember something about…" Chaco winced again. He pushed Margo's hand away and struggled to his feet. His legs felt like bands of melting rubber. His knees buckled, but he regained balance, and stood with one hand on a tree trunk, seeking stability.

"It's a terrible thang, Chaco, but Rocky didn't have no choice."

Jude's corpse sprawled in the dirt not far away, a chunk of his head missing. Blood splattered everywhere. Abigail knelt at the side of her son's corpse and no longer screamed, but her contorted facial features twisted in silent agony. Tears ran from her eyes to her nose, mixed with snot, and slipped down her chin. She didn't look like Abigail Walker, but like a bad caricature of the elegant woman Chaco had known. He ran to her side. He intended to lift her off the ground, pull her into his arms and comfort her, but a strong hand grabbed his shoulder and restrained him. "No," said Russell. "Leave her alone." Russell Walker had been crying, too. His eyes looked like twin dead piranhas, red, slippery and dangerous. "Please. Leave her alone."

Rocky held the two little girls, one in each arm. They hung like rag dolls, neither crying nor trying to wriggle free. He had turned so that they could not see their father. He carried them into the forest, their legs limp and dangling.

"Poor little thangs," Margo said. "First their mama, then… I'm tellin' ya, they was screamin' their little heads off like I ain't never heard when they saw their daddy fall down dead like that, but Rocky dropped his rifle quick and got to 'em before they could see much more…you know…of the blood and their daddy's head partly off. It's jist good Rocky got to 'em before they saw all that."

"This is my fault," Chaco said. "If I had been more careful, more…"

"It isn't your fault," Russell said. He still held Chaco, digging his fingers into his shoulder so hard Chaco felt bruises forming.

The younger man made no attempt to move away from the older man's grip, to wrench away from the pain of Russell's vice-like fingers.

"I'm so sorry, Mr. Walker, I am so…"

"You did not shoot my son, and none of this is your fault." Russell released his grasp. "I have to tend to Abigail and find Rocky and the girls. Let Margo take care of that scalp and your ear. You'll need stitches."

Russell moved stiffly like a man-sized wind-up automaton. He pulled off his jacket and approached Jude's lifeless body. He covered his son's face, then picked up a piece of Jude's blood slicked cranium that had blown off when the bullet struck. A bit of scalp, a bit of dark hair, a bit of brain clung to the bone. Russell pushed the piece of his son's head under the jacket, as though doing that would somehow make things better. He put his arm around his wife and lifted her to her feet as if she were a child. She turned to him, buried her face into his chest, and wailed.

Chaco took a step toward the Walkers, the people he knew as family. He wanted to hold them both, to apologize to Abigail, to embrace them, to cry with them.

"No. Let 'em be," whispered Margo. "Plenty of time for that later. Let's git you cleaned up and stitched, then Rocky and me will need your help to dig a grave tonight, and find some rocks to put over it."

Margo led Chaco to the riverbank. She had with her a small bag tied with a leather strap. She ordered Chaco to sit, then pulled open the bag and extracted a needle, a spool of thread, a book of matches and some kind of paste at the bottom of a tin cup. The concoction, a vile greenish goop, smelled of rotted leaves and pungent English tea.

"What is that?" Chaco asked. He leaned against a tree stump. His head throbbed, and his ear stung.

"It's a mixture of a few herbs includin' yarrow, all mixed up together. It'll help take away the pain and prevent infection."

With two fingers, she scooped some of the goo from the cup and plastered it on Chaco's scalp wound and his ear. "That'll help a bit. Don't wash it off or nuthin'. Jist leave it be." She threaded the needle and lit a match. She passed the sharp end of the needle through the flame until the metal turned black. She held up the needle and thread. "Ya know this is gonna hurt a lot, but I'll do it fast. Do you want to bite down on a twig or somethin' while I sew up yer head?"

"No. Just do it." Chaco braced his back against the tree, clenched his hands, and dug his nails into his palm. She worked with skill and speed, but the needle stabbed into Chaco's skin and scraped against his skull. With each repeated tug and yank of the thread, he jabbed his fingernails into his palms with such ferocity that he drew blood.

When finished, with one clean jerk, she bit the needle from the thread. "That'll do it. I'll take them stitches out in about ten days."

"Thanks."

"It ain't me you need to thank. It's Rocky. If it weren't fer him, you'd be the one we'd be buryin', not Jude."

"I don't want you to think that I'm not grateful but…"

"I have some thoughts about all this." Margo had already stowed her things back into the bag. She rinsed her hands in the river, stood and dried them against the rough fabric of her jeans. "Why didn't Jude git you? He was so close to you, and he's a damn good shot. That boy couldn't have missed, less he did it intentional." She put her hands on her hips and leaned back on her heels. "But here's the thang. If Jude missed on purpose, why was he fixin' to shoot again? Anyway you look at it, don't make much sense."

The throbbing and stinging in Chaco's scalp and ear had eased a bit. Now, the self-inflicted wounds in his palms hurt the most. Most of all, he felt tired, so tired. Even his bones were tired. He yawned, then yawned again. "Remember when we talked a while back about the numbers of returning soldiers with PTSD who commit suicide?"

"Yeah, I remember…wait, your hands is bleedin'." She extracted the cup of green stuff from her bag and put it on a rock. "Lemme see your palms." Chaco held out both hands. "You poked your nails through yer skin, didn't you?" She dampened a rag in the river water and brought it back to Chaco. "Wash those wounds out before they git infected."

He did as she ordered, then she applied some of the goop from the cup. With thin strips of the sheet she also had in the bag, she wrapped both of Chaco's palms and tied them into knots at the back of his hands. "Try not to git these too dirty. I only have a few, and I'm gonna have to wash 'em fer you to use again. Now…what was that about suicide? Are you sayin' you think that's the reason Jude missed ya?"

"Maybe."

"So, yer thinkin' Jude set Rocky up to kill him, like that death-by-cop thang you told me about."

"He counted on someone putting him down."

"And 'a course he wouldn't think his own daddy would shoot. Jude had to know it was Rocky, which, now that I think it over, kinda figures in a different way, too."

"Why do you say that? How does that make sense, Margo?"

"Cause Rocky warned him to stay clear a' you."

"He did?"

"Yup. He told Jude we was keepin' our eyes on him." She wiped her forehead with the back of one hand. "And Jude was plain mad about that. He might a' wanted to git back at Rocky some way. I told ya already twice that me and Rocky was watchin' Jude 'cause we didn't trust him anywheres near you. Don't you listen to nobody?"

"Sorry…I never thought Rocky…"

"You never thought Rocky what? Rocky kin be a big, blustery idiot, but I told you, deep down he's a good man. 'Cause of the way he is, you jist never could see it. What I don't git is Jude. He wudda known that Rocky wudda kilt him right in front of his mama, his daddy, and his little girls." She stood and offered a hand up to Chaco. "I don't git how he could hurt his own family like that, especially them children, his own little girls."

"When someone is in that much pain, rational thinking flies out the window and disappears, Margo."

"He was a damned coward. That's what he was."

"I wouldn't call Jude a coward. Suicide is an act of absolute despair. We can't judge."

"If he weren't a coward he wudda gone off somewhere private and did hisself in rather than hurt his family like that. I would never say so to Russ or Abby, but their son was a weakling."

"I wouldn't say…" A close shotgun blast startled a murder of crows roosting in a nearby tree. The birds took to the sky in a mass of black feathers and screeches. Frantic, Chaco groped the dirt for his gun.

"Honey, we ain't got no gun here," Margo whispered. "Do you think that might be Russ or Rocky? Let's go see."

Chaco grabbed Margo and pulled her to the ground. "No. I don't know who it is, but we are going to lay low and out of sight until we *do* know."

A man's voice, unfamiliar, echoed through the narrow canyon. "I think I gut-shot her. We'll have to track her and finish her."

"What the fuck?" another man responded. "You had a clean shot. How could you miss?"

"It wasn't my damned fault. She moved at the last minute, okay? Don't be bustin' my chops, dickhead."

"You two quit shittin' around and let's go get her," said a third. "I want me some doe steak tonight. She looked pregnant. Maybe we get two deer for one shot." The man laughed.

Chaco motioned for Margo to get down behind a boulder. He crawled toward the voices, and there, between the trunks of old growth pine, he saw three men, hunters, one in a camo hat with a peace sign embroidered on the front, one dressed in bright red, and the third with a limp in a long black oiled coat.

Oh no.

CHAPTER 28

Chaco, Margo, and Rocky dug a grave. Russell, weak from grief, clung to his wife and granddaughters and watched. The men swaddled Jude in a blanket, pushed him into the hole, and covered him with shovelfuls of soil. They piled stones and logs high over the mound.

"We need to make certain coyotes can't get to Jude's body," Chaco said.

Rocky stripped two slender branches, and bound together with a bootlace, fashioning a cross. On a separate piece of flat wood hewn from the trunk of a cedar, he carved a message. *Here lies Jude Walker, beloved son, husband, father, and a veteran who served his country.* He nestled the wood among the rocks on the mound.

Abigail refused to see her son's body shoved into a grave. "No, I can't. And I don't want the children to see it, either. They've been through too much already," she'd said to Margo. She took her granddaughters to the river to wait. Once Chaco and Rocky had interred Jude, Margo gathered the family and led them to the burial place.

Russell, who would have ordinarily been the one to say a few words over the body, had no words to say. He could not speak. Chaco stepped in to take Russell's place. "Jude Walker was a good man who loved his family. May at last his soul rest forever in peace." He crossed himself.

The others, their heads bowed, said, "Amen."

"Is that where Daddy is?" Olivia pointed to the burial mound, tears streaming down her face. "No, sweetheart." Abigail stroked her granddaughter's hair. "Only his empty body is under those rocks. He's with your mommy, and they are together with the angels now."

"Do they have big angel wings?" Lacy asked.

"Maybe so." Abigail pulled both of her granddaughters closer.

"Thank you," Russell whispered to the men who had buried his son.

In heavy silence, the group packed for their continued journey.

***

Later, Margo fed and put the girls to bed for the evening. Abigail and Russell ate nothing. Once the children fell asleep, Abigail drug herself to the edge of camp to perch on a stump of a long ago felled oak, and grieved alone. Her husband stood guard, rifle slung over his shoulder. He shooed away Chaco and Rocky's attempts to relieve him of guard duty. "I need to do this by myself," he said. "Make sure the girls are okay. They've been crying all day and if they wake up, they'll need some comfort, and get Margo to fix you something to eat."

No one wanted to eat. Chaco picked at dried berries and pine nuts to keep his energy high. "Rocky, before you turn in, I need to talk to you," Chaco whispered, handing a fistful of nuts to the bigger man.

Rocky shook his head. "Nope. Don't want anything to eat. What is it, little hombre? Anything to do with that shot I heard when Margo was fixing you up yesterday afternoon? She said hunters. I meant to ask you about it."

"Let's get away from here for a minute." Chaco, rifle in hand and wary as a cat, walked to the river bank. Rocky stayed ahead by a few steps with his flashlight and illuminated the way.

When far enough to talk without being overheard, Chaco propped the Remington against a tree. "Cannibals."

"Are you sure?" Rocky wiped his forehead with the back of the hand holding the lit flashlight. The beam of light bounced off boulders and tree limbs in a zig zag pattern. "Damn." Rocky steadied the flashlight and set it upright on a flat boulder, under-lighting both men's faces. "We gotta do something. Did they see you?"

"They'd wounded a doe and were after her. They were in a hurry, so didn't even know Margo and I were nearby."

"That's one good thing, at least." Rocky paused. "We should tell Russ."

"Maybe not. He's so distraught right now."

Rocky let out a sound like a wolf pup caught in a trap. The big man struggled to retain his composure. "I killed my best friend's son." He bit his lip, then sunk down into the dirt onto his haunches and put his head in his hands. Even in the darkness, Chaco could see the hulking man's shoulders heave as he sobbed. "I did that. I killed my best friend's son…right in front of him. He'll never forgive me. And Abigail, and those little girls…they saw everything. Oh God."

Chaco kneeled and put his hand on Rocky's arm. "You did what you had to do. I will never forget you saved my life. Thank you."

***

Margo's screams woke Chaco from a sound sleep. Although barely dawn, and the temperature frigid, he bounced out of his bed sack, not bothering to pull his jeans over his undershorts or put on shoes. He ran to Margo. "What happened?"

By then, Russell, Abigail, and the girls were also awake. The little girls, their hair in a mess of tangles, barefooted despite the cold, tried to run to Margo. Abigail restrained them.

"Gramma, let go," Olivia cried. "Something bad happened to Margo!"

"No. Honey, stay with me. Grandpa and Chaco will take care of it."

Chaco sprinted to Margo's side, Russell a few steps behind. "Where's Rocky?"

Margo, eyes watery, and face pale as the inside of a tuber, threw her hands into the air. "That's jist it. I ain't gotta clue. He took off...and he left a note sayin' he ain't never comin' back."

"Let me read the note," Chaco said. "Maybe I can figure out where he's gone."

"Suit yerself, but I ain't got time to dick around. I gotta go find him. That fool is bound to die out there by hisself." She grabbed her coat and rifle.

"No, Margo, wait, please." Chaco put his hand on her upper arm. "Let's think this through."

"The longer he's gone, the more he's gonna be in trouble. He could git hisself kilt." When certain there'd be no danger, Abigail herded the girls closer to the fray. Margo's eyes, frantic with worry, darted from Chaco to Russell, but when she saw the faces of frightened little girls, she relaxed a little.

"Uncle Rocky left?" Olivia's eyes widened with concern.

Margo managed a wan smile. "Don't you worry 'bout yer Uncle Rocky. He kin take care of hisself, and we'll find him, or he jist might show up on his own."

Chaco released his grip on Margo's arm and repeated his request. "Let me read the note."

Margo dug a wadded piece of paper from her jeans pocket and handed it to Chaco. He opened it, put it on a rock and smoothed the creases. Then he picked it up with both hands and read it in silence.

Margo, honey, I love you more than anything, but I killed my best friend's son. I can't be here and see his pain every day. I can't even look at Abby or the girls knowing what I did. You are a strong woman. Stick with Chaco. I know the two of you will work together and lead Russ, Abby and those two little ones to Moonforest Sanctuary where you will all be safe. One day, maybe, you'll find a good-looking cowboy and the two of you will make a life together. Until that happens, keep me in your heart, as I will always keep you in mine. I love you, Rocky.

P.S. I made something for you, and the horses are for Olivia and Lacy.

He handed the note to Russell. After reading it, he returned the note to Margo. She folded it and tucked it into her back pocket. Russell reached for Margo and put his hand on her shoulder. "I hope you know both Abigail and I understand that Rocky did what he had to."

"I do," she said." Thank you fer sayin' so. I'm terrible sorry. I feel jist awful about Jude."

Russ shook his head. "Don't.... you can't.... we will help you find Rocky. I don't want him out there any more than you do. Now, what is this about horses for Olivia and Lacy?"

Olivia's voice chirped like a little bird. "Horses? Uncle Rocky got us horses?" She and Lacy looked one way and the other. "Where?"

Margo bent down, "They ain't real horses, honey. He made somethin' 'specially fer you two because yer Uncle Rocky loves you a whole lot, and wanted you to have somethin' nice to play with." She walked into her tent and came back holding two carved horses, one of birch and the other of oak. Each horse was approximately eight inches in length, perfect in proportion, long manes, and tales. One looked as though running, the other, the one of birch, stood on its hind legs. Each line, each cut, intricate in detail. Every muscle, every strand of hair, the details of the hooves, the eyelashes, perfect. The wooden horses looked alive, as though once put on the forest floor they would whinny and gallop through the conifers. Chaco held one in his hand turning it over, examining it. "I've never seen anything quite so beautiful." He gave the horse to Olivia. Lacy had already made herself busy playing with the other.

Margo slipped a wooden bracelet off her wrist and handed it to Chaco. Its edges were finely burnished, with tiny connecting hearts chiseled around the circumference, so perfect each little heart, and so uniform in size, they could have been machine engraved. Inside the bracelet, an inscription: "ROCKY + MARGO 4 EVER".

Margo extended her hand, and Chaco placed the bracelet in her palm. She folded her fingers around it, held it to her chest, and burst into sobs.

Abigail put her arms around Margo and rocked her like an infant. The two women had a good long cry together. Once spent of tears, and their embrace broken, Chaco stepped in. "I'm sorry, Margo. I know this is tough, but I'm curious about what Rocky took with him."

Margo sniffed. "Is it important?"

"Could be."

"Well, let's see. His rifle, and maybe fifty rounds of ammo. His big ol' huntin' knife that I got him last year for Christmas. A sleepin' bag, a little food and a water canteen, some water purifyin' pellets, waterproof matches, fishin' line and hooks, a change of clothes, and his big fur lined coat. I think that's it. That huntin' knife was real special to him. I bought it from Indians who made it by their own hands. It's heavy, too. Probably stuck it in his big ol' belt. He's lookin' like a mountain man now."

"Sounds like he's got enough survival gear. If he has good skills, he'll be great on his own for a long while. I think we need to take inventory to see what else…" A crackle and snap of someone, or something, stepping on a fallen limb echoed through the camp, followed by footsteps of someone, or something, bounding through the woods.

"Rocky, is that you?" Margo started toward the sound. Russell grabbed her shoulder. "Stay here with Abby and the kids. We'll check this out."

Chaco picked up his rifle and started after Russell. *Please let it be a buck or even a bear.*

CHAPTER 29

It wasn't a buck or a bear. Sets of booted footprints left deep tracks in the loam. Chaco squatted to inspect more closely.

"Can you tell anything from those footprints?" Russell asked.

"Yeah. The impressions are too big and too deep not to be from good-sized men. There are several sets. See?" He pointed at the prints and picked up an empty plastic water bottle nearby. "Four distinct sole patterns, and different sizes. From the way the pine needles are disturbed, looks like they were sitting, or maybe even reclining. They were here for a long time, maybe all afternoon."

"You think they were spying on us?"

"Possibly."

"How long do you say they were watching?"

"For a bit. Look, there's toilet paper and feces. Food wrappers. They were probably attracted by…" Chaco had turned to look at Russell taken aback by the intensity of the older man's grief. The spry, distinguished gentleman looked 100-years-old.

"You mean, to say, Chaco --- you think they were attracted by the gun blasts last night."

"I'm sorry, Mr. Walker. I know losing Jude that way…"

"No, Chaco. Not now…please." He set his jaw. "Looks like the men headed north. Do we know for sure if they are the cannibals?"

"Not north. They circled behind us." Chaco pointed at footprints leading away, and a pine sapling among the thick copse of trees a few yards due south. From a higher branch, about six feet off the ground, a camo hat with an embroidered peace sign hung by its strap. "They are the cannibals for certain. I will remember that hat in every nightmare I have for the rest of my life."

"Jesus." Russell's face blanched.

"And Mr. Walker?"

"Yes."

"I hate to tell you this, but I'm certain they are stalking us. We are their prey."

CHAPTER 30

When they returned to camp, Chaco sought out Margo. "I need to talk to you. It's important."

"Sure. Let me get the girls their breakfast, and…"

"No. Now."

"Abby says that weren't nuthin' but a buck in the bushes a while ago. Anyway, that's what Russ told her." She looked at him sideways and clucked her tongue. "It was sumpin' else, weren't it?

Chaco looked around and put his finger to his lips. "Shhhhh…let's get away from camp for a minute."

"I jist knew it!" Margo threw down the towel she had in her hand and called out. "Abby, I gotta go with Chaco to get kindling to make a fire for the girls' hot cocoa. We'll be back in a minute."

Chaco led Margo to the outskirts of camp to where the cannibals had taken their spy post.

"Oh, no," Margo said. "Are those foot tracks of robbers?"

"Something much worse, I'm afraid, Margo." Chaco told her the story of the cannibals, of how Russell and Rocky and he had found the camp and discovered they had cooked and partially eaten the bodies of the young hikers. He told her about how they'd decided to staunch the fear factor by not saying anything.

"Oh, that's plain horrible. But…. dammit, Chaco Rodriquez. You think I didn't know sumpin' was up? I knew y'all was lyin' when you came back from checkin' that supposed fire. And I thought it weird that y'all were doublin' up on guard duty all of a sudden. Y'all saw a mountain lion, you said. A mountain lion my butt!" Margo shook her head, her expression determined. "We sure as shit ain't gonna tell Abby. It'll scare the ever lovin' poop outta her. 'Sides, she's been through way too much pain to find out those kids were kilt like that. They represented hope fer her, and I don't want to scare her none, or them little girls…and…"

"What do think will scare me? And what represents 'hope'?"

Chaco and Margo swung around to find Abigail only a few feet away, listening.

Chaco stepped forward to keep Abigail from advancing close enough to see the tracks. "A bear came into camp last night, not a buck. And I enlisted Margo's help to…you know…since she's good a shot, and since Rocky's gone, to help us keep guard."

"A bear. Really? And you weren't going to tell me so I could maybe be a little more cautious when going to the forest to use the toilet, or to get water at the river? And you still haven't explained what you think gives me *hope*." She looked from Chaco to Abigail. "You two do realize I'm a little miffed, don't you?"

Margo smiled. "We jist didn't want to put more worry on ya…and, well, we thought you was feelin'…hope…that even with Rocky gone, about how we'd all pitch in and take measures to make sure ever 'one stays safe…you know, hon. You've already been through more hurtin' than any woman has in a lifetime, and…"

"And therefore, you think I need to be coddled? Is that it?"

Margo took a step toward her friend.

Abigail put up both hands to stop Margo. "Listen to me." She pointed at herself with both forefingers. "I'm in a world of hurt, yes. I saw my son get his head practically blown off, and I was so close his blood splattered on me." She choked back a sob, then regained her composure "I loved my daughter-in-law, and she died a horrible death also almost right in front of my eyes." She dropped her hand and clasped both arms in a self-hug. "Now, I've got two little girls to care for who have lost everything, their home, their parents, even their dog. Oh yes, I've been through a lot. I've seen a lot. But, I don't need to be babied by anyone. If there is a bear lurking nearby, I need to know it so I can help protect my granddaughters. If there is any danger whatsoever, don't keep it from me. Are we clear?"

"Yes, Mrs. Walker," Chaco said.

"Abby, we're real sorry, ain't we, Chaco?"

Chaco nodded his head.

"I'll come right back with the kindling," Margo said, "and make breakfast fer us all."

"Thank you. Now, it's Russ's turn to get a piece of my mind." Abigail turned and, still hugging herself, marched back to camp.

After Abigail left, Margo turned to Chaco. "That was way too close fer me."

"You handled it well."

"Thanks, Chaco, but now I guess we cain't go traipsin' around looking for Rocky, kin we?"

"I'm afraid not. We all must stick together, and under the circumstances, we need to get to Moonforest Sanctuary as fast as we can with or without Rocky. I'm sorry."

"Well, then, I gotta trust the good Lord will keep my man safe, and he'll come back to me someday. I kin hardly believe that fool idiot ran off like that."

***

After breakfast clean up, Chaco called the group together. "It's spring now. The weather is warming and we'll probably have clear skies, making it easier to get to the Sanctuary. By my calculations, we could be there in a couple of weeks or less if we hurry. But we also should be aware that in the Cascades sometimes the most brutal storms hit in spring. We have no way of knowing if another blizzard might...a substantial snowfall will delay us."

"When do you think we should head out?" Abigail asked.

"Right away."

"I have to agree with Chaco," Russell said. "Today is not too soon. We should get moving now."

"What about Rocky? Aren't we going to look for him?" Abigail threw her hands into the air. "I thought Margo was dedicated to finding her husband. I know I would be."

"It's all right, Abby," Margo said. "I thought better of it. If the knucklehead wants to go off by himself, that's jist fine. He's picked up good survival and huntin' skills. If he don't show up by the time we git to Moonforest, we kin send out a search party from there."

Nonetheless, Margo walked into the woods and called for him. "Rocky, yer worryin' ever-one. C'mon on back, baby."

**

As the group packed, Chaco's thoughts wandered to Fiona. *Soon, mi amor, and we'll be together.*

Bit by bit, the days grew longer. The Sun sat higher in the sky, and the wheels of the constellations turned. In a short while, Orion's Belt would disappear. Last night, as he stargazed, Chaco made out Leo Minor, Ursa Major, and Gemini. Tonight, he'd check the night sky again. He loved the spring constellations the best. More complex, more interesting than those of summer, winter, and autumn.

By late afternoon they'd loaded the remaining goods and were ready to travel. Margo went to the edge of the forest to call out for Rocky again. Abigail and Russell went to Jude's grave to say a last goodbye. Chaco ached for them. In his sorrow, he struggled against a fleeting desire to give up. *Those pinche cannibals can kill and eat me right now for all I care.*

Instead, he focused on his thoughts of Fiona. His love for her motivated him, fueled him with energy and kept his will to survive consistent and powerful. Chaco decided to throw one last pail of water over the cold campfire as insurance against a hidden ember. As he leaned forward to set down the empty bucket, a rifle blast split the air. Had he been standing upright, a high-powered bullet would have passed through his skull and ended his life. The bullet shattered the bark of a Douglas fir behind him.

"Drop to the ground!" Chaco shouted. "Everybody. Drop." The little girls cried and clung to their grandmother who pulled them to the ground and held them close. Chaco motioned for Russell and Margo to escort Abigail and the girls to safety behind a boulder. On his belly, with his rifle across his back, he inched toward the direction of the blast. He advanced within two or three yards from his destination when he heard a scuffle, a man cry out, then an "oomph." By the time Chaco reached the site, there were blood splatters everywhere. The cannibal in the long black oil cloth coat kicked his feet in his death throws, his head half severed from his neck by what could have only been a large hunting knife.

CHAPTER 31

Chaco told Abigail the shot came from a hunter who had probably mistaken their movement for game. He told her when he'd investigated he found no trace of them.

"Well, then, I suppose we need to be careful, maybe clang pots together or talk in loud voices to make sure whoever is hunting will know we are people, not deer."

"Good idea, Mrs. Walker." Worst idea ever. We'd make our presence known to the cannibals.

Russell, of course, knew where the shot had come from. "I am not going anywhere without a firearm."

"Excellent idea, Mr. Walker." And this time Chaco meant it.

He found Margo at the river bank. She sat in the dirt with her head in her hands, sobbing. He put an arm around her, pulling her close. "Your husband is a hero. He saved my life, maybe twice. First Jude, then that cannibalistic bastard before he could get off a second shot. I'll always be grateful to Rocky."

Margo sniffed and wiped her eyes with the back of her hand. "He's a complete idiot. I cain't believe he'd jist up and leave me like that. You don't leave someone when ya truly love 'em, do ya?"

A pang of guilt shot through Chaco's gut. Like I left my family and Mirabella behind in El Salvador to save my own life?

"But Rocky is a good man or I wouldn't a' married him and stayed all these years, the dumb brute that he kin be. I know he kin take care of hisself, and I take comfort in thinkin' he might be close by lookin' out after us, but to tell you the damned truth, I'm scared for him. And we don't know exactly if it were Rocky that kilt that man."

"Who else could it be?"

Margo shrugged her shoulders. "We've seen others around

here, and it ain't like Rocky not to git credit when he done somethin' good like that. He'd be all puffed up comin' into camp sayin' somethin' to you like 'You cain't survive without me. I told ya I was better 'n you, little hombre.' You, know how he is."

Chaco laughed.

***

A tearful Margo that morning, then Abigail's turn in the evening. Chaco had mistaken Abigail's stoicism for valor and dignity. She'd helped Margo with breakfast and the clean-up, and when Margo left to grieve by the river, Abigail kept a calm demeanor through the day, even managing lunch for everyone by herself, and scrounging an afternoon snack for the girls. She'd just put on a night time pot of coffee when it happened. Without warning, she dropped to her knees, threw back her head and wailed like a wounded bear cub. Yes, she had cried when they found Rufus dead. And she cried when Bethany died, but Jude was her son. It was as though his death had robbed her of her last scrap of hope and left her in a world of despair. She experienced a complete meltdown in front of her horrified grandchildren, in front of everyone. She rolled around in the dirt like a Pentecostal filled with the Holy Spirit and muttered incomprehensible insanities. She tore at her flesh, gouged her face, then with her fingers she ripped her blouse into shreds. Even Russell could not calm her.

Margo ushered the children into her tent. "Let's git your play horses and pretend they is galloping free in the wild west."

Chaco struggled to say something. This woman, with all her grace, always clean and prim, had never shown anything but strength. Here she wallowed in the dirt, baying and salivating, covering herself in tear-soaked ashes and filth. Chaco's heart broke for her. Yet, he stood helplessly by. "It's okay, Mrs. Walker. Let it out. Let it all out."

Then she stood, held her head high, and brushed herself off. Russell put his arm around her and walked her to their tent. She leaned against him as though too weak to make it the few steps from the campfire. A few minutes later, she emerged with Russell behind her. She'd cleaned herself, brushed her hair and changed her blouse. Her eyes were swollen and bloodshot. The scratches on her face had swelled, but otherwise, she looked much like her dignified, classy, beautiful self.

Chaco reached to her. She smiled, took his hand and squeezed it.

"You look better, Mrs. Walker."

"I'm fine now, Chaco. Thank you." Still holding Chaco's hand, she raised her voice so she could be heard by everyone. "I'm sorry I lost it there for a few minutes. I hope I didn't make anyone too uncomfortable."

That was the last time Chaco saw Abigail Walker shed a tear.

***

The way to Pine was clear, the air chilly but the skies cornflower blue. Everything smelled fresh and green. Sometimes, they'd pass the remains of a farmhouse. When they called out to the inhabitants and inspected the grounds and outbuilding, the properties appeared vacant, and most were looted. Some had been burned. Once they found an emaciated horse, still alive but with ribs protruding from its hide. Chaco opened the gate and the horse galloped into the forest. They followed creeks and ravines and went up and down hills and mountainsides. Sometimes they'd catch a glimpse of what used to be a town or city. Sometimes they walked paved roads littered by abandoned cars and trash. Cement and asphalt cracked open and grasses and grains forced their way through those impossible places. There were field mice, raccoons, skunks, grey squirrels, deer, fox, and an occasional bear. They shot rabbits and got another buck. This time, Chaco tanned the hide while Margo made jerky. Once the girls found a tabby cat, but it had gone feral and ran from them when they tried to catch it. Now and again, Chaco had the eerie feeling the cannibals followed them. He kept a sharp eye out for them, but whenever he investigated a strange noise or the sound of a breaking twig or branch, he found nothing untoward. Then they crested a ridge, and in the distance, there standing proud, a magnificent white capped mountain.

"Everyone, look!" Chaco pointed. "That's Pine Mountain."

The group cheered. Abigail brought the two girls a little further onto the ridge so they could get a better view. She knelt beside them. "See that mountain?" she said pointing. "We're going to be with your Auntie Fiona and your cousins real soon."

Russell looked to the sky. "We made it. Thank God."

By then, Chaco had the field glasses to his eyes.

"Do you see anything?" Russell said.

"I see where Redville is…or used to be, and looks like some other town."

"Maybe Estherville, Anders or White Bluff?" Abigail said. "Trailridge?"

"No. We're further northeast of those areas," Chaco said. "We'll have to get the map and check."

The little girls squealed and clapped their hands. "We get to see our auntie and our cousins. Yay!"

"Kin ya take a look around to see if there's a sign a Rocky anywheres?" Margo asked.

With the glasses in place, Chaco swiveled his head to search. "I don't see him, but that doesn't mean he isn't near."

"We ain't seen nothin' of him for a bit now. I jist hope he's alive, the goober." She lowered her voice to a whisper. "No sign of them cannibals, either?"

"Not for a long while, no."

The little girls had left their grandmother's side and now clung to Margo. "Have you been to the moon place, Aunt

Margo?" Olivia asked.

"No, but Chaco has. Kin ya tell the girls what it's like?"

Chaco nodded and squatted down next to them. "Moonforest Sanctuary is a fairy tale land. There are all kind of animals there like chickens, and goats, and sheep, and horses, and…"

"Real horses?" Lacy asked.

"Yes. Real horses. And there are gardens and flowers everywhere, and fruit you can pick right off the trees, apples, and pears, and…"

"Are there lots of children?" Olivia asked. "I mean, like our age, who are girls? Our cousins are boys. They're okay, but we don't like boys."

"Oh, yes. Lots of children, and many girls. There are streams and creeks where children play, and tree swings, and outdoor games, and even a school."

"School? We have to go to school?" Olivia wrinkled her nose.

"Everyone goes to school. Don't you like school?"

Olivia shook her head. "I had a mean teacher, Mrs. Erickson, and she said I wasn't smart because I'm better at reading than math."

"I can assure you that you are very smart, and that Mrs. Erickson won't be at Moonforest Sanctuary."

Lacy raised her hand and waved it. "I like school a lot. A whole lot."

"How do you know?" Olivia said. "You haven't been to real school. You're too young."

"I have so. I have been to pre-kindergarten and I'm ready for kindergarten, so there."

Abigail and Russell were a short distance away holding hands like teenagers. She leaned her head against his shoulder, and he kissed the top of her head. Chaco had not seen them that relaxed in months. Abigail called to them. "Margo, Chaco, keep an eye on the girls. Russell is going to escort me to that cliff over there so I can…take care of my personal…business… you know. We'll be right back."

Chaco's heart expanded with gratitude and affection as he watched them disappear together over the ridge of the shale bluff, then the earthquake hit.

CHAPTER 32

Except for his years studying in Bonn, Germany, and his travels through Europe, Chaco had spent his entire life in the Americas. He'd lived mostly in El Salvador, a year in Mexico as a visiting student, a summer hiking through Brazil, and the past five, going on six, in the United States. He had survived some terrible quakes, including the 2016 Riverside Quake that killed twenty-seven people, injured hundreds more, and caused extensive damage to the Walker and Pennymons' neighborhood. He spent the better part of the year helping Russell repair sections of his house and outbuildings. The barn and shed had to be rebuilt from the ground up. Although the new deck on the cottage needed extensive repairs, and every dish or breakable thing in the guest house had broken, the quake had caused no other damage. Chaco surmised the old guest house had been built far better than the big modern houses surrounding it. But that earthquake paled in comparison to this one.

The ground shook with such violence it slammed everyone to the ground. Margo concussed her head on a rock. Chaco feared her dead, but crawled to her and found her breathing. The girls, who were with Margo when the quake hit, screamed and screamed and screamed. He managed to grab them and hold them while the ground shook and shook and shook. It must have been two, three minutes, longer. The noise. Sounded like a volcano had erupted, a hydrogen bomb had exploded, the earth had split in two. And when the shaking ceased, the earth *had* split. A new rift, a long, wide, deep crack in the ground snaked for miles between the group and Pine Mountain. Chaco's ears rang and his legs went weak. "At least I don't have to deal with coyotes, evil wraiths, vipers, or the chupacabra."

When he checked on the girls, neither were injured badly. Lacy had split her lip and Olivia sustained a few bruises. Both cried as though they were dying. Margo sat upright when Chaco made his way back to her. She rubbed a bump on the side of her head where it had struck the rock. "Oh, that's a big 'ole knot," she said. "That'll leave a mark. Everyone okay? How's Russ and Abby? Sure hope Rocky made it. I hope he's…" She ceased talking and struggled to her feet.

"You know Rocky is fine. He's a survivor. Stay here with the girls. I'll check on the Walkers," Chaco said.

"You girls c'mon closer," Margo said. "Yer Uncle Chaco will go find Grandma and Grandpa. C'mon, sweeties. It'll be fine." The still sobbing girls climbed into Margo's lap, and clung to her.

Chaco walked in the direction he'd last seen Russell and Abigail, and crested the ridge. Boulders and rocks had rolled everywhere, some so large they had knocked over 100-foot firs and snapped them in two like they were dried pasta. What he found at the base of what had been a rocky overhang stopped his heart.

The earthquake had loosened and broken off a piece of the ledge. Most of it had landed on Russell. Only his left foot and his right forearm were visible from beneath the tons of rock. Chaco imagined or hoped, that Russell died quickly. But then a sound. Abigail cried out, her voice so weak Chaco couldn't quite make out what her words.

Ru..what…I..oh…oh…Russ…"

He followed her whimpers and found her a few yards away, pinned from the waist down by an enormous boulder. Her eyes were opened, glassy. Blood trickled from her nose and mouth. She was alive, but barely, and she shivered. Chaco assessed the problem. Even with Margo's help, there would be no way to remove the boulder, and even if they could manage it, without proper emergency medical care, Abigail would die anyway. Chaco kneeled next to her. "Mrs. Walker, it's me, Chaco."

"Where…Russ…is? …It's…cold…so cold."

"Mrs. Walker. You're in shock. Let's take care of you first, then we'll take care of Mr. Walker." He removed his shirt, wiped the blood from her face with a sleeve, and covered her arms and chest to help warm her. "I'll be right back. Don't worry."

"No..please...no..plea...don't..." She fell unconscious.

Chaco ran, stumbled over felled trees, stumps, limbs, rocks. When he reached Margo, the two girls were asleep in her arms.

"What happened? Where's Russ and Abby? What happened to yer shirt? Yer shakin' so hard."

Chaco sat beside her and whispered to her what he'd found.

"Mother of Jesus! Gawd, no." She squeezed shut her eyes and put her hand over her mouth, but she could hold back the sobs.

Olivia woke. "What's wrong, Aunt Margo? Why are you crying?"

"It's okay, darlin'. Don't wake up yer sister, jist put yer head back down. Thatta girl. Shhhhh."

"I'm going to put a tent around her," Chaco whispered. "I'll build a fire and stay with her tonight. You need to take care of the girls."

"What about that boulder on her?"

"It's...huge....it would take machinery and manpower to lift it ...I'm afraid there is nothing we can do."

"We cain't jist leave her there like that!" Margo shook her head. "We cain't."

Lacy whimpered and tucked her head further into Margo's lap.

"She's dying. We will stay with her until...she no longer needs us," Chaco said.

"Sweet Jesus." Margo hung her head, and tears spilled down her cheeks. Chaco put his hand on her shoulder, gave it a squeeze, then left to fetch his tent.

By the time he got back to Abigail, she was alert, still delusional, but speaking in complete sentences.

"Seems like I'm stuck under something, Chaco. Can you get it off, please?"

"I'll try."

"Russell was here. He said he was going for help. He said the strangest thing, that he loved me, always will, and he'll be waiting. Waiting for what, I wonder?"

Chaco looked to the pile of rocks, under which his other father lie. One foot and arm still protruded from beneath.

"Are you in pain, Mrs. Walker?"

"No, dear. I don't feel anything, but maybe I'm a little cold. Do me one favor, please?"

"Sure, anything."

"Call me Abby."

"Okay...Abby."

She smiled. "That's better."

He stroked her forehead, clammy and cold.

"There were Indians here."

"Indians, Mrs...Abby?"

"Yes, Native Americans. They were almost invisible, or I could kind of see through them. They were dancing. They were trying to be nice. I didn't understand their language, though, when they spoke and sang. I rather liked them."

He continued to stroke her forehead.

She smiled again. "That feels nice. Oh, did I tell you Rocky was here? He looked so funny, his hair all scruffy, and that beard! Looked like Grizzly Adams. Of course, you don't know who Grizzly Adams is. They probably didn't have that old TV show in El Salvador. Rocky said he would figure out how to get that big thing off me. He really is pretty nice when you get to know him." She was quiet for a moment. She closed her eyes and smiled. Chaco continued to stroke her forehead. Then she opened her eyes, "Before I forget, there are two things..."

"What two things?"

"First, when Russell visited me a moment ago he reminded me that it was important that we tell you this."

"What, Abby?"

"We love you. We never said so, but you are family to us, like a son. You know I saw Jude here, too? He's perfectly all right. I don't know what all that to-do was about. And the other thing is I want a hamburger. I want a double-double cheeseburger, with everything on it, and a pile of French fries. Can you go down the hill to In 'N Out and get me a burger and fries, and a big cola, too? Buy one for yourself, and one for Russ and Jude, too. The money is in my purse on the dresser. I'm going to rest here for a minute." She closed her eyes and died.

Chaco tugged on the collar of the shirt he'd put over her arms and pulled it over her face. At first nothing, then the tears came, the tears of his lifetime, more tears than he'd cried in front of Fiona, more tears than he had in him. He cried until his stomach, and his chest and his eyes were empty of tears. After a long while, he stood and whispered, "God be with you Abby, and with you, Russ. I love you, too." But before stowing the tent he'd brought with him, and walking away, he noticed something…boot tracks pressed into the dirt around Abigail, too big to be Chaco's, size twelve at least. And a branch. One end was lodged under the huge rock, forced there. Someone had attempted to use it as a lever to move the boulder off Abigail.

CHAPTER 33

Chaco piled rocks on the visible remains of Russell and Abigail Walker. "May you go with God, Mama and Papa Walker. I will take good care of our family. I promise." He crossed himself and returned to Margo.

The children napped under a blanket beneath the branches of a Douglas fir.

Margo sat cross-legged in the dirt, looking off into the distance. As Chaco approached, she stood and faced him. He read the pain and worry in her eyes. She took a step toward him and whispered, "Abby?"

"Gone."

"Jesus, forgive me." She hung her head. "I didn't even git a chance to say goodbye to my best friend in the world." Margo walked to Chaco. He folded her into his arms, and let her cry it out.

She pulled away. "Them little girls. Whadda we say? They jist lost their grandma and grandpa." She wiped her eyes with her sleeve. "On top of everthang else they seen and been through, it jist ain't fair."

"I don't think we should tell them."

"Whadda ya mean? We have to tell 'em. They gotta know the truth."

"Let's get them to safety first. We don't have to tell them right away."

"What are we gonna say in the meantime?"

"We can say their grandfather and grandmother decided to go on ahead so they could make sure everything is ready for our arrival. And we can say they wanted to get started right away, so that's why they left in such a hurry."

"That'll work. I'll say that their grandma and grandpa came 'round and kissed them whilst they was nappin'." She paused. "I'll tell 'em they said I should say how very much they love 'em both." Margo's voice broke. She bit her lower lip. Despite her best efforts, tears spilled onto her cheeks. Chaco reached for her, pulled her in close again, and rocked her in his arms.

The first of many strong aftershocks pitched the Earth. The girls jumped from their blankets and ran to Margo's side.

"I want my mommy." Lacy sobbed. "Where's Grandma?"

Olivia patted her little sister on the head. "It's okay. Grandpa took her to go potty before the big earthquake. Where are they?"

Margo turned her back so the girls could not see her cry.

***

Chaco built a robust fire and put the largest of the available tents near it. After a meager dinner, both girls, Margo, and Chaco crowded into it. They slept the best they could. Every so often, the Earth beneath them buckled and rocked, waking the little girls who clung to the adults.

***

Margo stretched as she crawled from the tent at dawn. "I'm sure glad you thought to put the tent out in the open away from them trees."

Chaco tended the fire. "Well, yes. We don't want anything falling on us during aftershocks."

"Ya mean like them?" Margo pointed to two large branches that had broken from the same Douglas fir the girls had napped under the day before. "If we'd put the tent over there, we'd all be certain dead."

Margo pulled together breakfast as the children slept. When they, at last emerged from the tent, rubbing the sleep from their eyes, Marco rummaged through the boxes to find what little cocoa remained. "You two up fer some hot chocolate this mornin'?"

"Goody," Olivia clapped her hands.

"But this is all we have left, so y'all drink it slow."

"Will there be hot cocoa when we get to the moon place?" Olivia asked.

"I don't know," Margo said. "We'll jist have to git there and find out."

"What if this is the last chocolate in the whole world?" Olivia said.

"I bet we'll find more. Drink it up. I'll fix ya some dried apples cut up in oatmeal, then after a bit, we'll git goin'."

Olivia nodded. "We need to catch up with Grandma and Grandpa, and hurry to see if there's chocolate at the moon place."

Margo sent the girls to the edge of camp with their horses stuck in their jacket pockets, their cocoa and bowls of oatmeal in-hand, while she and Chaco packed the remaining gear. "Y'all stay close where me and Chaco kin see ya, now. I'll call ya when we are ready to hit the road."

"Okay, Aunt Margo," Lacy said, and the two little girls scampered away.

They'd finished packing, and were ready to depart. Margo called for the girls. "C'mon, you two. We gotta find a way 'round that big crack and git to…" She stepped into a clearing near where she'd sent the girls. The empty oatmeal bowls and cocoa cups were upturned in the dirt. She shielded her eyes with one hand against the morning Sun and searched one way, then the other. "Where are you? Olivia? Lacy? Told y'all to stay where we kin see ya." She put two fingers to her lips and whistled.

Chaco came running from behind a boulder where he'd gone to relieve himself. "What's going on?"

"I'm jist frantic," Margo said. "Them girls went off and they ain't answerin' when I call."

"I'll find them. Stay here in case they return." He grabbed the Remington and trotted in the direction where Margo had last seen the girls. He'd gotten no more than thirty feet when the little girls burst through the bushes, running to him, wild-eyed. "Uncle Chaco! There were men," Olivia said. "What do you mean? You saw men?" Chaco dropped to his knees and put the rifle on the ground within reach.

"They came right up to us when we were playing with our horses and talked to us. One said if we went with them, they would show us something really pretty and they said they heard we liked chocolate, and they had some."

Chaco froze then grabbed Olivia's arms. *Hijo de puta...the cannibals. They've been here watching and listening.* "What did the men look like?"

"Ouch, Uncle Chaco. You're hurting me."

Chaco relaxed his grip. "I'm sorry. Just tell me. What did they look like?"

"Well, they were big."

"And had hair on their faces, lots," Lacy said.

"You mean beards?" Chaco said.

"Yeah," said Olivia. "Beards. Like Santa, only dark. One was a little bit behind in the trees and we didn't see him too good. But one was in red, and the other was in that stuff hunters wear."

"Camouflage."

"Yeah," said Olivia. "I think there was another one, but we couldn't see him too good. And I wouldn't talk to them at all because Mommy and Daddy told us we can't talk to grown ups we don't know, but Lacy wanted to go with them. I told her she couldn't, and she got mad at me."

"They had chocolate! You said there might not be any chocolate left in the whole world." Lacy began to cry. "You're just dumb. They were going to show us something pretty and give us chocolate."

"They could be bad men," Olivia said. "Couldn't they, Uncle Chaco?"

"Yes. They could be very bad men. What happened? Where did they go?"

"Another man, someone else, yelled at them," Olivia said. "He said a really, really bad word and told them to get away from us."

"Another man? Olivia, did you see the other man?"

"No, but he was real mad. And he threw a big knife and it missed the guy in red because the red guy ducked. Then they all three ran away into the forest that way." Olivia pointed toward a thick copse of pine.

"Can you tell me anything about the other man? The different one?"

Lacy held her hand up. "I know, I know. I can tell you something."

"What?" Chaco said.

"He kinda sounded like someone I know…I'm not sure…"

"You girls did the right thing by not going with those men."

By that time, Margo had appeared at Chaco's side. "Did you say a man yelled?"

Lacy nodded. "Yeah. He did, but not too loud." She put her hands up, palms down as though to hush a noise. "He was real close but in the bushes where we couldn't see him. And he said some bad words to those other men, and…"

Olivia said, "The other guy told the guys to get the…well, a really, really bad word…. away from us or he'd kill them! Everything happened fast, and there was a big knife from nowhere flying at the red guy, and it stuck in a tree, and all the big men left fast, and we ran here."

"That's jist fine," Margo smiled. "Jist fine. Let's go on over where y'all kin help me finish up packin' and let Uncle Chaco check thangs out. Then we'll go on to Moonforest Sanctuary."

"To see Aunt Fiona, our cousins, and Grandma and Grandpa, right?"

Margo didn't respond. She grabbed the two girls by their hands, and they walked toward the fire ring. She enlisted the girl's help in kicking dirt over the dying embers, a game they thought great fun. "Can we help you put out the fire every morning?" Olivia asked.

"You betcha, honey." Margo kneeled and embraced both little girls. "You betcha."

Where the girls had been playing, Chaco discovered footprints. And in the bark of a pine, a deep, long slash.

CHAPTER 34

Finding a way around the rift proved more of a challenge than Chaco anticipated. The new rip in the earth spread for miles, and from what he could tell, too wide to cross. It blocked their way to Pine Mountain.

Chaco put the field glasses to his eyes. "*Hijo de puta*. So close."

"What's so close?" Margo had been standing by Chaco. She leaned her head toward his. "If that eee-ho day puutaw thang is what I think it means, you best not be sayin' that around them little girls."

"They don't know what it means."

"Don't be so sure, smarty pants." Margo gave Chaco a playful shove and laughed.

"You know? That's the first time I've heard you laugh since…"

Margo's countenance darkened, and she stepped back. "Since Rocky took off on me? Since m'best friend and her husband was crushed to death under rocks? What exact time did I stop laughin' and…"

"What rocks? Who got killed?" Olivia materialized from nowhere.

"I thought you kids was playin'." Margo dropped to her knees to meet Olivia eye-to-eye. "Honey, what…"

"We got hungry, and that's why I came, so I could get something to eat for me and Lacy. Who got killed? You and Chaco treat me like I'm a baby, and I'm not." She pointed to herself with both forefingers. "I know more than you think. You're talking about Grandma and Grandpa, aren't you, and don't tell me a lie."

"Honey. I'm so sorry." Margo sunk further into the dirt and pulled Olivia to her. "I'm so dang sorry. I loved yer grandma like a sister, and I loved yer grandpa, too. I am so, so sorry."

Olivia broke into a wail. She sat down and covered her eyes with her hands. Her little body shook so hard with grief, she convulsed. When Margo reached to comfort her, Olivia jerked away.

Chaco raised his hand to his forehead to shield his eyes against the dying sunlight and gazed into the forest. "Olivia, where's Lacy?"

The little girl coughed and sniffed back her tears. "She said she saw some doggies and wanted to find them."

"What did you say she saw?"

"Doggies."

"Oh, no. Margo, stay with Olivia. I have to get Lacy."

Coyotes. Please, no. If they're hungry enough…and game is scarce…. within a few minutes a hungry pack can kill a full-grown man, let alone a child. It had happened once in a small village a few kilometers outside of Soyapango when Chaco was a small boy. El Indio, just a poor laborer, had been walking home to his village on a remote path at dusk when a pack set upon him. Some said they could hear the man's screams a mile away. Some reported the yips of the killer coyotes reverberated through the arroyos for hours.

The authorities found the remains of the man, only pieces, an arm without a hand, his head with a cheek and one ear eaten off, a femur with some muscle and tendon still attached. The grisly discovery of the man's body made all the newspapers, accompanied by graphic photos and detailed descriptions.

For months, El Indio's death was the talk of Plaza Mundo in Soyapango, and even in San Salvador. The tales spread, and grew, sparking rumors the goat-sucking chupacabra had turned into a man-eating beast, a cross between werewolf and vampire. After that, Chaco developed a deep-seated fear of coyotes, and El Indio's hideous demise cemented his terror of the mythical beast, as well.

Dusk had settled over the mountains like a plum colored blanket, and near dark is when coyotes are most active. *Oh no, oh no. Please, please.* Chaco ran, tripped now and again over rocks, stumbled into gopher holes, recovered, and ran faster. "Lacy! Where are you?"

Chaco recalled an incident in 2009 when coyotes tore nineteen-year-old Canadian singer-songwriter, Taylor Mitchell, to pieces. She'd been hiking on a path through the Cape Breton Highlands National Park in Nova Scotia. The news devastated Chaco. He'd become a fan, and had memorized every lyric to her songs, "Don't know how I got here," and her Gordon Lightfoot cover, "Love and Maple Syrup." After her death, he played her CDs until he wore them out. "*Pobrecita.* Horrible way to die, and she was so young, so talented." Then there was news of the children attacked and killed by coyotes in California and Maine.

Lacy screamed, then screamed again. Chaco ran faster.

With her back against a white oak, against all odds, the tiny girl stood her ground against three coyotes who circled her. "Go away, doggies! Go!" She held a branch in both hands, and did her best to beat them off, swinging wildly. As they closed in, she swung and hit one coyote on the snout. It yipped and shook its head.

Chaco reached for the Remington. "Lacy. I'm here. Keep swinging that stick. *Mierda.* My rifle!" Always one to be cautious, and as a skilled guerrilla fighter, Chaco would never be so careless as to leave his weapon anywhere. But he'd been so frightened for Lacy, and in such a panic, he left it on the boulder where he'd stood gazing through his binoculars at Pine Mountain. "*Mierda,*" he said again. Keeping his eyes locked onto the eyes of the alpha male, Chaco whistled low. "C'mon to me, Mr. Coyote. Away from the *niña. Ven acá.*" In a controlled, even voice, Chaco cajoled the animal. "Come here, *Señor Jefe.* Mr. Boss." He felt for his knife. No knife. In his peripheral vision, Chaco noticed loose rocks on the dirt. He edged sideways toward them, never once averting his gaze from the coyote's eyes. He stooped to lift one in one hand. "*Ven acá, boy.* I'm right here."

The coyote growled and bared his teeth, his hackles stiff. He lowered his head, took a tentative step toward Chaco, and as the beast prepared to charge, Chaco drew back his arm, took aim, and threw the rock. It connected with its target, hit the big male between the eyes. The coyote yelped and leaped into the air. When he landed, the coyote shook his head and retreated a short way from Chaco and the girl. The others followed, giving Chaco enough time to sprint the few yards to Lacy. He scrambled up the oak onto a low limb and grabbed the little girl at the moment the coyotes returned and closed in for the kill.

As Chaco pulled the screaming girl into the tree, one of the coyotes snapped at Lacy's dangling leg, but missed. From what Chaco could tell, a female, smaller than the alpha, she had not waited for the larger male to attack first. She would certainly pay for her impertinence later. Why he hesitated for a split second to ponder the coyote hierarchy, he didn't know. It would be a decision Chaco would regret. The female snapped again, and this time, snatched a tennis shoe from Lacy's foot and shook it as though killing a rat. This was the first time Chaco appreciated that the little one never tied her shoes. Chaco yanked hard on the child's arm to move her out of harm's way, then he heard the revolting splintering of bone, and Lacy screamed in pain.

Chaco held Lacy as they huddled close together on the branch. They were less than seven feet from the snapping jaws of the alpha male, angry, vicious and persistent. The child cried in pain and fear and cradled her injured arm.

Then….an explosion of a rifle shot and the female who had stolen Lacy's shoe twisted into an arc and fell to the dirt, twitched, and kicked her forelegs and paws. Margo had shown up, fired, and with a single shot, the bullet hit the coyote in the chest and passed through the animal's body. Blood mixed with fur spurted from the animal's torso and sprayed the trees. The other coyotes scrambled into the woods, the alpha at the lead.

"Hand me down Lacy, and you climb on outta that tree,"

Margo said and held up her arms to receive Lacy.

"Careful. Her arm is injured."

"Oh, fer gawdsake. How did *that* happen?"

"I'll explain later." Chaco lowered Lacy to Margo. As she reached for Margo, the little girl winced and cried out. "Owie, Aunt Margo. He hurt my arm. Uncle Chaco did it. He pulled hard and hurt me."

Chaco leapt from the branch. "Here. Let's take a look." The arm swelled fast and turned purple. "I'm afraid it is broken."

"Let's git her on back to camp. Olivia's waitin' there. I told her she had to stay in the tent until we got back. We'll set it, and I'll splint it there."

"Without anesthesia? I guess we have no choice."

"I'll git her somethin' to help with the pain. We'll do it quick."

***

"Aunt Margo, Uncle Chaco! What's wrong with Lacy?"

"Uncle Chaco broke my arm. It hurts, too."

Chaco shook his head. "I had to pull her into a tree to get her away from the coyotes."

"Are coyotes what Lacy thought were dogs? Do coyotes hurt people, Uncle Chaco?" Olivia asked.

"Not often, but if they are real hungry and there is no food…"

"You mean, they were gonna eat Lacy?"

"Olivia, there is no way I would let you or your sister get hurt. Not ever."

"I mean…. but Uncle Chaco…. first my mommy, then my daddy, Grandma, Grandpa, Rufus…everything is awful. Everyone is dying." Olivia devolved into tears and ran to her sister. "Lacy! I'm so glad you're here."

Lacy, still in Margo's arms, held out her uninjured hand to her older sister.

"Uh oh" Olivia said to her little sister. "Your other arm looks really bad. I'm so sorry you got hurt."

Margo set Lacy on a rock, and said, "You stay right here fer a minute, darlin'. Uncle Chaco and I have to take care of that arm fer ya."

"What are you going to do?" Olivia asked. "We don't have Neosporin or anything."

"I'm gonna fix your sister a little drink that'll help with the pain a bit. Then we gotta set her arm and put somethin' on it, like sticks, to keep it from movin'. Both you girls need to be real brave fer me while we do this." Then she turned to Chaco. "Uncle Chaco is gonna fix some wood pieces for me. Ain't ya, Chaco? Okay, girls?"

"Okay," the girls said in unison.

Margo made a paste of white willow bark powder and blended it into hot water with a hearty shot of Christian Brothers from a bottle she kept in her sack of medicines and potions.

"I didn't know you had more of that," Chaco said. "I finished my last bottle of wine weeks ago. I could use a drink."

"Y'all never mind. It's only for thangs like this. If ya git yer arm broke, I'll give ya some."

She removed the spoon and held the hot brew to the little girl's lips. "Take a sip, sweetheart."

"Ewwww. It tastes icky."

"I know. But, ya have to drink it all up fer me anyways. Will ya? You'll get a little sleepy, you'll feel real good all over, and yer arm won't hurt so bad."

The little girl took another sip, made a face, and took another sip. Within a few minutes, her eyelids grew heavy, and she yawned.

"Thatta girl. Jist rest here. Chaco, git on over here. I'm gonna need yer help." Chaco held Lacy and stroked her brow while Margo grabbed the little girl's arm in both hands, one placed below the break, one above it, and yanked, snapping the bone into place. Lacy screamed.

"What are you doing? You're hurting her. Stop!" Olivia cried.

"We had to put her broken arm into place, sweetie, or it wudda healed all wrong and she'd be a cripple forever."

Chaco handed Margo torn pieces of a pillow case, and two splints made from narrow branches smoothed with the edge of his knife. With speed and impressive expertise, Margo splinted Lacy's arm. "I had to do this fer my little brother when he slipped on rocks in the crick a few miles from the ranch." She made a sling and hung it around the little girl's neck. "Put yer broke arm in here and don't move it or bump it, and in a few weeks, it'll be good as new."

Chaco built a fire and Margo found pieces of venison jerky and a stale box of raisins. "It's getting' too late to make a stew of any kind or find any greens. I know it ain't much, but this'll have to do 'til breakfast." She handed a piece of jerky to Olivia.

Olivia's face brightened. "Oh, I almost forgot to tell you, Uncle Chaco and Aunt Margo. I saw those men again."

Margo froze, her face filled with terror. "What do you mean, sweetie?"

"You know. The ones that wanted me and Lacy to come and have chocolate."

"Where did you see them? WHERE?" Chaco said.

"Don't yell at me. While you and Aunt Margo were getting Lacy, and I was waiting, I decided to look through your binoculars. The men were over there." Olivia pointed toward the southeast. "And you know what?"

"What?" Chaco said.

"One of them, the guy in the camo stuff?"

"Yes? Go on."

"He had binoculars, too. He looked straight at me while I looked at him. And he waved at me even, but I didn't wave back."

Hijo de... "Thank you. I'm really glad you didn't wave back. You were smart not to. Show me again where you saw the men."

Olivia pointed.

***

That night, the girls and Margo climbed into the tent. Chaco sat outside in the dirt, his rifle across his lap, his knife tucked into his belt. He would not sleep. He would guard. He pulled his jacket around him and scooted closer to the fire. The little girls cried, Olivia, because she grieved for her family and her dog, and Lacy because her arm hurt. Margo sang *Amazing Grace* to them in a voice so sweet it took Chaco by surprise. A slip of a waning moon hung in the sky, but, slightly overcast, this would not be a good night for stargazing. Instead, as he listened to Margo, *"Amazing grace, how sweet the sound, that saved a wretch like me,"* he thought of Fiona. He composed a poem. He would not write it. He would burn it into his brain, and when he next held her, he would whisper it to her.

Mi Amor,
My love,
For me,
You are all that is,
All that will ever be.

Your smile, the open sky of my being,
Your eyes, the wild ocean of my heart,
The scent of your skin, my entire world,
More sweet,
More exquisite,
Than music
From the throats of angels.

You, my salvation.
My amazing grace.

In the distance, a coyote howled, then the pack yipped and bawled. They had killed something. Chaco tensed and shivered, but not because of the cold.

CHAPTER 35

They'd walked miles, skirting the chasm, searching for a place narrow enough to cross. They'd gone through most of their food and had pared down everything else so the remaining supplies and goods would fit onto one of the two travoises. They used the other to pull the girls over hills and rough terrain. They decided when they reached another plateau, and it looked like the girls could make it the rest of the way without a struggle, they could break the second sled into firewood.

With his rifle across his back, Chaco pulled the one travois, piled with goods, behind him. Margo walked alongside, pulling the other sled with the girls and their remaining food. Now and again, an aftershock hit and clumps of dirt and rocks tumbled down the mountain toward them. One rock hit Olivia and bruised her knee. After comforting the crying child, Margo hoisted the little girl from the travois onto her shoulders.

"What are ya thinkin'?" Margo asked Chaco.

"I'm thinking about the weather. It's late March, so there will be rain, and could be more snow." Chaco looked toward the threatening thunderheads.

They made camp near a stream. Margo shot a squirrel, gutted, and skinned it. "It's pretty darn skinny and surely tough. Fer some reason, ain't much game now, and that's probably why them coyotes are so desperate. We kin try for a crow tomorrow. They ain't bad in a pinch." She crafted a makeshift spit, and as she turned the rodent over a fire, Chaco told the girls stories about Moonforest Sanctuary.

"Besides the orchards and gardens, there are many greenhouses."

"What are greenhouses, Uncle Chaco? Are they houses that are green?" Lacy asked.

"No. They are big tent-like things that you grow vegetables and fruit in year-round, so there's always fresh food."

"Like strawberries?" Olivia asked.

"Maybe."

"What about candy?" Lacy asked rubbing at her injured arm. Since the break, she'd been whimpering off and on, and sometimes she cried. Chaco had promised Abigail and Russell to protect their family, not to break their limbs. Beyond that, seeing either of the little girls in pain tore at his heart. *Pobrecita.*

"Ouch, Aunt Margo. Can I have some of that drink? My arm hurts me so bad."

"Sure, honey." Margo reached into her bag to retrieve the white birch powder and a cup.

"Hey, don't you want to know about sweets at the sanctuary?" Chaco asked.

Lacy nodded.

"They have bee hives."

"Bee hives? Bees bite." Lacy shook her head. "A bee bit me once when I was little and it really hurt bad."

"Bees also make honey."

"Everyone knows bees make honey." Olivia climbed into Chaco's lap and sniffed at her sister.

"Well, I didn't know that," Lacy said and scowled back.

"But," said Chaco, "what do you think you can make with honey?"

"You can eat it with peanut butter. That's how I like it, anyway," Olivia said.

Her little sister laughed. "And if you eat too much, you can throw up, too."

"Be quiet, Lacy!" Olivia jumped off Chaco's lap. "You just shush."

Lacy laughed again, "Yeah, like when you snuck the jar of honey from the cupboard and ate half of it, and had to go out in the back yard and throw up in the grass, and Rufus licked it up. Ewwwww. Mommy was so mad."

"I said, shush."

"Girls. No arguing," Chaco said. "Come back here and tell me what you can make with honey." Olivia climbed back onto Chaco's knee.

Both girls shrugged their shoulders, and when they did, Lacy winced, tearing at Chaco's heart again. "With honey, you can make cookies, cakes….and, guess what else? Candy."

"You can make candy with honey?" Olivia said, putting her arm around Chaco's neck.

"Indeed you can," said Chaco. "In fact, in El Salvador where I grew up, my *abuela*, my grandma, used to make honey candy for me all the time. It was my favorite."

"Goodie," Lacy said. "There is candy at the moon place!"

A crack of a limb and rustle of brush at the edge of camp caught Chaco's attention. He put his finger to his mouth to silence the girls. Margo picked up her rifle and motioned for the girls to get behind her. Olivia hopped off Chaco's knee, and she and her sister crowded behind Margo.

The brush rustled again, and another twig cracked. Crouching low, weapon at the ready, Chaco made his way toward the noise. *Cannibals. I'll blow their pinche brains into chunks.* Before Chaco could raise his rifle, the bear charged.

***

"Margo, why didn't you let me kill that bear? We are low on food, and bear meat is good."

The second the bear appeared, Margo had fired into the air. The bear turned tail and ran into the forest. Chaco had started to give chase and kill it, but Margo yelled. "No. Let it go! Chaco! No."

"Why? We need the food, Margo. What we have won't last us three days."

"That was most likely a she-bear, and she probably has cubs.

She cudda jist come outta her den and smelled the cookin' squirrel. She's real hungry, poor thang. If we kilt her, then her babies would die, too. Sides, ain't I done a respectable job teachin' y'all about findin' greens and shootin' birds and squirrels? And, you got that buck not long ago. Plenty of jerky left fer a while longer than three days."

"Yes, but...." Another snap of a branch caught Chaco's words in his throat. "Margo, if that bear has come back, I *am* going to kill her. I don't want you to try to stop me."

"Go on. Git. Do whatcha have to do." She called to the girls and said, "Y'all stay here close to me in case it's that bear again."

Instead of a bear, Chaco found tracks. Human tracks. Boot tracks.

CHAPTER 36

On noon of the third day skirting the chasm, Chaco discovered a possible crossing point. "We can get to the other side from here."

"Don't think so," Margo said. "That's gotta be darn near thirty feet between the edge of this cliff and that far side."

"We can build a bridge."

"Are you outta yer mind? How? With what, smarty pants?"

"With that." Chaco pointed to a sturdy Douglas fir with a thick trunk perched on the edge of the chasm. "We cut it so it lands on the other side, and we walk over."

"I suppose it'll work, that is if we kin git it to fall the exact right way and land jist so."

"We can do that."

"Let's git to it, then. We ain't got but a few hours of good light. We gotta unbury that saw and hatchet, and whatever else we got on that sled thang we kin use to cut down a big tree."

With a small axe and a handsaw, it took Chaco and Margo most of the afternoon to cut through the trunk. Chaco had marked calculations in the dirt and figured the angle they'd need to cut through the tree so it would fall directly over the chasm and land where they needed it to.

"What's that yer doin'?" Margo had asked when she saw the lines and angles he'd made in the compacted dirt.

"Calculus."

"I almost fergot yer fancy science degree."

"I suppose right now my education is coming in handy."

"Well, you sure didn't look like no college professor scientist when that bear was comin' atcha. You shoulda seen the look on yer face when that bear runs outta them bushes." Margo slapped her knee and laughed.

Chaco, who once thought her guffaws more grating than the screech of fingernails against a tin sheet, now found the sound of Margo's laughter like music. "I suppose I didn't look too dignified, did I?"

When the tree fell and landed exactly where Chaco had estimated it would, Margo and the little girls clapped their hands. Chaco, pleased beyond measure with himself, whispered. "I told you, Mama and Papa Walker, I'd take care of our family."

Chaco crawled out onto the felled tree to test its stability. "Feels secure," he shouted. "I'm going to cut some of these limbs so we can get over." He sawed through the smaller branches with ease. The larger branches were more of a challenge, but one by one, he got through them. When he reached the other side, night had fallen.

Margo had lit a fire, pulled a pile of dandelion greens and some wild onions, and created a kind of squirrel ragu. The fragrance wafted through the evening air and made Chaco's mouth water.

"C'mon back. Food's ready. I got the flashlight. Down to our last batteries, so be careful but come on quick."

She flipped on the light, then froze. "Oh no, Chaco. Got yer rifle?"

"No. I couldn't carry it and the saw, too."

"Then you best git on over here right away."

"Why?"

"Jist turn around real slow and look."

Chaco turned his head over his shoulder. Not more than a dozen yards behind, a pack of coyotes with their heads down stepped quietly as snowfall toward the man who had his back to them.

***

Although young, nimble and strong, Chaco had never been fast on his feet. But just then he thought he could have broken an Olympic record with the speed in which he ran over that log. Chaco slipped once and struggled to regain his balance.

"Don't you dare fall and break yer neck!" Margo yelled. "Jist keep comin'. I don't wanna scare ya, but one's on the log already. I'm gonna fire my rifle to scare it off. Ready?"

"Do it, Margo. Now!"

"Jist keep runnin, but fer gawdsake, don't you trip again 'cause if the fall don't kill ya, I will." She pulled the trigger.

Chaco made it to the last four feet of the log. From there, he jumped onto the dirt, fell and rolled, panting. Margo fired again, and the coyotes retreated.

***

His years as a freedom fighter served Chaco in many ways, but right now, he was most grateful he'd been trained how to stay awake for days, alert, with only catnaps here and there. Otherwise, so exhausted he'd have a tough time staying awake that night to guard against not only cannibals but coyotes. There would be nothing stopping the mangy dog-beasts from crossing the log bridge and getting to Margo, the girls, and him…if they were hungry enough. He kept a sharp eye for even the slightest movement and listened for the faintest of sounds.

The following morning, Chaco and Margo prepared for the crossing. "I'll be back in a few minutes to help finish packing," he said to Margo. He walked away to a private spot and found a beautiful blue spruce. He kneeled, crossed himself, and addressed the spirits of Russell and Abigail Walker. *"Adios, mis padres.* Goodbye, my parents. May angels keep you."

He stood and surveyed the land. In the distance, snow-capped Pine Mountain had turned the color of roses where the early sunlight brushed against it. Chaco thought it the most beautiful sight he'd ever laid eyes on next to his Fiona. He leaned back, and using his thigh as a table, took a pencil stub to a half of a brown paper bag he'd earlier stuffed in his back pocket, and wrote a letter.

Mi preciosa, Fiona,

A journey I had hoped would take two to three months, has taken almost seven. I'm sorry to have made you wait so long. But in a few days, I will be with you again. My greatest fear is after all this time apart, you assume me dead and have moved on with someone else. If that is so, I will keep you forever in my soul. I will always wish for you the best life has to offer, and all the love in the universe.

I am so sorry your dear mother and father are no longer with us. I am sorry your brother and sister-in-law did not make it. I did my best to keep everyone alive on the journey. I'm afraid I failed. I grieve most the loss of my second parents, whom I grew to love as though born to them. In the end, your mother told me that she and your father, loved me, too. I know now with certainty they would have blessed our union, my dearest one. In seeing us together, their hearts would be filled with joy.

I fervently hope the good people of Moonforest Sanctuary will welcome us, feed us, and shelter us. With luck, the commune leaders will find us worthy enough to assign to us meaningful responsibilities. Between us, we have so many useful skills, Fiona. You may not believe it, but Margo will impress you.

Your nieces are beautiful, and I've grown exceptionally fond of them both. In my mind's eye, I see their eager faces as they sit at the tables in the commune school. In the afternoons and on weekends, they will play with your boys by the creek, eat honey candy, and thrive. They have been through so much, and have lost so much, yet through unimaginable horrors and heartaches, both have demonstrated extraordinary strength, grace, and resilience. I am proud of them.

Mostly, I dream of reuniting with you, of feeling you close to me, covering your neck with kisses. If you are still free and will have me, I would be honored if you would consent to be my wife. Your sons will be my sons. Your nieces will be my daughters. And, God willing, we will have children of our own one day. As I promised your mother and father, I will take care of our family, protect and provide, and love you all for as long as I draw breath.

I love you, *mi amor, mi* Fiona.

Chaco

He read the letter to himself. Smiled. *If fate or God will it, it shall be so.* Chaco tore the letter into confetti pieces, and with a glad shout, threw them into the air and watched as they fluttered through the air like tiny brown moths.

CHAPTER 37

Crossing the abyss was easy enough for everyone except Olivia. Chaco thought she'd scamper over the log like a ferret, and it would be her little sister with her arm in a sling who would have trouble. Olivia balked. He hadn't counted on her being afraid of heights.

"No, no. I can't do it. I can't. Please don't make me, Uncle Chaco. I'll fall."

"Jist take my hand, and don't look down. Put one foot in front of the other, and you'll be fine," Margo said. "Trust me. I ain't gonna let you fall."

"Yes, you will. If I slip, you can't catch me, and I'll go way down there and die!"

After nearly an hour of cajoling, and several failed attempts, during which the child would take a tentative step then pull back, Chaco lost patience. When Olivia tugged in fright at Margo's hand once too often, nearly causing Margo to lose her balance and tumble off the log, Chaco stepped in. "That's it." He grabbed Olivia and threw her over his shoulder. With her screaming and beating on his back, he ran with her over the log and deposited her on the other side. "You almost caused Margo to fall, and because of you, we're delayed another hour."

"Please don't be mad at me, Uncle Chaco," Olivia cried. "I was so scared. That's all. I wanted to go across, but…I couldn't." She buried her head in her hands and sobbed. "I'm sorry."

Chaco kneeled beside the little girl, pulled her into his lap, and rocked her. "You have to trust Aunt Margo and me. I promised your grandma and grandpa I'd take care of you, and I will."

The child wiped her eyes with the back of her hand. "I love you, Uncle Chaco."

"I love you, too."

***

With each step toward Pine Mountain, the atmosphere grew lighter. They travelled a well-worn path through a pass. "I'm reasonably sure this leads directly to the commune," Chaco said to Margo. On the level portions of the path, the little girls skipped. Margo hummed Willie Nelson's "On the Road Again." Chaco had not seen her that happy in a long while.

"You seem in good spirits," Chaco said.

"Given that Rocky ain't here, I'm managin' all right, I suppose," she said. "If he was with me, I'd be singin' a whole lot louder." She cupped her hands around her mouth and shouted, "Rocky, are you around somewheres? Time to quit foolin' and c'mon back to me now."

Chaco's heart pounded in anticipation. *Almost there, mi amor, mi Fiona.* Although he'd lost count of the exact number of weeks they'd travelled, from the position of the stars, he knew spring would soon arrive. "*La primavera es maravillosa.* Spring is wonderful." He took a deep breath. "Smell that?"

"What?" said Olivia.

"The sweet smell of new beginnings. The perfume of hope. Spring."

"Is *maravillosa* the word in Spanish for spring, Uncle Chaco?" Lacy asked.

"No, *mi hija,* my daughter. *Primavera* means spring. The word sounds like a song, doesn't it?" He broke into a Salvadoran folk song for children, "*Las estrellitas.* The Little Stars." His singing voice, not much better than his love poetry, made both little girls break out into loud guffaws.

Still, even with his spirits high, Chaco remained vigilant. *Animals, cannibals, and who knows what else is before us still.* He maintained the point position with his rifle at the ready. Margo walked the rear with her firearm. Whether bouncing their way down the trail, clamoring over rocks, or crawling up steep hills, the girls remained sandwiched between the safe bookends of Chaco and Margo. Several times, Chaco discovered bear scat, deer droppings, as well some ominous tracks. He bent over and measured a set of lion tracks with the span of his hand. He held his hand up to halt the girls, walked back to Margo and whispered in her ear. "There is a puma nearby. A big one. Keep sharp."

By Chaco's estimation, they were now less than twenty or so miles from the commune. He would have pushed through and walked the remaining distance without stopping, but the little girls grew too tired and hungry to continue. It had started to rain, too.

While Margo made camp, Chaco fixed his binoculars to his eyes and guarded the perimeter. He'd been on watch for less than an hour when men on horseback came into view. From what he could see there were two of them headed toward him from the opposite direction. He tracked them as they closed in. *Yes, from the sanctuary!* Chaco recognized the bigger African American bald man at once, the cobbler with the gold earring he'd met when Fiona had taken him on that tour so very long ago. Chaco picked up his rifle and waved it in the air. He jumped up and down. "Hello, hello!"

The men halted their horses. The bald one held a pair of field glasses to his eyes and looked through them. He stowed the binoculars, said something to the other rider, then the men spurred their mounts and galloped full speed toward Chaco.

"Margo!" Chaco shouted. "Men from Moonforest Sanctuary. On horseback. Will be here any minute."

Margo put the girls in the tent. "You two stay here outta the rain. I'll be right back." Before she joined Chaco, she pulled the hood of her jacket over her head to protect against the weather. "I don't see 'em."

"You will. I wager they'll be here to greet us in five minutes at most."

Chaco put his firearm on a nearby rock and danced a few steps of Salsa. The sound of hoof beats preceded the sight of the men. When they approached the camp, they halted, drew their weapons, and aimed them at Margo and Chaco.

Chaco took a step back and put his hands in the air. "Glad to see you," he said. "We've travelled a long way." He nodded toward their guns. "No need for those rifles."

"I'll be the judge of that," the bald man said and scowled. "Who are you and what are you doing here?"

"Is it all right if I lower my hands?" Chaco said.

"Yeah, but keep away from that." The bald one motioned to Chaco's weapon.

"I'm Chaco Rodriguez. This is Margo Pennymon. In that tent behind me are two little girls, Olivia and Lacy Walker. We have come to seek shelter at Moonforest Sanctuary."

The men looked at one another, and the black man shifted in his saddle.

"We have met," Chaco said to the bald man. "Several years ago, Fiona MacDougal took me on a tour of the sanctuary. You make sandals."

"That's right. I do make shoes. But I don't recognize you, and I don't recall ever meeting you."

"It was a long while ago. A brief meeting. And I looked a little different." Chaco had grown a full black beard and had lost weight on the journey. His clothes were worn, dirty, and tattered.

The other man spoke. "You didn't say how you know Fiona."

"I worked for her parents, Russell and Abigail Walker."

"And the Walkers are…where?"

Chaco shuffled uncomfortably and looked at his feet. "They didn't make it."

"What do you mean?"

"They are both deceased."

"You mean you killed them," the bald man said.

"I did not kill them! I loved…look, we only want to join the commune."

"I don't think so. We've had a lot of trouble with people just like you...nice folk on the outside with kids and dogs, who repaid our kindness by stealing our food and threatening us with violence. Several of our commune members have been murdered by marauders and thieves who came to us seeking shelter. Our job is to protect the sanctuary. Unless someone can corroborate your stories, you will turn around and go back to wherever you come from, or we'll kill you right where you stand."

"Aunt Margo?" Olivia emerged from the tent and came within a few paces of the adults.

"Olivia! Git back in that tent right now. Go take care of your little sister. Git. I mean it!" Olivia retreated with a pout on her face. By the time Margo turned back to the men, her face had morphed from soft white to vivid red. "You ain't got no call to threaten us and be so hostile. We came a long ways and been through a whole lot, and we ain't going back nowheres. Fiona kin tell you we are who we say we are. Go ask her. And, fer gawdsake, put down yer damned rifles. One might go off and you could hurt one of them little girls."

The men looked at one another again. The bald man spoke. "Fiona isn't at the sanctuary."

Chaco's heart caught in his throat. "What do you mean? Where is she? She is okay, isn't she?" His gut burned with anxiety. His eyes darted from one horseman to the other. "Tell me she's okay."

"Settle down," the bald man said. "She's on a trading expedition. She'll be back in a few days. Who else at Moonforest can corroborate your story?"

Chaco let out a breath.

The bald man spoke again. "No one?"

"I've only met a few people at the Sanctuary, and can't even recall their names. Margo has never been there."

The bald man scratched his chin. "This is what we'll do. You all stay put. When Fiona returns, we'll ask her about you. What is your name again?"

"Chaco Rodriguez."

"If you come anywhere near the commune before we can check you out, we'll shoot you. Understood?"

Chaco nodded.

The men wheeled their horses about and trotted back toward the sanctuary.

"Well ain't that the special warm greetin' we was expecting?"

Chaco didn't respond, so Margo raised her voice. "Cat got yer tongue, Chaco? Whaddaya make of them hostile guys with them guns pointed at us?"

"I can't blame them for protecting the commune," Chaco said. "Given their situation, I'd do the same."

For a minute, the patter of rainfall was the only sound, then two guns blasted in quick succession.

Chaco pulled Margo to the ground. She gasped. "Oh Lord."

The sanctuary guards lurched forward. Blood bloomed like grotesque flowers on their backs. The bald man cried out in pain, and a third shot finished him. First, one guard, then the other, slid off their horses as the animals bolted. Before Chaco could react, two men, one in red and the other in camouflage emerged from the forest canopy, grabbed the dead men by their feet, and dragged them into the woods.

The cannibals were less than eighty yards from where Chaco and Margo stood. One came out of the forest but kept cover behind a cedar. "Hey, you!" he shouted. "We got ourselves some good meat now, boy howdy, but we're gonna get you, too. Those little girls will be perfect over a spit, and once we're done having a little fun with that woman, we're gonna cut her into some sweet steaks. As for you, you little beaner, we're gonna skin you alive and make jerky out of your muscle meat. Yum, yum, yum."

The other cannibals laughed. One sounded like a hyena.

"Those are the men!" Olivia said. At the sound of the shots, both girls had run to Chaco and Margo. "The ones with the chocolate and stuff. The bad guys we saw."

"What's a spit?" Lacy asked.

CHAPTER 38

"Margo, stay here with the girls."

"Are ya goin' after them men?"

Chaco shook his head. "No. I think they're going to be busy for a while…with…"

"Skinnin' and guttin' those two guards?" Margo whispered.

Looking around to make sure the girls couldn't hear him, and keeping his voice as low as Margo's, Chaco responded. "Yes, I think they'll take care of their most recent …er, business… before coming after us. I'm going for the horses. Keep your firearm loaded and within reach."

It took Chaco over an hour to round up the horses. He found them on their way back to the Sanctuary where they'd stopped to graze. Chaco clicked his tongue and called to them. He held out a pinecone hoping the horses might think it fruit. It took some tries, but the ploy worked. Both horses were tame and curious enough to approach Chaco. He led them back to camp.

"Ya know, I thought them horses would run from ya. They'd be back at the commune by now, and you'd be draggin' yerself back here on foot." Margo said.

"I have a way with horses. Always have."

"Horse whisperin' wasn't somethin' I figured you fer," Margo said. "That's more what I do."

"I wasn't exactly horse whispering. You could say I handled them."

"I suppose a guy with a college education could be smarter than a horse. Maybe not by much, but some anyways." Margo threw back her head and let out a hearty laugh.

"Any sign of those men?"

"Nope. I imagine you was right. I bet they're still a little busy with them guards."

"They'll be back, Margo. They have been tracking us for weeks, and they're not letting up. We can't let the girls out of our sight."

"Horses!" Olivia, who had gone back into the tent to play with her little sister, re-emerged with Lacy behind her. "Are those the ones those sanctuary guys had? Can we ride them, Uncle Chaco?"

"We're going to ride them to Moonforest Sanctuary, *mi hija*."

"Really? Lacy, did you hear we get to ride horses all the way to the moon place?"

Lacy squealed. She braced her broken arm with the opposing hand, and bounced up and down then spun on one foot like a wooden top.

***

By dark, they'd reached the sanctuary wall. Chaco road the appaloosa gelding with Lacy in front grasping the saddle horn, and Olivia in back with her little arms wrapped around him.

Margo rode the smaller horse, a bay mare with a jaunty step. Chaco thought the horse suited her just fine.

They came within thirty-fifty feet of the commune entrance before halting the horses. Chaco had remembered it a different way. When he'd last been here, there had been a sign: "Moonforest Sanctuary" carved into a solid wooden beam spanning a graceful wrought iron gate, a gate more decorative than utilitarian. The commune left it ajar for anyone to enter. Everyone welcome. There were flower gardens in the front, and a Koi pond, and dozens of dogwoods that bloomed pink and white in the spring. But there were no flowers now, no dogwood. The pond had been filled in with rubble. Rocks had been piled into a rough eight-foot wall creating a barrier between the commune and the outside world. Someone, probably workers in the commune, had cemented the rocks in an odd and untidy fashion. It looked as though, in great haste, someone had dumped wet cement over the barrier without any pattern or reason. But, the wall, crooked and ugly, served its purpose. The peaceful, idyllic sanctuary had become a fortress. Chaco imagined that instead of gentle people behind the walls, there were armed warriors, and if threatened, they were prepared to defend their property and themselves with intense ferocity and ruthlessness.

A rusted metal door creaked on its hinges as it opened, and three humorless, armed men stepped through. The door closed behind them.

The largest of the men, a huge blonde reminding Chaco of an ancient Viking, stepped forward. He had to be six feet four inches, or taller, with broad shoulders and the largest biceps of any man Chaco had met. "Who are you and where did you get those horses?" he said.

"I'm Chaco Rodriguez."

The blonde man took a step back, and without changing his expression, looked over Chaco, eyeing him from head to foot. "So, you're Chaco."

"Yes," Chaco said. "I don't believe we've met."

"I'm Zachary MacDougal. Fiona's husband."

CHAPTER 39

Chaco went cold. He willed his heart to stop beating. He no longer wanted to breathe, to exist, not if Fiona was lost to him. Although weak and sick with grief, he maintained self-control. He managed to keep his face impassive as he stared into the cool grey eyes of the Viking. *The man is talking to me. I can see his mouth moving, but I can't hear the words. Maybe the man switched to Danish or Swedish or some ancient Viking language that I cannot understand. Why a Celtic last name? He should be Leif Sörengaard, or some such thing. Zach MacDougal, really? Fiona's husband. She'd gave up and went back to him. Why didn't she wait for me?*

This isn't "heartbreak." No. Heartbreak is something else. This is "soulbreak." My soul is gone from my body, ripped out, torn into pieces, and I am nothing now.

"I said, do…you…understand?" The Viking spoke to Chaco in perfect English.

"Sorry. I've been thinking about something, and I…"

"I said, we have limited resources, and I'm afraid we'll have to turn you away."

One of the other men, the quiet one, began to speak, but the Viking put his hand up to silence him. "There are many people who have come to our gates seeking shelter, safety, food. At first, we took in as many as we had room for. It was to our detriment that we did. We can no longer accept others into the compound. No exceptions."

"But what about Aunt Fiona and our cousins? Can't we see them?" Olivia said.

The Viking leaned to one side to get a better view of the little girl on the back of the horse, then turned back to Chaco. "This is Fiona's niece?"

"Me, too," Lacy said pointing to herself. "She's our auntie, and we have cousins, and we came a long, long way to see them. And we're supposed to get honey candy, too."

The Viking stroked his beard, then spoke to Chaco again. "You didn't say how you got those horses."

"Those horses belong to Jack and Mike," one of the other men said, one with red curly hair who reminded Chaco of a circus clown. "Just how in the hell did you come by their horses, and where are Jack and Mike?"

Chaco told about how overjoyed he'd been to see the two men, and how one had promised to check out their story with Fiona. "He said, if Fiona could verify our story, we'd be admitted to the Sanctuary."

"Did he, now?" said the Viking. "No one is authorized to make the decision to admit anyone."

"He told us Fiona was on a trading mission…"

"….and that she is. I think she'll be back in a day or two." The Viking looked off into the distance, and his shoulders drooped.

Chaco felt satisfaction witnessing the big man's discomfort, *no, not discomfort, misery. Something is up between them.* Chaco's mood brightened. "You didn't accompany her? You are her husband, no? Lots of wild animals and murdering thieves out there. Wouldn't you want to make sure your wife would get to her destination unharmed, and return safely?"

The Viking's eyes narrowed into steal slits. "That is none of your concern."

"How do you know who I am?" Chaco said. He knows about me and Fiona. The pendejo, the idiot, is jealous. Ha! He's still her ex-husband, not her husband. He felt his soul return to him. It filled his head, his throat, his chest.

Chaco smiled and released the tension in his shoulders. "The guard did promise if we were to stay where we were, once Fiona returned, he'd ask her about us."

"Never mind how I know who you are. And I don't really

care what anyone else said, you aren't coming in. Now, tell us what happened to Mike and Jack, and how you ended up here on their horses." The Viking put his hand on a firearm he had tucked into his belt.

"Yeah," said the clown. He'd raised his rifle.

Chaco told the story of the cannibals, how they shot the two men and dragged them into the forest, and how afterward he'd been able to round up the horses.

"Cannibals?" As the Viking spoke, he didn't look quite so big, not quite so formidable.

"Yes. They killed and ate some hikers, and have been tracking us since. We've had a few run-ins with them."

"They ate the hikers?" Olivia said. "People don't eat people. Icky." She started to tear up.

"Now, now, Olivia. No need to cry. You need to watch what yer sayin'," she said to Chaco.

"I don't believe that story. Nope," the Viking said. "This is what I think happened. You killed Mike and Jack after they told you there was no way you'd ever get inside the walls of Moonforest Sanctuary. You stole their horses and came here with some bullshit story that they promised you would be admitted."

Margo leapt from her horse and strode toward the big man. "You listen here. Chaco ain't kilt nobody unless in the protection of hisself or someone he loves." She jutted her chin. "He ain't lyin' 'bout nothin'. He knows Fiona. He's got her little nieces with him, and those two men, rest their souls, did say if Fiona knows us, we'd git in." She stepped closer to him. "We mostly walked on foot fer near 800 miles, with wild animals, and snakes, and m'best friend died. You kin see that one of them little girls is hurt. Now, it's gittin' dark and cold. We are low on food. We're hungry, we're bone tired, we're gittin' damned mad, and we expect you to show us some Christian charity."

The Viking lifted a brow and nodded. "I'll tell you what. We'll give you some food and some water. You give us back the horses. Then you can camp outside the walls for tonight. Tomorrow, you be on your way. And we'll take the children in, but not you, and not him." He pointed at Chaco. The Viking stepped to the Appaloosa and held out his arms. "Give me the children, then dismount." The other men drew their weapons.

Olivia cried, "You want us to leave Uncle Chaco and Aunt Margo? No. No. I won't go."

"Me, neither." Lacy wailed, then turned to Chaco and clasped her uninjured arm around his neck.

"Don't let that man take us, Uncle Chaco. Please." Olivia leaned her head into Chaco's back and dampened his jacket with her tears.

Margo reached up and patted Olivia's leg. "Look, sweetie. You need to go inside where you'll be safe, kin git some food, and have a warm bed to sleep in. I'll tell you what. You go with this man, who is actually married to your Aunt Fiona, so he's kinda yer uncle, too. And as soon as we kin see our way clear we'll come back."

"No." Olivia shook her head.

"But, honey, it's the best thang fer you and yer little sister, and she's still hurt and maybe needs a doctor."

"I don't care…I'm not…"

The gun shot from the forest startled everyone. Chaco whipped his head around to the source of the rifle fire, then the clown let out a scream. Before the second blast, Chaco jumped from the horse and pulled the girls with him. The girls cried out.

The clown had caught a bullet in the shoulder, dropped to his knees and pressed his hand to the wound. Blood seeped between his fingers. Another blast. A man let out a scream from somewhere in the forest. A second man from the forest screamed, screamed again, and again…and all fell silent.

"Stay on the ground," Chaco said to the girls. "Don't move." From a crouched position, he reached to the saddle and pulled down the Remington.

The guards took cover behind boulders and trees and had aimed their weapons in preparation to fire at...someone. *Who?* The Appaloosa blocked Chaco's view.

Then Margo called out. "No. Don't shoot. Hold yer fire!" The horse moved to one side, enabling Chaco a clear view. Margo ran to...that someone, a big man who had emerged from the forest, thin, gaunt, with a huge bushy beard, covered in skins sewn together in a patchwork pattern, with tufts of fur sticking out here and there. He wore on his head what appeared to be a sleeping squirrel. The rodent's legs dangled down the sides of his face, and with each of the man's steps, the squirrel's snout bounced against the man's forehead.

The gaunt man held a bloodied hunting knife in one hand, but when he saw Margo, he dropped it. She ran, stumbling into his arms. With both hands, he lifted her as though she were a child.

She folded her arms around his neck and wrapped her legs around his torso. "Oh, fer gawdsake, Rocky!"

CHAPTER 40

The moment the little girls recognized Rocky, they ran to him squealing. Rocky kneeled and grabbed them both into his arms and held them to his chest. He hugged them for a good long while until the always impatient Lacy squirmed her way free. "Every single day we play with the horses you made us," she said to him.

Chaco greeted him. "Good to see you, Rocky. Hey, ah, what happened back there?"

"Let's just say no one need worry about some of those cannibals again. A couple got away, but they won't be coming around after what they saw me do to their buddies." With a forefinger, Rocky made a slicing motion across his throat. He lowered his voice to a whisper. "I strangled one of the bastards with his own intestines."

Although the Viking objected, the door into the sanctuary opened, admitting everyone. The silent guard helped the bleeding clown to his feet, and they all made their way into the grounds of Moonforest Sanctuary.

Relieved, Chaco saw the commune much as he'd remembered it. The yurts, the orchards, and the barn still there. The greenhouses stood, and fields looked good. All the people were still there. Some he recognized. Most of the residents halted their work to watch the curious procession led by their leaders and the Viking.

The Sanctuary physician ordered the clown to lie down and secured a tourniquet to staunch the bleeding. He called for a gurney, and two buff men carried the clown to the infirmary. Then the doctor turned his attention to the visitors. "Let me see that arm," he said to Lacy. The little girl extracted her arm from the sling and held it to the doctor.

He examined the small limb, turned it, removed the splint and felt the muscle and bone. "Someone did an impressive job splinting this. Of course, we don't have x-ray equipment, but from what I can see, it looks good." He prodded the arm again. "Does it hurt, sweetie?"

"No, not really," Lacy said. "Not even when I bump it."

"When did you hurt it?"

"A long, long time ago. Chaco broke it."

Margo intervened. "It happened when he pulled her into a tree to git her away from coyotes and yanked too hard."

"Then, Chaco splinted the arm?"

Margo smiled and pointed to herself. "Heck no. It were me. I have lots of healin' ways with herbs, and poultices, and I kin birth babies and I kin set bones."

"I could really use your help in the infirmary, if you would be interested."

"Yes, sir, Doctor. I'd be plenty glad to be of use. Do ya need me right now? I only jist reunited with my jackass husband who took off in the forest and only today got back. Me and him need to have us a talk, that bull-headed son of a…"

The doctor threw his head back and broke into a hearty wholesome laugh, and Chaco couldn't help but laugh with him. The doctor, still chuckling, nodded. "When you are ready, ask anyone where the infirmary is. I'll be there."

Chaco thought Margo might want to sit with Rocky away from the curious crowd gathered around them. He suggested a quiet place for them to talk in privacy near the creek.

"Nope. We're havin' it out right here in front of Gawd and ever 'one." She folded her arms and spun to face her husband. "Rocky Pennymon, why did you take off like that and not come back fer so long? You made me, and ever 'one else, worried fer no good reason."

"Hon. I never really left. I was always close by, you know that. And…" he looked at the ground, "I thought maybe you'd be better off with Chaco. I can tell you like him, and I didn't want to come in between you two. I mean, if that's who you really want to be with."

She unfolded her arms. "You knucklehead! I ain't never loved no man but you. Chaco is a friend, a good friend, and that's all there is 'tween us. What in Gawd's name is wrong with you? Don't you love me no more? Are ya sick a' me? You wantin' to pawn me off on someone else? Is that it?" She drew back her fist and punched him hard on the bicep, and he flinched. Someone in the crowd tittered. Margo turned to the offender. "You jist shut up. This ain't funny." Then she turned back to Rocky. "You big ole' idiot. Cain't you tell I love you and no one else?"

Rocky rubbed his wounded arm. "You know it was more than that...the whole thing with Jude."

"Jist shut yer mouth. You did what you had to do, and you saved Chaco's life."

Rocky turned his attention to Chaco and sneered. "Speaking of that, looks like I had to save your bacon a few times there, little hombre. That Ph.D. and all your time as a big freedom fighter doesn't do you a hell of a lot of good out in the real world. Does it, boy?"

Chaco advanced toward the man, who stepped back. "Hold on there, you little wetback. Don't you get too close, or I'll have to kick your brown ass."

Chaco ignored him, advanced closer, and threw his arms around the big man. Rocky stumbled, then recovered and reciprocated the embrace. He lifted Chaco from the ground, hugged him tightly, and whispered, "Thanks for taking care of Margo and the girls, Chaco." The bigger man set the smaller man back on the ground. "That's enough of that. I don't want anyone thinking I'm a faggot or anything."

***

The travelers met with the Sanctuary elders. Chaco was not too surprised to learn before inheriting his millions, Rocky had been a licensed general contractor who could build anything. The elders were delighted.

"By the way," he told them, "that so-called security wall of yours is a piece of crap. It won't hold. I'll build a new one for you that will last a thousand years, and it will look a hell of a lot better, too. We have enough straw and mud around here to make bricks."

The leaders assigned Chaco to Commune Security duty, and because of his years of experience in handyman work and gardening, he would be a floater. The elders assigned Margo to the infirmary. Everyone would work the grounds as required, helping with building, planting, harvesting, and foraging.

The girls opted to stay with Margo and Rocky in their yurt. Later, they would move in with their aunt and cousins, but not tonight. As a temporary measure, Chaco ended up with a canvas tent. Good. He needed to be alone and pitched the tent as far away from the others as possible so he might enjoy the quiet, happy to be in the company of cicadas and frogs.

That night, Chaco fell into his sleeping bag exhausted. As he fell into a dream, footsteps outside his tent woke him. A dog? A chupacabra? A chill gripped him. He unzipped his sleeping bag and grabbed his firearm. When he opened the tent flap, there stood the Viking.

"I want to talk to you right now," the Viking said.

"Look, Zack. I'm exhausted. I haven't slept much in weeks. Can this wait?"

"You don't call me Zack. You call me Zachary." The bigger man's eyes narrowed.

"All right, *Zachary.* Can this wait?"

"No, it can't. We need to get something straight between us."

Chaco pulled his rifle to the opening of the tent within reach, then yanked on his boots and emerged, leaving the tent flap open and his rifle in sight. He faced the Viking.

The bigger man stepped forward and leaned down within inches of Chaco's face.

Chaco stood his ground.

The Viking jabbed a finger at Chaco. "You! Stay the fuck away from Fiona and my sons."

Chaco didn't flinch. "Don't you think that's Fiona's decision?"

"She's my wife, you little fucker. I'm warning you. Stay away."

"And if I don't?" Chaco assessed the man. *Big, muscular, but clumsy. Maybe slow. Enraged. His anger will hamper his judgment.*

"I'll break your scrawny little neck. You better hear me. Stay away from my wife!" The veins on the Viking's neck protruded, pulsed.

Chaco grinned and said, "You mean…your *ex*-wife?"

The Viking shifted, pulled back his arm, and swung a fist, but Chaco twisted and avoided the punch. He swung his leg in a low arc, tripping the big man. The Viking fell hard on his back with a "whoomph," the air knocked out of him.

Before he recovered enough to stand, Chaco stomped him hard in the ribs. Bones splintered.

The Viking yelped in pain and rolled in the dirt, grasping his side.

As the big man curled to protect his torso, Chaco kicked the side of the Viking's head with a blow that left him dazed.

Blood spurted from the deep cut in his scalp delivered by Chaco's boot heel.

Chaco kneeled, grabbed the man's arm and in one smooth movement, twisted it behind him, yanking. "Move, and I'll break your arm."

The wounded Viking lie in the dirt, moaning, blood spilling from his head.

"Okay, okay. Just get off me."

Chaco stood and left the man in the dirt still gasping. "Jesus. You broke my ribs, you little prick. What the fuck did you do to my head?"

"I'll do more than that if you ever threaten me again, *Zachary*."

***

The young Asian woman he'd met on the trail before, the one with the cattails, told Chaco she'd seen a robin's nest. There were patches of snow in the shade. Most of the sanctuary residents still wore their heavy coats and wool wraps, but as sunlight spread over the meadow Chaco saw the first green leaf buds of the white oak.

Chaco worked in the barn with Rocky and Margo and several others when Fiona returned from her excursion. She burst into the barn, her sons close behind. "Where's my family?" She called out. "Mom? Dad? Jude? I'm here. Is Chaco with you?"

He had been in the rafters and couldn't climb down fast enough to reach Fiona before Rocky and Margo intercepted her. He called out, but over the din of the other voices, Fiona couldn't hear him.

Margo embraced Fiona.

"It's so good to see you, Margo. Where's Mom?" Fiona broke the embrace and cast an eye over the barn. Chaco stood in the crowd behind her, waiting for his moment to make himself known. He could scarcely breathe from want of her.

"My gosh! Is that really *you*, Rocky? You've lost so much weight…and that beard. You look like a real mountain man." Fiona laughed, then craned her neck, searching. "Mom?"

Margo kneeled on the barn floor and spoke to Fiona's sons. "You boys, go outside fer a minute and play with yer cousins, Lacy and Olivia. They're out by the crick. I've got somethin' I gotta talk to yer mama about."

The boys looked to their mother, who nodded her permission. Still on her knees, Margo watched the little boys retreat from earshot. She stood, and put her arm around Fiona.

"What's up?" Fiona asked. "What's going on?"

"I've got some real bad news fer ya, honey."

By the time Chaco managed to get close to Fiona, she sat on a bench, sobbing. A wall of people crowded in around her.

Rocky waived them away. "Give her some space."

Overcome with grief and shock, and with her head hung low, she could not see that Chaco had worked his way through the crowd and stood by the bench close enough for her to touch him. Margo and Rocky sat with Fiona and did their best to comfort her.

Rocky tapped Fiona on the shoulder. "Someone else is here, honey." Fiona looked up, and the second she saw Chaco, her eyes widened. She began to cry anew, but this time from joy. She stood to fling her arms around Chaco, and that's when he saw it. She'd worn a long heavy cape to stave off the spring cold. Bulky and colorful in a busy pattern like a crazy quilt, it hid her figure. As she rose to her feet, the front of the cape parted. Her belly, swollen with the child within. Chaco stepped back and gaped at her bulging midsection in all its ripeness. He reflexively grasped his chest to prevent his heart from shattering into brittle fragments. *The Viking. She's having his baby.*

She put her hands on her belly, and her face warmed with a smile. "It won't be long before you meet your son, Chaco."

He whooped and pulled her into to him. But as he held her, he became aware of something, or someone, else. The hairs on the back of his neck prickled. He pulled Fiona closer and looked over her shoulder. At the entrance of the barn stood a figure, a big man backlit by the afternoon Sun. His head bandaged, the Viking frozen in place like a metal sculpture, his legs apart, stared at the Salvadoran with more cold hate than Chaco had ever seen in any man's eyes. He smiled at the big man, then nuzzled Fiona and covered her face in petite kisses. *"Mi amor, mi amor. Te quiero mucho."* He slid his hand under her shawl to her abdomen, and when Chaco felt his baby move, he buried his face in her hair and inhaled the spring of her.